THE TEXIAN PRISONERS

A Biographical Novel of Old New Mexico

Loretta Miles Tollefson

PALO FLECHADO PRESS

ISBN: 978-1-952026-08-9

Library of Congress Control Number: 2023923458

Excerpts from "to the echo of my guitar" and "El Valse Chiqueado" from *New Mexico Folk Music : Treasures of a People,* by Cipriano Frederico Vigil, University of New Mexico Press, 2014.

Spanish-language proverbs from *Refranes, Southwestern Spanish Proverbs,* collected and translated by Rubén Cobos, Museum of New Mexico Press, 1985.

This novel uses only historical characters and strives to provide an accurate depiction of past events as far as they are known. However, the thoughts, words, and motivations of the people portrayed in this book are products of the author's imagination and interpretation of the historical materials. This book is a work of fiction. References in it to historical events, real people, or real places are used fictitiously.

Palo Flechado Press, Santa Fe, New Mexico

Other Books by Loretta Miles Tollefson

Old New Mexico Fiction
Not Just Any Man
Not My Father's House
No Secret Too Small
There Will Be Consequences
The Pain and The Sorrow
Old One Eye Pete (short stories)
Valley of the Eagles (micro fiction)

Other Fiction
The Ticket
The Streets of Seattle

Poetry
But Still My Child

THE TEXIAN PRISONERS

Loretta Miles Tollefson

EPIGRAPH

Todo es según el color del cristal con que se mira.
(Everything is according to the crystal in which you see
yourself.) Charles Aranda, *Dichos: Proverbs and Sayings
from the Spanish.*

De la suerte y de la muerte no hay quien se escape.
(From fate and death, no one escapes.) Rubén Cobos,
Refranes: Southwestern Spanish Proverbs

PREFACE

They called themselves "Texians." In Fall 1841, a ragged and malnourished band of roughly three hundred men straggled into New Mexico after a grueling crossing from Austin, most of it on foot. They had intended to assert the Texan Republic's claim to everything east of the Rio Grande. Instead, they found themselves captured by New Mexican militia and sent south to Mexico City.

The first leg of this journey took the Texians from eastern New Mexico to El Paso del Norte, today's Ciudad Juárez. The largest group, which included New Orleans journalist George Wilkins Kendall, was escorted by militia Captain Damasio Salazar. Five prisoners died on the way.

Kendall was released from Mexican prison in April 1842 and back in New Orleans the following month. He immediately began writing a book that accused Salazar of food deprivation, mutilation, and murder, and expressed contempt for Mexicans in general and the Mexican Army in particular, calling them weak and poorly armed. The resulting *Narrative of an Expedition Across the Great Southwestern Prairies, from Texas to Santa Fe* was a best seller in the U.S. and did much to rally support for the 1846-47 aggression now known as the Mexican-American War.

The Texian Prisoners is a carefully researched biographical fictional account of the twenty-day journey Salazar and his prisoners made from eastern New Mexico to El Paso del Norte. It explores both what did and what is likely to have occurred as they traveled through New Mexico's pueblos and settlements, then across the barren plains known regionally as El Jornada del Muerto, or The Journey of Death.

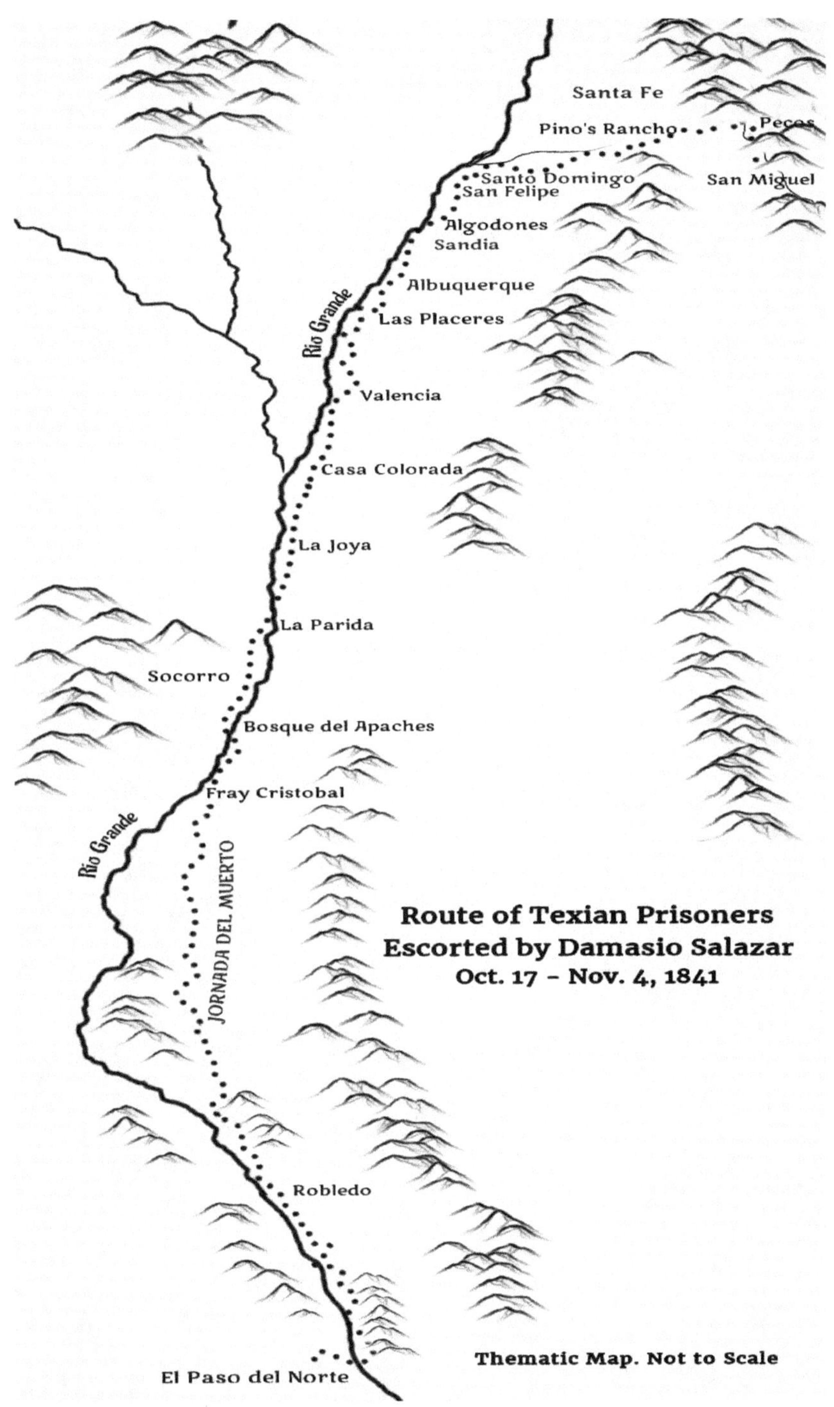

Santa Fe
Pino's Rancho
Pecos
Santo Domingo
San Felipe
San Miguel
Algodones
Sandia
Albuquerque
Las Placeres
Río Grande
Valencia
Casa Colorada
La Joya
La Parida
Socorro
Bosque del Apaches
Fray Cristobal
Río Grande
JORNADA DEL MUERTO
Route of Texian Prisoners
Escorted by Damasio Salazar
Oct. 17 – Nov. 4, 1841
Robledo
El Paso del Norte
Thematic Map. Not to Scale

CHAPTER 1
Saturday, October 16, 1841
San Miguel del Bado, New Mexico

The guard outside the open-air window stirred sleepily as Fitzgerald, Kendall, and I peered through its carved wooden bars. Above San Miguel del Bado's flat adobe roofs, the sky was just beginning to brighten toward sunrise. At the lower end of the plaza, General McLeod moved wearily to a cluster of horses. A Mexican soldier gave him a leg up. A handful of other Texian officers appeared and were assisted onto their mounts. Then the soldiers closed in. Bridles jingled as they moved up the plaza and past our cell. No one acknowledged us.

"Damnation!" Kendall muttered. "Without McLeod, the Texian Expedition is leaderless."I nodded absently. The General and his guard angled away from us toward the square bell towers of the village church and the road beyond. The one that connected to the route south to Mexico City and retribution. The silver on their high-pommeled saddles was a dull gray. No one looked back.

I straightened and turned to our unpainted adobe walls and little corner fireplace. "To think we came all this way only to be captured and imprisoned. Texians defeated by Mexicans, and without a shot being fired."

"It is difficult to grasp," Fitzgerald said as he leaned forward to study the plaza. "That being said, I'm not sure how to define 'Texian.' Many of our company were American. And as an Englishman born in Ireland and educated in France, I don't feel I truly have a country to call my own."

"A Texian is anyone who has declared himself to be one," Kendall said. "A statement which I personally have not made." He pushed away from the window, slapped the wall and limped toward the fireplace, hands on his hips. "I'm an American tourist! I informed that damnable Damasio Salazar of my status when he captured us. And Governor Armijo as well, when he condescended to favor us with his presence!"

He wheeled toward me. "And Van Ness, you vouched for my statements! They know it's true!" He waved his hands in the air, repeating what he'd been saying for the last month. "Yet here I am. Incarcerated!"

"I did vouch for you," I said. "However, the fact remains that you accompanied an Expedition to claim the lands east of the Río Grande for Texas."

"Spoken like a lawyer," he sniffed.

Fitzgerald grinned at me, then gave Kendall a grave look. "Our visitors yesterday did say you were to be released."

Kendall nodded reluctantly and ran his fingers through his wavy shoulder-length brown hair. "True, my friend. Very true." Then his face changed. "I pray to God it is so. That I will never again hear these damned Mexican guards calling '¡Centinela, alerta!' every thirty minutes throughout the night!"

Fitzgerald laughed and Kendall's expression soured again. "'Alert, sentinel' indeed. As if they could have stopped us from escaping if we'd known where McLeod and the others were." His chin went up. "As co-owner and editor of the *New Orleans*

Picayune, I intend to begin agitating for the General's safe return immediately upon my return home."

Fitzgerald's hazel eyes glinted with amusement. "Ours as well, I hope."

"Certainly." The newsman flexed his fingers. "It will be a relief to write again, to smell the ink-wet sheets, to see my thoughts in print." He shook his head. "It's mid-October already. When I left New Orleans in May, I thought I'd be in Mexico City by now. I haven't even seen Santa Fe yet!"

I raised my eyebrows. "Do you still plan to visit it?"

He shrugged. "If Governor Armijo extends me the courtesy to which I'm entitled, I expect that I shall. We're late in the season for a return East via the Santa Fe Trail. All the American merchants who plan to do so will surely be well on their way by now." He pushed his hair away from his face. "I certainly don't plan to return the way we came."

Fitzgerald chuckled at this, but Kendall ignored him. "It would undoubtedly be best to continue west and then south, at least to Chihuahua. From there, I can head for the Mexican coast and ship home to New Orleans." As if the thought of the upcoming journey reminded him of the time, he tugged at the gold chain draped across his chest, pulled out the gold-cased watch attached to it, and began carefully winding it.

I moved back to the window and bent down to look out. The square was waking into activity. Personally, if I were released I would find my back to San Antonio as quickly as possible. Back to where I had some right to be.

We'd called ourselves the Santa Fe Pioneers when we'd left Austin in June, three hundred strong. We'd had such high hopes and expectations—the glory of creating a new route to Santa Fe, the riches that would come as a result. However, the journey had disintegrated into a series of misadventures, hunger, and thirst. Then, in the eastern reaches of New Mexico, our real troubles began.

We three, sent ahead to find supplies, had been quickly captured and locked up in an adobe-walled room on San Miguel's plaza. We'd spent almost a month in suspense before the remaining Expedition members had been rounded up. A good third, including our leader Hugh McLeod, were now on their way to Mexico City and the tender mercies of President Santa Anna, a man known for his hatred of rebel Texians. The 340 men captured at Goliad in 1836 had experienced the penultimate effect of that hatred. He'd had all of them executed.

It was possible that we would face a similar fate. The remaining Santa Fe Expeditionaries had arrived in San Miguel four days ago and been shut up on the other side of the plaza in the big building with the tall walls and narrow gate. None of the villagers or guards seemed to know what was going to happen next, although Kendall had been assured by our higher-ranking visitors that he'd be released.

Perhaps Governor Armijo was taking the newsman's status as a tourist seriously. But then, given the *Picayune's* support of Texian independence, Armijo might feel a little antagonistic toward Kendall, and not inclined to treat him gently. There was also the matter of the news piece last January that described the governor's wife as shaped like a tobacco hogshead and waltzing like an elephant dancing.

I shook my head, pushed away from the window, and went to investigate the various earthenware pots of food the village women had brought us. Kendall was now sitting on his bedroll. He'd laid his money out on the floor and was calculating how much it might cost him to continue south.

"I'll need to find a mount, of course," he said. He glanced at his right foot. "Walking any distance would be nigh unto impossible. My ankle hasn't been the same since I took that fall outside Austin just before we left."

Fitzgerald turned from the window, ran his hands through his shoulder-length black hair, and grinned at the newsman. "I never have understood how you managed that."

"It was dark and I was in a hurry."

"That's clear enough. I have some experience myself of the way a bank edge can appear at one's feet on moonless nights. What I don't understand is how you managed to fall hard enough to break your ankle. Most people would merely slide to a stop. You seem to have gone end over end."

"The slope was rather precipitous." Kendall flexed his foot. "It's healed quite well since then, but it still twinges. I wouldn't want to have to walk a full day's journey on it." He began placing his coins into neat stacks. "I wonder where my horse is. Salazar undoubtedly passed him on to one of Governor Armijo's relatives. Even if I can locate him, I'll almost certainly be compelled to buy him back." His mouth twisted. "Not that I should be required to do so, since the animal was stolen from me, along with my papers."

"You'd be better off with a mule," I said, heading off another diatribe about his missing papers and passport. "An animal like your Molly would do nicely."

Kendall shook his head. "She's big and sturdy, but she's a pack mule. That sideways gait of hers would make sitting astride her back mighty uncomfortable." He shrugged. "That being said, I have no idea where she is. I'll undoubtedly find it necessary to purchase a mount, while doing my best not to get cheated too outrageously." He turned back to contemplating his resources.

He was at it again when I woke the next morning and lifted my straw-colored head. He'd stowed the coins and placed his bedroll, walking stick, water gourd, and tin cup in a neat pile against the wall, and was now contemplating his various pieces of jewelry, including the ornate silver breastpin he was particularly fond of. He moved the pieces here and there thoughtfully, then fastened the pin inside his waistband, separated the watch and chain, and distributed them and the other items into his deepest pockets.

When he noticed me watching, he gave a little shrug. "I won't be wearing any of these until I get home. There's simply too much risk." He tapped the pocket that held his watch. "This timepiece was the first item of jewelry I purchased when I began to earn a professional income. I managed to hide it from Salazar when he captured us and I'm damned if I'm going to let some other Mexican purloin it from me."

Before I could point out that the captain had confiscated only our paperwork, Kendall touched his bare throat. "There's no point in keeping the breastpin out, anyway, since my cravats are all scattered between here and Austin."

His eyes went to my upper chest. My one remaining cravat, badly wrinkled but relatively clean, was knotted securely around my long throat, protecting it against the morning chill. "You look very much the lawyer," he said lightly.

I grinned and pushed my blanket aside. "One who sleeps in his clothes."

Kendall chuckled and turned to the fireplace, where Fitzgerald was carefully warming the tortillas and beans the village shoemaker's wife had brought us the day before.

The newsman patted his pockets, as if making sure everything was secure, then grabbed his tin cup, crouched down beside the mica-flecked bean pot, and lifted the lid. "More hot chiles," he grumbled. "I'll certainly be glad to see the last of those." He shook his head as he ladled food into his cup, then reached for a tortilla.

There was a knock at the door and the guard entered. Kendall tossed his tortilla to one side and jumped to his feet. "Give me just one moment and I'll be ready to go," he said, moving toward his gear.

The guard turned to me. "Todos ustedes," he said. He waved a hand, indicating we were to bring our belongings with us.

Kendall put his hands on his hips and gave me a questioning look. "All of us," I translated.

Kendall blinked, then clapped his hands. "That's undoubtedly as it should be! Yes, let us be freed together!"

The guard raised an eyebrow at him, then turned studiously away to wait on the threshold while we gathered our things. As we filed past and outside, I gave him a quizzical look, but his gaze was fixed firmly on a knot in the wooden door frame.

We paused on the covered porch, breathing in fresh air and the smoke of morning fires. Although the sun was well hidden behind our building, the village leader's low-slung house on the other side of the plaza was well lit. The guard moved toward it. We followed hopefully.

"I suppose the old man has something to say to us before we depart," Kendall murmured. "Is it too much to hope that he'll apologize for his testy attitude while we've been in residence?"

But then our guard veered left, toward the building beside the alcalde's house where our compatriots were incarcerated. Two men, one tall, one short, stood in front of its battered gate, lances held across their bodies.

"No guns, as usual," Kendall muttered. The rest of us ignored him. Our guard halted ten feet from the gate and we lined up beside him. The men with the lances looked us over, then the shorter one turned his head and barked a single word at the gate.

For a long moment, nothing happened. I glanced around the plaza. A small boy with his arms full of firewood stood near the well, studying us. When he saw me looking, he ducked his head, turned, and scampered out of sight.

The gate hinges squealed. Board scraped across dirt. The men with the lances stepped aside and our fellow Expeditionaries streamed into the sunlight. They also had their gear hung about them and blanket rolls over their shoulders.

Kendall turned toward me. "Surely we aren't all going to be freed."

I didn't have time to respond. The newcomers surrounded us. Men I barely knew greeted me joyfully, pushing straggling hair away from deeply tanned bearded faces, and grabbing my hands with delight in their tired eyes.

"Van Ness!" a British voice said from behind me. "And Kendall and Fitzgerald too! How are you?"

"Falconer!" Kendall exclaimed. "How scrawny you are!"

The rangy, sandy-haired British lawyer turned to me. "Van Ness! My fellow lawyer!" He grinned at Kendall. "I'm not as thin as he is, and our guards told us you've been here a whole month!"

Kendall laughed. "Van Ness is always thin!"

I opened my mouth to protest but was interrupted by another voice, this one a good fifteen years younger than Falconer's. "Herr Van Ness!"

I turned to find nineteen-year-old Cayton Erhard. He was small for his age and his pale blond hair stuck out at odd angles, giving his thin face a waifish look and somehow emphasizing his orphan state. "Erhard!" I said.

As we shook hands, Felix Ernest appeared. He was a short, narrow-chested man with a patient air about him. "Good mornin'," he said in his soft Tennessee accent. "Certainly is good t'see all ya'll's friendly faces."

"And yours!" I looked from him to the boy. "How are you both? How do you fare?"

Ernest shrugged and showed me the back of his hands. They were covered with weeping sores. "Well enough."

Cayton's mouth drooped. "Bread only to eat."

Ernest's eyes twinkled. "The Mexicans give us mutton meat twice after we surrendered, and a deal of soup, but it's mostly been bread since." He grinned at Erhard, then me. "The young uns is always the hungriest."

Cayton's hand went to his stomach. "Hungrig most times," he said gloomily.

Falconer reappeared at my side. "The guards told us General McLeod was sent south yesterday." He combed his fingers through his hair and beard, the way he tended to do when he was agitated. "Are we to follow? Do you know?"

"I—"

"Not all of us," Kendall said. "I am a tourist with an American passport, I am to be freed."

Falconer's face fell for an instant, then he said heartily, "Let me congratulate you!"

"I'll do my best to get word to your families, of course," the newsman told him. "And agitate for your release."

The British lawyer nodded. "Yes, I expect that will be useful."

"Are there any injured among you?" I asked.

"Amos Golpin and Edward Griffith. Governor Armijo allowed the jersey sick wagon to remain with us, so they haven't been forced to walk."

"I'm pleased to hear it. In what way were they hurt?"

"Kiowa," Anton Erhard said, coming up just then. Cayton's younger but sturdier cousin, he also had thin fair hair, but a wider face. There were open sores on the back of his hands, too, but he hid them when he saw me looking.

Falconer nodded, confirming his words. "The Indians harassed us a good deal. They shot Griffith in the right thigh."

I winced. "What about Golpin? I know his withered right hand was giving him difficulty within a day of our leaving Austin. Was he further injured?"

Falconer shook his head. "No, but he has been severely worn down by our experiences. We've had a truly frightful time of it." He glanced at the German boys, eyes flicking to Anton's hands. "As can be seen by how thin these young men have become."

Kendall laughed. "Yes, they're even thinner than you!"

"Or me," a reedy voice said from behind him. Thomas Gates, a small, thin-chested man with a narrow nose, smiled at us benignly and extended his hand.

As I shook it, a voice at the edge of the crowd shouted "¡Poneos en fila!"

The others looked at me.

"Line up," I translated.

We began forming into straggling rows that faced the gate, but each new rearrangement brought someone else I hadn't spoken to in many weeks, and stopped my movement forward. There was Hornsby in his blue lieutenant's coat, its brass buttons as shiny as ever, a neatly rolled red blanket slung over a broad shoulder. And black-haired John McAllister, thirty years old, as tall as I was, and still favoring his left ankle, weakened in a childhood accident.

And then our two invalids, the narrow-shouldered Griffith, and Golpin, the Mississippian who wasn't much taller than Cayton Erhard. He gripped my forearm with his good hand and looked into my face. "We done thought you all was dead," he said. "It sure is a relief to find our conclusions untrue."

I grinned. "It's a relief to us as well."

"¡Poneos en línea!" the voice bellowed again.

Golpin chuckled. "He sounds a mite aggravated."

We began to form up in earnest now, but then another group of Texians entered the plaza. "Curtis!" Anton Erhard yelped as Golpin exclaimed "Old Paint!"

"Is it true?" Kendall asked from behind me. I craned my head over the crowd and then nodded. The newcomers did include thirteen-year-old Curtis Caldwell, the youngest member of our Expedition, and his father Matthew, the grizzled Indian fighter otherwise known as "Old Paint".

Kendall shoved past me, eager to greet them, and we all followed. As we crowded around the newcomers, we also found other Expeditionaries we hadn't spoken to yet. The voices of the Erhard boys and Curtis were high with excitement even as they tried to maintain a more manly demeanor.

Things were just starting to settle again when more Texians arrived. These were accompanied by the man they'd been billeted with. A pretty, brown-haired young woman rode pillion behind him. As the prisoners moved to join us, the girl slipped off and ran after them, wrapping her arms around the waist of the tallest and blondest of the men.

The Texian's face reddened, but he gave her a tender kiss and turned her gently toward the man on the horse. "Go to your brother, querida."

She shook her head, dark curly hair wild, but when he kissed her again, she went quietly enough, cheeks wet with tears. Her brother reached down to swing her up behind him, then sat studying the crowd. I caught his eye and he nodded somberly.

A hush fell, quiet enough to hear the girl's weeping and Kendall saying, "I am a tourist! I am to be freed!"

Then the door to the alcalde's house opened. Governor Armijo appeared, followed by his host and a small group of officers. Silence fell.

Armijo was a tall man, taller than me, and he towered over those around him. He paused on the porch to tuck his hand into his jacket, Napoleon style. He was in full uniform, with shining brass buttons and epaulettes that made his shoulders seem even broader than they were. The white feather on his bicorne hat brushed the underside of the porch roof. As he looked us over, a smile flicked his lips. Then his gaze reached Kendall, in the center of the front line, and his handsome face turned to stone.

The people of the village had come out of their houses while we Texians greeted each other. They stood on the porches that circled the plaza, watching silently. Armijo turned slowly, taking them in, then returned to us Texians. And Kendall.

The man could be an irritating bastard, but he was still one of us. I edged forward, thinking he might need my help with the language. Falconer stood next to him, with Fitzgerald just beyond. They moved aside as I reached them and Fitzgerald gave me a grateful look. We both knew his Spanish was too thin for any extensive interchange between Kendall and the governor.

But Armijo's gaze had moved on. He motioned to a man who'd been leaning against a post at the end of the porch and fingering the thick-handled Spanish pistol at his waist.

"Sargento!" the governor snapped. This was apparently a prearranged signal, because the man straightened, snapped off a salute, then began moving between the rows of prisoners, counting loudly as he came to each of us.

When he finished, he returned to the porch and saluted again. "¡Ciento ochenta y siete prisioneros rebeldes!" he reported.

Kendall looked at me.

"One hundred eighty-seven rebel prisoners," I translated.

He frowned. "But he counted me as well. I am an American tourist and am to be released."

I put on my blankest lawyerly face, the one I used for clients when the judge had ruled against us. "That's what he said."

Kendall frowned and looked toward the house. "There must be a mistake."

I followed his gaze. Armijo was staring straight at him with a small, triumphant smile.

"So it was all lies, after all. I am not to be a tourist, but a prisoner." Kendall's face hardened. "He will pay for this. The entire world will know of his perfidy."

Falconer glanced at him. "Had he told you that you would be freed?"

"He didn't condescend to inform me himself, but others did, and on more than one occasion," Kendall said without turning. "Men who are said to be close to him. He undoubtedly bade them to tell me lies." His eyes narrowed as his fists went to his hips. "He will pay."

On the porch, the governor's smile deepened. Then he turned, eyes roving the plaza. He frowned impatiently and said something to the sergeant who'd counted us. The man nodded and hurried out of the square.

A few minutes later, he returned, still on foot, with Damasio Salazar, in a blue cloak and a hand on his sword hilt, riding close behind. An older man with a thin, irritable face trailed after them on a small black mule.

The captain's mount was a tall block-headed chestnut mule whose muzzle jerked to one side as she walked. Kendall's breath hissed between his teeth when he saw her.

Falconer gave him a quizzical look. "Do you know them?"

"I know both the men and the mount," the newsman said bitterly. "The men are the bastards who captured Van Ness, Fitzgerald, and me. The one with the sword is Captain Damasio Salazar and he's riding my molly mule, damn him. The other man is called Don Jesús."

Falconer's eyebrows went up at the name, but there was no time for further discussion. The two riders had reached the porch.

The governor acknowledged them with a nod, tucked his right hand further into his jacket and turned to us prisoners again. His head turned from side to side as he studied us with an expression that was equal parts contempt, triumph, and relief.

Finally, he took a step forward and flourished his free hand toward Salazar, as if introducing him to us. "Señores, este hombre los acompañará hasta El Paso."

Kendall and Falconer glanced sideways at me. "Gentlemen, this man will escort you as far as El Paso," I translated softly.

"That bastard?" Kendall growled.

The governor gestured toward Don Jesús. "Y también alférez Jesús Lucero."

"And also Ensign Jesús Lucero," I added.

Falconer's brows contracted. "Yaysus?" he muttered. "Truly? As in Jesus?"

Kendall chuckled. "Truly. Although one look at his dark-visaged face makes it quite clear that he is indisputably un-Christlike."

But Armijo had started talking again, explaining at length and with a satisfied smirk that from El Paso we would be taken to Mexico City, capitol of the great republic of the United Mexican States. There, His Excellency President Santa Anna de López would determine what was to be done with us.

There was a hiss, not from us but from the villagers. A movement on the far side of the plaza caught my eye. It was the thick-shouldered man who'd acted as our purchasing agent in San Miguel. His arms were crossed over his broad chest and his dark eyes held an anxious expression.

Kendall saw him too. "Even Bustamante looks anxious for us, and not only for the loss of our money." Then he seemed to realize the implications of what he'd said. His shoulders drooped. "Anxious for all of us."

On the porch, Governor Armijo took another step forward and spoke to Captain Salazar. Something about a translator.

Irritation flashed across the other man's face and was quickly replaced by a courteous blandness. "Si, señor."

Armijo gave him an irritated look, then turned to the alcalde. He said something in a low voice. The village leader pointed begrudgingly in my direction. Armijo nodded, looked at Salazar, and indicated me with a jerk of the chin.

Again the captain said, "Si, señor," but it was clear that he didn't think a translator would be necessary.

Armijo's face tightened, then he shrugged, made a dismissive gesture, and turned back to the alcalde.

Captain Salazar's chin jerked, then he turned Kendall's mule and began riding slowly past our front ranks, looking us over with a sour expression. When he'd surveyed us all, he trotted the big mule back to the porch and wheeled to face us.

Armijo had fallen silent and he and his companions were watching. Captain Armijo's shoulders snapped back and his chin surged forward, transforming his face into a mask of fierce determination. "¡Prisioneros!" he proclaimed. "¡El invierno está cerca! ¡Debemos marchar rápidamente!"

I muttered a translation out of the side of my mouth. "Prisoners, winter is at hand! We must march rapidly!"

Kendall sniffed. "The weather has been clear and dry for the last month. I'm from Vermont. Now those are winters."

Salazar had turned to Armijo, who nodded. The captain swung back to us. "¡Cualquiera que se demore será fusilado!"

I stiffened. Kendall glanced at me. "Any who delay will be shot," I said reluctantly.

But Salazar was continuing. "¡Si alguno intenta escapar, morirá!"

I frowned. But then, we were prisoners. It was probably not an unreasonable statement. "If any try to escape, they will die," I added.

Kendall huffed in irritation. Armijo's eyes swept toward him, his left hand tapping against his leg. Then the governor stepped forward and said something to Salazar that I couldn't catch.

The captain's head jerked toward the porch. He gave the governor a long look, then nodded and turned back to us. "Si mueres, te cortarán las orejas para demostrar que es así," he said flatly.

I blinked. Surely I hadn't heard that correctly. But Kendall was jogging my elbow. I glanced at him, then slowly translated. "If you die, your ears will be cut off to prove it is so."

Kendall's breath hissed between his teeth.

Falconer and Fitzgerald looked at each other. "That's certainly the most hyperbolic statement I've ever heard," the lawyer said.

I looked toward the porch. Armijo was deep in conversation with the alcalde. Captain Salazar's mule moved impatiently, but her rider's face was impassive.

"I believe the captain's statement is an exaggeration designed to capture our attention," I told my companions.

Kendall shook his head. "He undoubtedly means every word." He jerked his chin toward Armijo. "After all, the order came from the devil himself."

This seemed a little extreme, even for Kendall, but before I could formulate a response, the air was filled with the sound of bawling oxen. We all turned toward the plaza's southern entrance.

The animals were making a great deal of noise for such a small herd. Widespread horns tossed in the sunlight as they trotted into the square, a handful of Mexican men on horseback riding alongside.

"This is all that remains of our three hundred draft animals," Falconer said quietly. "These eighteen."The little herd moved closer. A cluster of loose mules followed them, then three wagons. Two were schooner types drawn by oxen, while the third was the high-wheeled mule-drawn one we'd used since Texas to convey the sick. Its white canvas cover was tattered and streaked with dirt.

"My old companion," Kendall muttered. "How many weeks did I lay within it while my ankle healed?" He shook his head. "I'm surprised that it's still functional."

Fitzgerald turned to Amos Golpin, who was just behind him and to his right. "Shouldn't you be riding in that?"

Golpin shook his head. "These last few days of no march in' have rested me right up. I'll be walkin' alongside the rest o' you, long as I can. It's my hand that's ruined, not my feet."

"Good man!" Falconer said heartily.

Kendall flexed his ankle as he stared at the cart. "I wonder how long it will be before I'm forced to ride in it."

Golpin glanced at him. "You'll hafta ask the Cap'n for the privilege."

"The captain?"

"Salazar, yes. Anyone wantin' to ride has t' ask his permission."

Kendall sniffed in disgust. I was about to point out that this had been the case under McLeod, when more Mexican men rode into the square. They stopped abruptly, blocking the way south. What I could see of the road beyond was crowded with them. "Militia," Kendall muttered.

I nodded. The newcomers positively bristled with bows, arrows, lances, and muzzle loaders. They sat looking us over until Don Jesús stood in his saddle and bellowed a command that overrode the bawling cattle and milling mules. The men in charge of the animals opened a corridor through the herd, and the newcomers spurred across to us and snapped into formation at our sides and back, three and four men deep.

Fitzgerald looked at them uneasily. "There must be a hundred fifty of them."

"Armed with muzzle loaders," Kendall jeered under his breath. "They're truly not much of a match for Texians."

The rest of us ignored him and watched Don Jesús, who stood in his stirrups, glaring at his men. Finally, he dropped back into the saddle and snapped a salute to Salazar, who turned and saluted the governor. Armijo nodded, wheeled, and disappeared inside, the alcalde and others trailing behind.

The captain gazed at the house for a long moment, then his face changed, hardening, and his shoulders straightened. He wheeled his mount. "¡Vámonos!" he shouted.

"Let's go,'" I translated.

Falconer grinned. "Yes, we've already become well acquainted with the term."

As we shared a companionable chuckle, a young man on a small brown mule trotted up and positioned himself beside the captain. He lifted a shiny but battered trumpet and blasted a series of notes. The guards moved forward, us with them.

We wheeled right and moved around the church, then stopped abruptly. The long lines we'd been standing in needed to break into smaller rows of three or four men each if we were to fit onto the westward road.

Our formation broke down completely while we waited for the men ahead to sort themselves out. The villagers who'd been watching from the plaza's edges took the opportunity to slip into our ranks, the women pressing food into our hands, the men speaking politely into Texian ears.

The man who'd provided us with meat and firewood while we were incarcerated came up to me. "¡Tomás!" I said as we exchanged the customary sideways Mexican hug of greeting or farewell. "Thank you for all your help."

He grinned at me and rubbed his forefinger against his thumb. "You pay well." Then his smile was replaced with a look of warning. "Salazar es un hombre difícil. Se frustra fácilmente."

Salazar hadn't been easy to deal with when he'd captured Kendall, Fitzgerald, and I a month before. "Yes, he does seem easily frustrated," I said.

The shoemaker's young wife came up just then. She nodded in agreement, her eyes searching mine. "Ten cuidado de hacer lo que dice."

I smiled at her. She'd been giving me advice since the day we met. "Yes, I will be careful to do as he says."

I could see from her answering smile that she didn't need this turned into Spanish. She stretched herself up to kiss my cheek. "Dios le guarde." She gave me another long look, then turned and slipped away.

"Ah Van Ness, you devil," Fitzgerald teased. "And her another man's wife."

I touched my cheek, sealing in the kiss. "Mexican girls are the sweetest of all women."

"They're the one redeeming feature in this benighted land," Kendall muttered. "It strains credulity that Armijo didn't release me."

CHAPTER 2
Sunday, October 17, 1841
San Miguel del Bado to Pecos Pueblo

Finally, we were ranged along the road. The guards rode single file on either side while we prisoners took the center, marching steadily north and west, uphill and inland. The rutted track wound around hillsides of craggy red-brown sandstone and resinous pine trees, though we paid little attention to our surroundings.

I walked with Kendall, Falconer, and Cayton Erhard, with Fitzgerald, Anton, Golpin and McAllister behind us. "How far is it to Mexico City from here?" McAllister asked.

"Fifteen hundred miles, more or less," I said.

"And on foot," Kendall said. "My ankle aches at the very thought."

I glanced back at McAllister, who'd been lame since childhood. He gave me a wry smile and gestured toward his walking stick, thicker than most, with a fork on the top that turned it into a kind of crutch. I nodded and focused on the road ahead.

After that, there was little talking. A pall of gloom settled over us. The weather didn't help. It was sunny one moment, then raining the next, wind gusting like fists out of nowhere, pellets of moisture stinging our faces. We kept our heads down and moved steadily forward.

Around noon, the weather settled a little, and Falconer's endless curiosity about the landscape reasserted itself. "The soil here contains a good deal more red coloration than that of the Eastern plains," he noted. He patted the worn blanket folded over his shoulder. "It's darker than this."

"Red as blood," Kendall muttered.

"More orange, I think. I suspect it contains a good deal of iron."

Behind us, Fitzgerald leaned forward and gave Falconer a friendly poke in the shoulder. "You still haven't released yourself from the role of Expedition scientific observer, have you?"

The other man grinned. "I may be a lawyer by profession, but I am a naturalist by inclination. I doubt anything will ever change that." He glanced at Kendall. "This iron-rich soil and its tenacious pines rich with sap show me a rich country, despite its stony outcroppings."

The newsman scowled. "They show me the road Van Ness, Fitzgerald, and I undertook so hopefully only a month ago, when I was certain Governor Armijo would welcome us with open arms and acknowledge the Texas Republic's rightful claim to this country." He launched into a detailed description of our meeting with Armijo below the abandoned Pecos Pueblo, his resplendent uniform and fine blue cloak, the giant mule he'd been riding, the way he'd summarily turned us back to San Miguel, insisting that we return the same day, no matter how far the distance, how tired we were, or how late the hour.

He was elaborating on the slant of the sun when Fitzgerald leaned forward again. "Don't forget to describe your first encounter with a New Mexico donkey," he said.

Falconer looked back questioningly.

"His ankle was aching quite badly. One of the guards offered him a ride."

Kendall sniffed. "For a healthy remuneration, of course."

I chuckled. "You got your money back."

Kendall grinned sheepishly. Falconer turned to him. "Out with it!"

"Don't try your cross-questioning lawyer habits on me," Kendall said a little sulkily. Falconer gave him a friendly smile, and the newsman's expression softened. "Suffice it to say that the donkey believed it most unjust to require him to carry two men simultaneously."

Fitzgerald laughed. "It bucked the guard and him both off! With great enthusiasm!"

Kendall rubbed his rear end. "I felt that experience for quite some time thereafter." He gave Falconer an appraising look. "You truly have become thin as the proverbial rail."

The Englishman's smile thinned. "As I mentioned earlier, the open prairie did not provide us with a great deal to eat. However, I did learn to appreciate snake meat."

Cayton Erhard shuddered. "Und die Eidechse, der Iltis, und der hund."

Falconer grinned at him. "I also expanded my German vocabulary to include lizard, polecat, and dog."

Kendall frowned. "And yet eighteen oxen remained."

"They were all we had to pull the wagons." Falconer made a hopeless gesture. "When the others became too weak to travel, we ate them, right down to their hooves and hides." He shook his head. "It was an unpleasant decision, however, we had nothing else to sustain us."

"Stringy, that fleisch," Cayton said. "Salt none."

"The lack of salt was a real problem," the Englishman agreed. "Without it, we couldn't seem to get full value from the meat." His face changed. "We also saw a great deal of the Kiowa Indians. That is, anyone who strayed from camp searching for food saw them."

"And came back not," Erhard said grimly. "Kiowa there and us, horses none."

I gave him a surprised look. "I had assumed the Mexicans took your mounts when you were captured."

He shook his head. "Kiowa ansturm—" He frowned, searching for the right word, then nodded. "Stampede."

Falconer chuckled. "That stampede was quite a sight to behold." He glanced at me. "This was shortly after you all left us. A small group of Kiowa sent our horses straight through the camp. The animals were positively wild with terror and rampaged everywhere, scattering men, knocking over fires, and generally creating chaos before they took off over the prairie. We lost eighty-three. As a result, almost half our men were reduced to traveling on foot." He shook his head. "It was a difficult time."

Then he turned to Kendall. "And it was made more difficult by the fact that we hadn't heard a word from your own contingent. By mid-September, it seemed certain that you had been captured."

"We had been, in fact. On September 15th, to be precise."

"The same day General McLeod decided to up stakes and go in search of you." Falconer grinned ruefully. "Up stakes. You see, I'm learning American vocabulary." Then he sobered. "That was a difficult trek, with few horses and less food."

Cayton nodded. "And no—" he made a wiping motion over his torso. "Seife?"

"Soap?" I asked. "I have missed soap as well." I ran a hand through my hair. "I would give a great deal for a proper bath."

But Falconer's mind was still on food. "We were soon reduced to eating snakes, lizards, and bugs." He glanced at Erhard. "Not a diet for growing boys."

"Boy I am not!"

"You've certainly comported yourself like a man," Falconer said agreeably. He glanced behind us, where Anton Erhard trudged beside Fitzgerald, his hands tucked inside his coat. Falconer lowered his voice. "Our diet was so thin that some of the men developed scurvy festers and pustules on their hands."

"Light bread only they give at San Miguel," Cayton said gloomily. "One loaf to man." He glared at the nearest guard. "I need fleisch!"

Kendall frowned. "They gave you no meat?"

"We were fed both beef and mutton the day following our capture," Falconer said.

Cayton scowled. "Not enough."

We clearly needed a different topic. "Didn't General McLeod martial a defense against the Mexicans?" I asked.

"Ninety verhungern men, no horses," Erhard said.

Kendall glanced at Falconer. "Verhungern?"

"Starving," he said.

I frowned in confusion. "Ninety men?" I gestured at the column ahead. "Weren't all of these with you?"

Falconer nodded. "We were all together, all approximately one hundred seventy of us." He combed his fingers through his straight, sand-colored beard, then sighed and dropped his hand. "However, when it came time to face the Mexicans, the more urgent dilemma was that many of us no longer had weapons."

Kendall frowned. "Had you run out of ammunition?"

Falconer shook his head. "No, quite remarkably, we did still have some ammunition." His voice slowed, as if reluctant to continue. "Many of the men who'd lost horses were so weakened by the subsequent foot travel that they began to reduce the amount of gear they carried. They discarded their firearms."

I stared at him, then turned away, not wanting him to see the horror in my eyes. A man who discarded his weapon was a man without hope.

Kendall sniffed in disgust. "Guns which are doubtlessly now in the hands of the Kiowa."

Falconer nodded. "That's certainly a logical inference." There was a long silence as we absorbed this idea, then he added, "I believe General McLeod didn't know about the loss until we convened to assess our chances against the Mexican troops who had found us." His fingers went to his beard. "In any case, it's unlikely he could have prevented what had occurred. All discipline had long since fallen away."

"And, as a result, you were forced to surrender."

"There were those who still heartily wished to fight."

"Too weak we were," Cayton said. "Hands and knees for get up from ground.

Falconer nodded at him. "Yes, many of us were quite weak physically. Once down, it was surprisingly difficult to rise easily to a standing position." Then he grimaced. "However, regardless of whether we'd been stronger or had the weapons we needed, General McLeod informed us that he had strict instructions not to fight."

I raised an eyebrow. That's certainly not what I had understood when we left Austin. And, if it was true, why had the Expedition included almost three hundred Texian soldiers and a six-pound cannon?

"In that case, it appears that he didn't have a great many options available to him," Kendall said.

Falconer nodded. "We couldn't simply turn around and return to Austin. As Cayton said, we were entirely too weak, as were our few remaining animals."

"Und Kiowa." Erhard shuddered. "Überwachung."

"Yes, the Kiowa certainly were always watching. We knew they would pounce at the first opportunity. We were too weak, both in men and arms, to defend ourselves from them or anyone else." He gave me a wry look. "Our decision to surrender was made easier by the fact that the Mexican officers were quite polite and assured us we'd be well treated and provided with food. We were so emaciated by then that the promise of sustenance was quite a strong incentive." His face twisted. "They also said any confiscated personal effects would be returned to us as soon as possible."

"Liars," Erhard muttered. "Stolen. Alles."

"Confiscation is the right of the conqueror," I said gently.

"It's the way of the world," Falconer agreed. "Indeed, I believe the men who made the promise did so in good faith, not realizing their orders would be countermanded." His head tilted sideways. "Though I do sorely regret the loss of my telescope and the rocks and mineral samples I had collected since leaving Austin."

Kendall frowned. "The Mexicans took them all?"

Falconer touched the canteen at his side and the blanket on his shoulder. "Everything but our essentials. After we arrived at San Miguel, Governor Armijo distributed our goods to his militia members and their Indian allies."

Kendall nodded. "We saw that from our cell window, with Armijo arrayed in his full uniform and that ridiculous white feather in his ludicrous bicorne hat."

Falconer chuckled. "His Excellency seems to be quite a showy man. One who appreciates both his food and his accouterments."

"He is the governor," I pointed out mildly. "And responsible for the military as well as the administrative side of things. He has a certain position to maintain."

"Spoken like a lawyer," Kendall sniffed. He turned to Falconer. "And your notes? Did they escape confiscation?"

"They did not." Falconer pushed his hair away from his face and tapped his high forehead. "My observations, including distances traveled and the route we took, now reside solely in here." He raked his fingers through his beard again, then gave himself a little shake, stuck his hands in his pockets, and focused ahead on a sandstone boulder the size of a house. A tiny fir tree clung to its side. "However, I do wish I still had a bit of paper and a pencil. I would have liked to capture enough details for a worthwhile report to the Royal Geographical Society when I return home."

"If we return home," Kendall said gloomily.

We walked on in silence. After a while, Falconer began asking Kendall about our capture and subsequent stay in San Miguel. When the newsman described how Salazar had taken his own notes, Falconer nodded sympathetically. This triggered more complaints from Kendall, which ranged from our initial flea-bitten accommodation to the amount of chile in the food, but eventually even his vituperations ran out. The intermittent rains had muddied the road, and the men ahead of us had churned it thoroughly. We had to concentrate to stay upright.

We didn't stop for a midday break. As the hours passed, my stomach began to rumble loud enough to be heard by those near me. Cayton Erhard gave me a sympathetic look, then rubbed his own abdomen. "I hungrig also."

I grinned at him. "My belly does this when I've swallowed too much air. I'll be all right."

Erhard shook his head. "I not." His shoulders drooped. "Most hungrig."

I nodded sympathetically. "I've been sitting in San Miguel eating mutton and beans for a month, while you've been subsisting on snakes and bugs."

He shuddered and turned away, his face suddenly pale. His hand went to his throat. "Sick," he whispered.

This caught the attention of the guard riding on our right. He leaned forward and looked into the boy's face, then straightened and reached back to fumble with the flap on his leather saddle bag.

Worry twisted Erhard's lips. "What doing?" he muttered to me.

This was the first time I'd actually looked at the man on the horse. As I shook my head to tell Erhard I didn't know what he was up to, I continued to watch him. His merry face and sharp eyes seemed familiar.

He drew a piece of bread out of his bag and waved it at Erhard with a questioning look. When the boy nodded, the man tossed him the food, then looked at me and winked mischievously. I grinned, finally recognizing him. It was the guard whose donkey had sent him and Kendall into the dirt.

I glanced at Cayton. The bread had a dark brown crust on all four sides and looked inedible. The boy didn't seem to notice. He jammed one end into his mouth and bit sharply down.

The crust didn't respond. Erhard yanked the bread out of his mouth and looked at it in amazement. His teeth hadn't marked it at all.

"Verdammen!" the boy yelped. He glared at the guard. "Is rock!"

The man on the horse threw his head back, laughing heartily as his mount stepped sideways in response.

Cayton scowled and turned the bread over, studying it. "What is?"

The guard leaned forward. "Galleta."

"It's hard tack," I said. "Try sprinkling it with a little water."

Cayton twisted around to his cousin, who lifted the water gourd he was carrying over his head and handed it forward. Cayton pulled the wooden stopper out with his teeth and carefully dribbled liquid onto the bread as we walked, then returned the stopper to the gourd and the gourd to Anton.

Although the crust hadn't softened much yet, he was now able to nibble along its edges. Then his hunger got the best of him. He crunched noisily down, barely chewing in his haste to fill his belly. The entire piece was gone within a few minutes. He looked hopefully at the guard, who pointedly ignored him, though his eyes were still amused.

Kendall gave the man a hard look. "That was a stony excuse for bread."

Erhard nodded, then shook his head ruefully. "Die Menschen—the people—here so poor. Rich I thought."

I also had been surprised by the apparent poverty of New Mexico's inhabitants, but I felt compelled to ask the question. "Why did you think they would be rich?"

He gave me a surprised look. "Das mines! Gold. Und silber." He shrugged. "None I see. Poor bread only." He shook his head. "Falsch those stories. All falsch."

"That it is a poor country is evidenced by more than the poor bread and the lack of gold and silver," Kendall said. "The weapons they carry are mere bows and arrows. Many of the lances are tipped with some kind of black stone. Most of their guns are ancient, worn-out muskets."

I glanced at the guard. He apparently understood some of what Kendall had said, because when the newsman glanced toward him, the man grinned and shook his lance in his direction. Kendall turned away with a sniff.

"They certainly seem to know how to use the arms they have," Falconer observed.

Kendall snorted impatiently. "If we knew how to get out of these mountains and were assured of food on the return route, we could easily best them and escape."

"Those are two very large ifs," I said drily. He shot me an irritated look.

Cayton had his hands on his stomach again. The hard bread, eaten too quickly, had reached his gut. Our route was more open here, with scrub oak scattered among the rocks beside it. Cayton bent over, grimacing with pain, then jerked upright, looked around wildly, and ducked under the nose of the guard's horse to dash toward a bush.

"¡Oye!" the guard yelped. He spurred forward, easily passing the boy, then wheeled, blocking his way. "No run," he said sternly. "I shoot. En serio."

Beside me, Kendall muttered, "So they do know English."

"Bitte," Erhard said. He gripped his stomach with both hands and bent forward, grimacing. "Bitte."

The guard frowned, not understanding.

I glanced at Falconer.

"He's saying 'Please,'" the British lawyer said.

I moved forward, turning the word into Spanish. The guard's lips twisted in something between amusement and disgust, then he nodded, moved his horse to one side, and waved the boy toward the bushes.

We'd all stopped for this. Now someone behind us yelled impatiently and we moved on. A quarter of an hour later, Erhard returned, the guard riding close behind.

I gave the boy a sympathetic look. "Are you feeling better?"

He nodded, though his thin face was still somewhat drawn.

"I suggest you be more careful after this," Kendall told him. "You would do well to keep in mind that the guards have orders to shoot."

The boy glanced toward the man on the horse. "He freundlich seems."

"He may seem friendly enough at the moment, but it's impossible to predict what he might do on another occasion," Kendall said. "Even if it were possible to make such a forecast with any certainty, another man might not be so sympathetic." He sniffed. "Not that they truly seem like men."

I glanced at the guard, who shot me an irritated look. "As you noted, Kendall, he does understand English," I said quietly. "It might be best to consider your words before you speak them."

He glared at me. "I am an American! I can say what I like!"

Behind me, I heard a smothered laugh. I glanced around. Fitzgerald grinned at me, eyes dancing. My own lips twitched in spite of my concern. Kendall's attitude truly was funny. He was so damnably arrogant, so American. As I faced forward again, I tried to catch Falconer's eye, but his gaze was firmly fixed on the jagged boulders ahead. I could have sworn I saw his lips flicker in amusement before they tightened again.

The sun was well down before we stopped for the night. The western ridges ahead were black outlines against the pink tinge of falling night. We were near the spot where we'd first met Governor Armijo, but I was too tired to care. When the column halted, I didn't even lift my head.

Falconer didn't seem to be as affected by the lack of food and long walk. He moved around Kendall and nudged my shoulder. "Is that a church?" he asked, pointing uphill. "A church, in the middle of this wilderness?"

I looked up. The massive adobe walls and bell towers of the building on the nearest ridge top glowed red gold in the dying light. "We're at old Pecos Pueblo," I said. "There were Indians here at one time."

The Englishman nodded, his eyes fixed on the building. Then the trumpet sounded, signaling the order to move out. Kendall and Erhard groaned simultaneously. "Hungrig," the boy groaned.

But instead of continuing onward, we turned right onto a path that angled upward past the church. "At least we'll get a closer view of that building." Falconer said. He turned to Kendall. "It's made of adobe, isn't it? Is that possible? It's a good deal taller than the single-story buildings of San Miguel."

Kendall shrugged, concentrating on his feet. "Mud. Everything here is mud. Including this path, although it also contains a healthy number of stones, each one determined to complete the destruction of my damaged ankle."

I glanced at him. He really did seem to be in pain. His face was pale under his wavy brown beard. In the row behind us, McAllister leaned heavily on his walking stick, although he appeared less tired than Kendall did.

Fitzgerald moved forward and gave the newsman his arm, helping him up the path. At the summit we found a flattened space, perhaps fifty feet wide and two hundred long, which lay due north and south. At the southern end was the church. Beyond the northern tip were mountains, capped with snow and glowing pink in the fading light. An ice-tinged breeze bit my face and hands. I tucked my fingers under the edge of my blanket roll.

"I wonder how long this has been abandoned," Falconer murmured.

I dropped my gaze to follow his. Thigh-high stone walls crisscrossed the hilltop and formed small enclosures, perhaps ten by ten feet each. At the northern end, a handful of adobe structures still had part of their roofs. The collapsed timbers stuck out at odd angles. As we watched, a guard grabbed a particularly thin one, pulled it out, then proceeded to smash it against the ground, breaking the wood into fire lengths. As he gathered them up and moved off, the timbers he'd left behind settled further inward with a dull thud.

Fitzgerald came up to us. "These rock walls put me in mind of Ireland," he said. Then he chuckled. "That being said, the stones at home are covered with green moss. These appear to be quite dry."

A guard came up the path, motioning at us to move through a gap in the nearest wall. McAllister looked at the space, then the rest of us, shook his head, and moved on up the path. Those of us who remained crowded into the little room, sank to the ground, and looked around.

Falconer reached to touch the nearest stone. "These do seem to be quite dry," he said. "And they are carefully stacked. They should block a sufficient amount of the wind."

A guard peered in at us. "Food?" Cayton Erhard asked plaintively, but the man's face registered only confusion.

"¿Alimento?" I translated.

He made an impatient gesture. "Por la mañana. Para nosotros también."

I turned to the boy. "In the morning. For them also."

"You can be sure Salazar is eating tonight," Kendall grumbled. He stood, pulled his blanket roll from his shoulder, shook it out, draped it over his upper body, then sat back down, his back to the wall. "I very much doubt that I'll be able to sleep tonight."

"We've become soft these last few weeks, with four walls and a roof over our heads," Fitzgerald said. He dropped onto his back. "If we lie flat, the stones will protect us from the worst of the breeze."

"That's a wind, not a breeze," Kendall said. "And it's edged with ice. Even sheep and pigs wouldn't find these rock piles sufficient protection from its bite."

I glanced at Cayton Erhard, whose hands were wrapped around his belly again. "Are you still in pain?"

He nodded, his face a pale wedge in the gathering darkness.

I gestured toward the water gourd beside him. "Drink a little more water."

"Gone," his cousin said from his other side, his voice sharp.

I handed Cayton my canteen. He accepted it gratefully, took a swig, then sank down and covered his face with his blanket.

Falconer was lying nearby, head propped on his elbow. "He's sure to feel better in the morning."

"Only if food," Anton said.

"I wouldn't depend on getting any real sustenance between here and El Paso," Kendall said grimly. "Salazar undoubtedly has every intention of starving us to death." He yanked at the blanket around his shoulders, trying to stretch it down over his legs, then gave up and slumped closer to the ground, his head on a jutting rock.

We all closed our eyes and tried to sleep. Even out of the wind, the air was cold. The periodic sound of the guards calling "¡Centinela, alerta!" was muffled, as if they were also tucked behind the stones and making the best of a bad situation.

I woke to clear daylight and Fitzgerald standing on the wall, admiring the westward view. When I joined him, I saw that the slope on this side was a good deal steeper than the one we'd climbed the night before. Another ridge rose almost immediately to the west. Between them lay a narrow valley filled with golden-leaved cottonwoods. Tendrils of mist filtered upward through their gray branches.

"There must be a river down there," the Anglo-Irishman said. He turned to his right, toward the snow-capped northern mountains. "Be that as it may, I wonder what lies in that direction?"

A passing guard seemed to understand the question, because he paused to say, "La villa real de la Santa Fe de Francisco de Asís." He looked at Fitzgerald, then me, expectantly. When we didn't respond, he shrugged contemptuously and moved on.

Falconer had risen now. He'd heard the guard's response. He lifted a questioning brow in my direction as he came to stand beside us.

"The royal city of the holy faith of Saint Francis of Asisi," I translated. Then I grinned. "More succinctly, the city of Santa Fe, which apparently that particular man considers to be quite an important location."

"Ah, yes. Everything here references the church, does it not?"

"They're all a damnable bunch of papists," Kendall grumbled from his blanket. He lifted himself from his sideways sleeping position and began running his fingers through his hair. "I can't even begin to express what I would give for a haircut and a shave."

I ran my hand over my face. The stubble was more greasy than prickly. "I'd be satisfied with a bowl of warm water to wash in," I said.

Cayton Erhard sat up. "Warm water?" he asked hopefully. When we all chuckled and shook our heads, he lay back down and covered his face again.

CHAPTER 3
Monday, October 18, 1841
Pecos Pueblo to Galisteo

A guard came by, shouting for us all to line up. Cayton sat up and roused his cousin and we all gathered our gear and shuffled out to get into position. The guards directed us to face us away from the road, toward the mountains, then placed themselves beside us, waiting.

"It's too cold to simply stand here," Kendall muttered as he surreptitiously pulled out his watch and began winding it. "Why are they dallying?"

"Hurry up, then wait," Fitzgerald said cheerfully. "No matter what Army you're in, it's always the same."

Kendall sniffed impatiently and tucked his watch back into his pocket. He'd chosen not to roll his blanket and had draped it across his shoulders instead. Now he rearranged its folds, clutched them closer to his chest, and gave Fitzgerald an exasperated look. "We are most certainly not an Army. No, we are prisoners, incarcerated unjustly and sent to an uncertain fate." He jerked his head at the mountain peaks. "Though if Santa Fe is truly as close as I believe it to be, I may very well have the satisfaction of experiencing it after all."

"It's very beautiful," Fitzgerald said.

Kendall frowned. "Santa Fe?"

"This range of mountains." The Anglo-Irishman waved a hand north, then turned to take in the sweep of meadow on our eastern flank, where the guards' mounts and the Texian cattle were being rounded up for the day. A small fire burned in the space between the two supply wagons and the Jersey vehicle. Golpin had apparently returned to using it. He was crouched over the flames, hands out and shoulders hunched against the cold.

High overhead, sandhill cranes flew south in a ragged formation, sending gravelly calls to each other as they went. "It reminds me of the Spanish peaks above the Arga River and the little valleys that run off of it," Fitzgerald said. "They always seemed so wild and yet peaceful."

"I must admit it's very bucolic in a romantic way," Falconer said. "Even here in the mountains, the land seems to go on forever."

Fitzgerald nodded. "As does the sky. Even the constantly re-forming clouds can't diminish its immense clarity. And the shadows the clouds cast on the ground are quite fantastical, the way they turn the land black, then back to sunlight a moment later." He shook his head. "It's a veritable garden of Eden."

Kendall snorted impatiently and turned away. "How did you sleep?" he asked Cayton Erhard. The boy shook his head mournfully and clutched his belly, which seemed to improve Kendall's mood.

Up ahead, the count began and swept over and past us. Captain Salazar appeared, walking along the edge of the column. He was followed by Don Jesús and two guards, each carrying a large basket heaped with rounds of bread.

At the end of each line, the captain paused and turned to the men with the baskets. They handed him the bread, which he tossed to the prisoners. When he reached us, Falconer deftly caught two and handed one to me. Salazar tossed another piece. As Kendall lunged for it, his blanket slipped off one shoulder, and he almost fell. As he righted himself, clutching the food, Salazar chuckled and moved on.

"Bastard!" Kendall muttered.

The captain wheeled and stared at us each in turn, clearly trying to identify who had spoken. I put on my blandest, most lawyerly face, but something in Kendall's expression must have given him away.

Salazar's face twisted with narrow-eyed contempt. His gaze moved on to the rest of us. When it reached me, the irritation returned, then was quickly replaced by something else. Contrition? Calculation?

"Por favor, señor," he said politely. "Dile a tu amigo que sus vidas están en mis manos. Haría bien en recordar esto." Then he turned on his heel and was gone, handing out more food.

Falconer looked at me. "What did he say?"

I glanced at Kendall and away. "He said to please remind my friend that our lives are in his hands."

"And we would do well to remember this," Fitzgerald added.

I nodded. Kendall's breath hissed between his teeth. I didn't want to look at him just yet, so I focused on the Anglo-Irishman instead. "Your Spanish seems to be improving daily."

Fitzgerald's eyes twinkled. "My memory is being refreshed in a unique way." He looked at the loaf of bread

Kendall was holding, then Cayton and Anton Erhard, who were watching hungrily. "Didn't you get anything?"

They shook their heads.

"Here," Falconer said. He broke a section from his and gave it to them. "These are actually quite large."

Cayton nodded his thanks and began stuffing bread into his mouth. Kendall's gaze jerked to the loaf he'd been clutching. He broke it in two and handed the smaller half to Fitzgerald, who bobbed his head in thanks. We were all still chewing when the order came to turn to face the church. The trumpet sounded and we moved out, snaking down the path to the road.

When we reached it, the guard who'd given Cayton Erhard the twice-baked bread trotted up on his horse and settled in beside us. He seemed to be riding as stiffly as we walked. Everyone's muscles were sore from the trek the day before and stiff from the cold ground we'd slept on. When we reached the road and turned west, we found ourselves crossing the river we'd seen from the top of the ridge. Its cold, damp mist swirled around us.

"Maldición!" the guard muttered as he wiped moisture from his face.

I batted at the wisps of air, waving them away. I'd wished for a chance to wash, but now I was glad when the road tilted upward and away from the stream. The climb and the rising sun warmed our muscles nicely.

We hadn't been walking long before we topped another hill and spied a fork in the road ahead.

The guard pointed at the right-hand branch, where the dirt track sloped gently downhill. "Santa Fe ," he said. Then he grinned at Kendall and pointed left, toward another route that twisted upward into a mass of mesas and mountains. "Alburquerque." He seemed to roll the rr's with great satisfaction. "Adónde vamos."

Kendall raised an eyebrow at me.

"Alburquerque," I translated reluctantly. "Where we are going."

"Surely not," he said. "Why not Santa Fe?"

I glanced at the guard, but he shrugged and raised his hands, palms up, to indicate he didn't know.

"Bastards!" Kendall muttered.

Sure enough, as the men ahead reached the fork in the road, they swung left and began moving upward between steep sandstone banks topped with stubby pines.

When we reached the spot ourselves, Falconer inquired about the species of trees.

"Piñon" the guard said. "Good to eat."

Kendall groaned loudly at this information and the man laughed. He looked at me, black eyes twinkling, and pointed to his chest. "I Ramón."

"You know English."

He pinched two fingers together. "Un poco."

"I am George Van Ness."

He laughed. "We say 'hoorhay.'"

I nodded that I knew this pronunciation for my first name, but Kendall scrunched up his nose and looked disgusted. "That's almost as bad as 'heysus' for Jesus."

Behind us, Fitzgerald chuckled. "How were you planning to travel in Mexico as a tourist if you didn't know the language?"

"I would have managed well enough." Kendall rubbed two fingers together in the universal sign for money. "There's always a way if you have the right coin to distribute."

Ramón was watching him with a bemused expression.

Kendall gave him a superior look. "I Kendall."

Fitzgerald grinned at the guard. "Hoorhay Kendall."

Ramón burst into laughter. Kendall scowled at him, then twisted around to glare at Fitzgerald. "He didn't need to know that."

At this, the guard laughed louder. Up ahead, someone bellowed his name and he broke off and raised an arm in response. He gave us a cheerful salute, kicked his horse into motion, and trotted off, disappearing around a curve in the road.

We walked on. After a while, Kendall grew restless and went into newsman mode, mock-interviewing us. "Why did you choose to become members of the illustrious Texas Santa Fe Expedition?" he asked the Erhard cousins.

They exchanged glances. "I orphan," Cayton said with a quiet dignity beyond his years. "Nothing I have."

Anton looked down at the older boy and nodded somberly.

"And you? Kendall asked.

He shrugged. "Poor I am. Only land my parents."

"Your parents only have land, not monetary resources?"

The boy gave him an annoyed look, as if it didn't bear repeating, then nodded reluctantly.

Before Kendall could interrogate them further, Fitzgerald said, "As for myself, I joined for the adventure."

Falconer grinned at him. "I take it the military ruined you for a quiet life."

The Anglo-Irishman chuckled. "I had enough quiet life studying for the ministry in France. That's why I joined General Evans's Legion to support little Queen Isabella. Then, after Spain, I felt the urge to investigate other parts of the globe." Then he sobered. "That being said, I also hoped to ascertain whether the populace here was truly as oppressed as I had been led to believe."

I raised an eyebrow at him. "And what have you concluded?"

He shrugged. "Oppression comes in many guises. For example, in Texas, most people appear to be uniformly oppressed by the desire for wealth and status."

"Just like home," Falconer said.

Fitzgerald chuckled. "Yes, just like England. And France, for that matter. But here in New Mexico, I haven't sensed that anxiety as much." He shrugged. "That being said, I haven't had the opportunity to speak to a wide variety of people, and my Spanish is too poor to allow me to understand the subtleties of any conversation I do have."

"I think you're wrong," Kendall said abruptly, dropping his newsman manner. "The people here are so oppressed by Armijo and the likes of Salazar that they don't know they're oppressed."

I pursed my lips. "Or perhaps it's simply the human condition."

"Oppression?"

"Inequality of one kind or another."

He sniffed. "We Americans are equal."

Falconer gave him a sideways look as he ran his hands through his beard. "Except for your slaves."

"Und men land without," Cayton Erhard said. "Mein Vater—" He looked away, eyes blinking rapidly.

After a few minutes, Fitzgerald leaned toward him. "Is that why your family immigrated to Texas?" he asked gently. "To acquire land and status?"

"Land make equal," Anton said.

Cayton nodded, then frowned. "Until die." He returned his gaze to the rocky slope above the road. A pine tree stretched precariously from a cleft halfway up.

"Be that as it may, you are still here," Kendall said. He swung an arm, taking in the landscape. "When America's manifest destiny is fully exercised, all this land will undoubtedly be open for settlement and young men like you will have unlimited opportunities."

"I'm not sure I'd want this particular section of land," I said drily. "It doesn't appear to be of much use for agriculture or grazing."

"There are almost certainly other resources hidden in these clefts."

Falconer gave him a sharp look. "Is that why you joined the Expedition, Kendall? To look for those other resources?"

"No, no," he said, waving away the suggestion. "I am, after all, a newspaper man. I came looking for a story." He looked around, saw that the nearest guard was well behind us, then said more quietly. "And to report on the lay of the land."

"The lay of the land?"

"Any newspaper in the country—mine included—will tell you that war with Mexico is inevitable. America must, by rights, push ever westward until she reaches the Pacific. Mexico's rotten government has refused to negotiate more peaceful means of acquisition. If she persists in standing between us and our destiny, other measures will be necessary. For those measures to be effective, we must have information. Military capacities, travel routes, fortifications, and so forth." He gave Falconer a sideways look. "Who better to gather those details than a mere tourist?"

"But Texas claims this land."

Kendall nodded. "It does. However, the land Texas claims is actually part of the U.S. not Mexico."

"I've heard that assertion several times since I arrived in Texas, but I still don't understand the reasoning behind the statement."

"When La Salle reached the mouth of the Mississippi River in 1682, he landed on its west bank. Following ancient custom, he raised the French flag and claimed the land for King Louis."

"Louisiana," Fitzgerald said.

Kendall nodded. "And therefore a portion of America's subsequent Louisiana Purchase in 1803."

Falconer gave him a skeptical look. "My understanding is that the southern lands west of the Mississippi had already been claimed by Spain."

"I've examined a copy of a 1740s map which identifies France's New World possessions as extending all the way to the Río Bravo del Norte, the river we know as the Río Grande."

Falconer frowned. "Was this a map created under the auspices of either the French or Spanish government?"

The newsman shrugged. "It's lasted almost a hundred years. It would have doubtlessly fallen by the wayside if there was no truth to it."

"I suspect that argument would not stand in a court of law," Falconer said dryly. He turned to me. "What do you think?"

I grinned at him. "That depends on the location of the court. If it was in Texas or the United States, the idea would probably be accepted without question. If Mexico, perhaps not."

He chuckled and turned back to Kendall. "So you believe war will come."

"Oh, undoubtedly. Texas will inevitably add its star to the American flag." There was a long pause, then. "And you? Why are you here? Wealth? Adventure? Information? Let me guess. To forget a bad love affair?"

The British lawyer smiled. "Any of those reasons will suffice." He nodded at a particularly large sandstone outcropping beside the road. "My interest is primarily geological."

"Although you've lost your collection and your notes," I said sympathetically.

"Unfortunately. However, I do have a trained memory." He tapped the side of his forehead. "As you well know, legal training is composed primarily of memorizing capacious amounts of what appears to be useless bits of information. I am busily emptying those I deem most worthless out of my brain and replacing them with more interesting material." He tilted his head at me. "And you?"

"Me?"

"Why are you here? As I understand it, you and your brother are rising young lawyers in San Antonio. Why would you leave it to join an Expedition to Santa Fe?"

I jerked my chin toward Cayton. "He's not the only person in Texas who believes New Mexico is a land of plenty. The Republic is perennially short on cash. The Expedition was sent out to find a way to acquire both the resources of the mines here and of the Santa Fe Trade." I shrugged. "Texian citizens also often find themselves without coinage. My brother and I had plenty of work, but we received little monetary compensation."

"So here you are."

"So here I am." I grinned at him. "For a lawyer, you do know how to get to the point."

He laughed. "And the same could be said of yourself!"

We went on. The road was dry and we were starting to tire. A fine dust, from the movement of over three hundred men, rose above the road and coated our skins. I used a little of the water in my canteen to rinse my face, but it didn't make much of a difference.

Ramón reappeared in the early afternoon, as we trudged up yet another sandy slope, moving into place beside us just as we topped the hill. I jerked to a stop and stared in wonder.. Below us lay a broad golden plain bisected with red-sided gullies and interrupted by sudden flat-topped hills. The light lay like a blessing on the land, which was dotted with large flocks of sheep. On the western edge of the plain lay a series of small mountains that ran into taller and darker ones to the south. Ramón chuckled in appreciation of my wonder even as he urged me forward.

Kendall, however, was oblivious to our surroundings. In addition to his injured ankle, his feet, softened by four weeks of rest at San Miguel, were swollen and blistered. As we moved downhill toward the plain, he groaned and shook his head. "I've never before fully understood the notion that it was more difficult to walk down than up," he said.

Fitzgerald grinned. "That will be something to tell your readers."

The newsman grimaced. "I would prefer to have never acquired this particular first-hand knowledge."

When the trumpet finally sounded for a short afternoon rest, he immediately sank to the grass beside the road and pulled off his boots, then his socks. "Release!" he moaned. "What a truly glorious sensation!"

I eyed his right ankle. It appeared to be twice the size of the left. "Are you going to be able to get that foot gear back on?"

He shook his head. "I don't plan to even try to do so."

Fitzgerald knelt down beside him. "You have a nasty blister on the outside of your left heel."

"I knew that without looking. It hurts like all creation." Kendall closed his eyes, his mouth twisting. "I should be in Santa Fe right now, resting beside a roaring fire, smoking good

American tobacco, and writing up my adventures. I most definitely should not be sitting on this desolate plain with an injured ankle and blistering soles."

I opened my mouth to remind him that he'd joined the Expedition voluntarily, then thought better of it. I really didn't wish a reiteration of his argument that he was a mere tourist and Armijo and Salazar were both monsters.

We'd all sunk to the ground by now. We leaned back on the grass and closed our eyes.

"Hungrig," Cayton Erhard mumbled, but there was no point in replying to that statement either. When he peeled off his boots, the sock on his right foot was dark with blood.

"When did that occur?" I asked.

He frowned, concentrating on finding the correct English. "Day vor today."

I looked at Falconer. He smiled slightly. "Day before today," he translated.

I swung back to Erhard. "Yesterday? You should have changed to another pair."

"He doesn't have more," Falconer said quietly.

"He could have asked—"

Kendall snorted impatiently. "You truly believe that Salazar cares whether our feet are bleeding?"

I said no more, though I did offer Cayton a little water to dampen his sock so it wouldn't stick quite so quickly to the wound underneath. When the call came to move out, we reluctantly pushed ourselves upward. Kendall pulled on his socks, but didn't replace his boots.

I looked at him doubtfully. "That wool is going to fill with dirt quickly."

He gave me a mulish look. "At this moment, any other condition is preferable to the scrape of leather against my blistered skin." He knotted the laces together and draped them around his neck, boots dangling against his chest. I turned away.

We moved out. We passed several large flocks of sheep, each monitored by one or two men and a couple large dogs, but we saw no other sign of human occupation. Grass seed had drifted across the dirt road with the autumn winds. Within an hour, Kendall was hobbling miserably, barely able to keep up. "Every prickly object on this plain is trying to get into my hosiery," he grumbled.

Salazar trotted past. Kendall gave him a baleful look. "I should be riding that mule."

"Perhaps you can put the boots back on the next time we stop," Fitzgerald suggested.

But we didn't stop. Kendall hobbled along, leaning heavily on his walking stick, which bent dangerously under the pressure. When Fitzgerald offered his arm, he took it, his face white with strain. Even I began to feel sorry for him.

The road moved generally southwest across the plain, crossing wide waterless gullies Ramón called arroyos and skirting small hills. Even with these interruptions, the land seemed enormous. It appeared even broader as the sun began to descend and the resulting purple shadows caught and lengthened each small bush and cluster of grass.

The road now lay along the upper bank of a cottonwood-lined stream Ramón said was the Galisteo River and Kendall derisively called a creek. The little valley it had carved out was so deep that the tops of the trees beside it were level with our feet. Their leaves were turning and glowed golden in the dusk, as if immune to the falling shadows and gathering chill.

Suddenly, another hill loomed ahead, but this one was larger and had buildings on it: flat-roofed houses and a church that bulked firmly against the clear navy blue of the sky. The little river curled around its base, embracing its east and west sides and blocking our way. Light streamed from house windows and we could smell wood fires and the contents of cook pots.

"Food!" Cayton Erhard murmured.

"Shelter!" Kendall breathed.

But no one stirred on the hilltop, and we didn't head toward it. Instead, we turned slightly left toward a sprawling set of well-kept adobe buildings I hadn't noticed until now.

The compound was surrounded by tall brown walls topped with small cactus plants. A massive pair of closed, ornately-carved gates appeared to be the only ingress. Salazar had apparently reached the place well ahead of us. The big Molly mule stood nearby, nosing the grass.

Falconer frowned. "Where are we?"

Ramón looked down at him, his face lined with weariness and dust. "La hacienda del señor Nicolas Pino." He spread a hand, as if introducing the place and the man to us as a unit. "El patrón del pueblo de Galisteo."

"The house of Mr. Nicolas Pino," I translated. "The—" I frowned, not sure what 'patrón' meant. "The owner of the town of Galisteo."

Kendall craned his neck toward the hill. "And that is undoubtedly the town of Galisteo," he scoffed. "A mere hamlet, and not much of one, at that." He shifted his weight from one foot to the other and scowled at the mule and the gates. "It stands to reason that Salazar is already ensconced inside while, after walking all day, we stand here in the dark." He crossed his arms, hugging his boots closer to his chest. "And the cold."

The temperature dropped even further before the big gates swung open and the captain appeared. His eyes drooped wearily as he looked us over. Then he waved a hand at the guards, gesturing toward the side of the compound. "¡Vámonos!" he snapped. "¡Rápidamente!

We moved forward, following the wall to a large space fenced in with piles of thorny brush. Its single gate was so narrow that we were forced to enter single file. Guards stood on either side, counting us off.

The interior was flat, dry dirt. Clusters of round black manure pellets were scattered here and there. Kendall grimaced and poked at one with his stockinged toe.

"Sheep," Falconer said. He turned, studying the brush walls. "This enclosure must be used to keep them safe at night."

Fitzgerald bent down to take a closer look, then straightened. "Definitely sheep," he agreed. "That being said, the pieces are quite dry and have no smell to them. I believe it's been some time since this space has been used for that purpose."

"We're counted off like sheep and forced to bed down surrounded by their dung." Kendall's chin jerked, his mouth more dissatisfied than ever. "I will remember this. The entire United States of America will know what has happened here."

"Where else could they house so many of us?" I asked.

"The brush fence is really rather ingenious," Falconer said. "It's certainly taller than the stone walls we slept behind last night. It will be interesting to ascertain how effective it is against the wind."

Kendall sniffed impatiently and moved toward a guard who'd just arrived with a pot of cooked meal. More appeared, distributing the food into our tin mugs. It was a thicker version of the cornmeal mush we'd become accustomed to at San Miguel, but without miel as a sweetener.

"The syrup they call miel is quite tasty," I told Falconer. "It's a kind of molasses made from corn stalks—" There was a rustle of newcomers and the fragrance of tobacco at the enclosure gate. We turned. It was Don Jesús and a young, prosperous-looking Spanish man, both smoking cigars.

The stranger nodded to us politely. "Señores," he said. "Accept please my apologies por las condiciones primitivas."

We glanced at each other. How to respond?

"General McLeod más cómodo," he continued.

We all stiffened.

"'Más cómodo,' means 'more comfortable,'" I said automatically, though I wasn't really thinking about the words. It was the name that had caught my attention.

And Kendall's as well. "He has seen McLeod and the others?" he asked me.

The man smiled slightly and nodded, not waiting for my translation. "Anoche."

"Last night," I said.

"So they are well," Falconer said.

Kendall frowned. "We don't know that."

"At least they are well on their way," I said. "And apparently they slept inside last night, since their accommodations were more comfortable than ours." I turned to the stranger. "Mil gracias."

He nodded and turned away, Don Jesús trailing behind. We went back to our meal.

"A thousand thanks!" Kendall said indignantly. "What do you have to thank him for? Forcing us to sleep in a sheep fold?"

"For the news."

Kendall sniffed, reattached his tin cup to the thong at his side, and moved off, checking the ground for sheep droppings. When he found a spot that seemed a little clearer than the rest, he dropped cross-legged onto the dirt and began pulling at his socks, trying to locate the grass seed by feel rather than sight.

"If we were inside, I would undoubtedly have firelight to aid me in this task," he muttered. He gave me an impatient look. "A thousand thanks, indeed! At the very least, they could have taken us into the village and housed us in the church. Are we to spend every night from here to Mexico City in the open air?"

"There are a hundred and eighty-seven of us," I pointed out. "Galisteo appears to be quite a small place village. I doubt even the church could hold all of us."

"I'm not a common soldier or a member of the Expedition," he sniffed. "I should be afforded the respect due to a tourist whose report will carry weight back home."

I turned away, pulled my blanket from my shoulder, and began to look for a spot to pass the night.

It was a cold one. The brush fence did keep out the worst of the wind, but we could still feel it. Toward morning, the temperature dropped further. When dawn broke, there was a rim of frost on our blankets and I was glad when the call came to be up and moving. My cravat had worked loose during the night. I tucked it more securely around my throat, thankful for the bit of protection it provided, even though it was now streaked with dust and grit.

CHAPTER 4
Tuesday, October 19 - Wednesday, October 20, 1841
Galisteo to Algodones

We were well on the road again by the time the sun was fully up in the flawlessly blue sky. Although the warmth was welcome, none of us were in good shape. Kendall, his boots back on his feet, limped more than he had the day before. In the row ahead of us, John McAllister leaned on a crutch-shaped walking stick and walked lopsided. At first I thought this was because of his lameness, but when Falconer asked, he said his feet felt like blocks of wood just beginning to thaw.

"Frostbite!" Kendall said triumphantly. "That's undoubtedly what it is! We'll all be losing toes before this is over!"

"I certainly hope not," McAllister said. "I definitely have all mine. They feel like they're on fire."

We were still following the little Galisteo River, which now ran west from the village, its stream bed still well below us, and the road level with the treetops. Their massive gold crowns glittered in the October sun. Beyond them, flocks of sheep grazed peacefully.

"The sheep make it feel like home, but this sky is a far cry from the gray haze of England," Falconer said. He turned to Fitzgerald. "Or the clouds of Ireland."

"True enough," the other man said. "That being said, when the sun comes out there, it is more rare and therefore perhaps more brilliant. And this land can never match the green grass of Ireland."

"I would trade a great deal for a bit of soft green grass under my feet," Kendall moaned.

"The jersey wagon is still rolling," Fitzgerald observed.

Kendall's chin lifted. "Under no circumstances will I beg Salazar for any privilege whatsoever. If my feet were worn to bloody stubs, I would not do so."

"I wonder if there's green grass on the riverbank," I said. "There must be substantial water in that stream, given the size of the trees it's supporting."

"It seems unlikely that there would be grass growing this late in the season," Kendall said. "Be that as it may, I warrant we won't be allowed anywhere near that so-called river."

I refrained from reminding him of this prediction half an hour later, when the road dropped down the sandy slope to the stream under the golden trees. The river was a pretty sight, crystal clear over small rocks, the long green grass on its edges leaning down as if to drink. My own feet suddenly felt the need for a good soak.

Falconer tilted his head back as he walked, examining the big trees. From this angle, they seemed to touch the sky. "They appear to be a kind of poplar," he said. "They're really quite glorious."

"What would be glorious would be to soak my battered ankle," Kendall grumbled. "It's not much of a stream, but not being able to stop and enjoy the little water it contains is unadulterated torture."

It was several more hours before his yearning for a soak was gratified. Our road had continued beside the stream and when we finally stopped, Kendall was the first to its banks. He came back much refreshed. "I feel as if I could walk forever!" he said, lifting his foot and shaking it like a horse testing a new shoe. "In fact, I could walk all the way back to Austin!"

"Now that's the spirit!" Fitzgerald laughed.

Kendall looked down, studying his ankle. The leather below it was rippled and thin. "However, my foot gear would undoubtedly disintegrate completely before I made much progress in that direction," he said ruefully.

Just then, Ramón appeared with a basket of flat barley loaves. "Careful," he said, handing them out.

Cayton Erhard gave him a puzzled look, then bit into his piece and yelped with pain.

"Careful, indeed!" Kendall laughed. "Your teeth are still damaged from that trail bread two days ago!" Then he bit down on his own portion and his amusement became indignation. "This is harder than stone!"

Ramón jerked a chin toward the river. "Se ablandará."

Kendall gave me a questioning look.

"It will soften," I translated. "I think he means we should dip it in water."

The guard nodded. "Agua, sí."

Kendall grimaced. "Dip it in boiling water, you mean. Or boil it all night." He waved his bread in the air. "I say it again, this so-called sustenance is harder than rock!"

"We'll need to refill our water containers anyway," I said.

Kendall frowned. "You persist—" he began.

But just then Salazar stalked by. He clambered up the sandy slope above the river, then turned and stared down at us with an expression somewhere between exhaustion and irritation. After a long moment, he barked an order, and the guards and prisoners strung along the little river valley all turned to face him. He studied us in silence, then suddenly looked down at me and made an imperious motion to join him.

"Careful," Ramón said in a low voice as I brushed past. I scrambled as best I could up the slippery bank and made my way to the captain.

"Vas a interpretar," he snapped.

I nodded obediently, indicating that I was willing to interpret. For a brief moment, his face softened, then he refocused on the men below. His expression hardened and he began speaking in a commanding voice. I did my best to pitch my own so it, too, would carry, and went to work.

General Armijo had ordered him to tie the Texian prisoners up every night, Salazar said. Out of humanity and respect for our weariness he had not done so. However, we seemed to be less weary now. He looked directly at Kendall. If any one of us was foolish enough to go missing despite the strong guard placed over us, the rest of us would be shot.

I stumbled in translating this. Did he mean all of us would die? That seemed hardly feasible. But the men below clearly thought that is what he meant. Kendall's hands were on his hips, his eyes blazing. Everywhere I looked, prisoners stared defiantly up at us, while guards looked away.

Salazar's lips thinned. He sighed, shook his head, and muttered something about the governor's orders, then turned abruptly and walked away, along the top of the bank.

I worked my way back to my friends, where Fitzgerald had turned to Ramón. "Is it true?" he asked.

The guard gave him a quizzical look. The Anglo-Irishman gestured toward the spot where Salazar had made his pronouncement. "Will he do it?"

Ramón grinned and shrugged. He turned to me. "Agua?"

"Water, yes," I said, grateful for a change of subject. "My feet, face, and hands could all use a good wash."

"Ever the practical one," Kendall said, his hands still on his hips. "Like a good lawyer."

I gave him a puzzled look.

"That bastard threatened to shoot us all and you worry about washing your face, as if nothing is amiss!"

"Surely the captain spoke in hyperbole," Falconer said, running his hands through his beard. "Can you seriously entertain the notion of Ramón systematically shooting us one by one?"

Kendall slanted a look at the guard and lowered his voice. "I most certainly can. He has an evil visage and a cruel sense of humor." He tapped the bread in his hand. "The fact that this is unfit for consumption is a mere joke to him." He waved a hand toward Cayton Erhard. "He gave the boy food unfit for a dog, then laughed when it sent him to the bushes!"

"If he'd wanted to shoot someone, he could have done it when Cayton broke out of line," I pointed out.

Falconer nodded. "His decision not to do so certainly indicates a propensity to withhold fire."

Kendall looked from him to me and back again, his lips curling in disgust. "Lawyers! It's of absolutely no use to discuss anything of importance with you!" He shifted his weight, winced, and peered down at his ankle. "I'm going to go soak my feet." He hobbled off, still clutching his bread.

"I think I'll find another section of river in which to do the same," I said. "As well as other parts of my body."

"And I will attempt to find a portion of the stream which hasn't been polluted by the dirt from persons such as yourself." Falconer grinned and made a wry face. He hefted his loaf of bread. "It appears that more than a little moisture will be necessary to render this palatable."

~ ~ ~ ~

In the scramble to leave the next morning, our little group ended up in the front line of the column, directly behind Salazar on Kendall's big mule. He looked grim and tired in the morning light.

"No food this morning," Kendall grumbled as we waited for the rest of the prisoners to be counted. He reached into the pocket where he kept his watch, then eyed Salazar and removed his hand.

The captain had turned and was watching him contemptuously. His mouth twitched with something close to amusement, and he looked at me. "Dile que evitará que escape," he said.

I made a mental note that the captain apparently understood at least some English as I turned to Kendall. "He says to tell you it will keep you from escaping."

"What will keep me from escaping?"

I shrugged. "I presume he means not having any food at the beginning of the day."

Kendall sniffed disparagingly. "Given the state of my feet, it would be impossible for me to run any great distance."

Fitzgerald raised an eyebrow. "The river water didn't revive them after all?"

"They did for the moment, but now blisters have formed. I don't dare remove my stockings for fear of tearing off the skin." The trumpet sounded just then. "Such music!" Kendall said irritably as we moved forward.

Ramón, riding beside us, seemed to find this funny. He gave the newsman a sideways glance and began singing out of tune, "Al eco de mi guitarra voy a entonar yo mis tonos, para echarles sus versitos en este día de matrimonio."

Kendall scowled. He turned to me. "What is he howling about?"

"It seems to be a song, although I agree that his musical talent is somewhat lacking." I wrinkled my forehead, concentrating on the words. "To the echo of my guitar I'm going to sing my tunes," I translated. I gave Ramón a sideways glance, not sure why he'd chosen this particular tune. "To sing you some little verses on this wedding day."

The guard grinned at me mischievously.

Kendall sniffed. "The man is insane!"

Ramón laughed and sang the lines again. And again. He didn't stop until Salazar finally twisted around and gave him a black look. Even then, he shrugged cheerfully and winked at me as he subsided.

The road had climbed up from the river valley and we were alongside the treetops. We'd left the hills behind, moving steadily west through a wide grassland. More mountains lay ahead, a distant blue beyond a long band of golden-leaved cottonwoods that stretched north and south under the brilliant blue of the October sky.

"The trees must mark the course of the Río Grande," Falconer said.

Fitzgerald nodded. "It's quite magnificent, isn't it?"

"The trees are, at any rate," Kendall said. "If the stream that feeds them is anything like this trickle beside us, I don't expect it to be very grand."

Ramón chuckled and looked at me. "Our río he no like?"

I grinned and explained in Spanish that the Río Galisteo wasn't large at all compared to the one in New Orleans, where the newsman lived.

The guard nodded. "El Missipp?"

"The Mississippi, yes."

Ramón shrugged. "Aqua es preciosa, all streams impor tante."

Fitzgerald laughed. "I suppose that when water is precious and all streams important, every creek becomes a river."

When I translated this into Spanish, Ramón grinned and nodded. "Water all year, es un río."

Fitzgerald barked with laughter but Kendall scowled. "These people have no sense of proportion," he grumbled. "Hamlets are towns, mere trickles of water become rivers, and a tourist to Mexico is a Texian Expeditionary soldier."

Falconer's lips quirked. "If you would be so kind as to clarify something for me, I would find it most helpful."

Kendall gave him a sideways glance and nodded.

"The Texian Republic claims its boundaries extend as far as the Río Grande," Falconer said. "If that is the case, am I correct in concluding that you, as a tourist, are technically still in Texas, not Mexico?"

Kendall gave him an impatient look. "Yes, I suppose so."

"That being so, then you are not at this point in time actually a tourist in Mexico."

"I am en route to Mexico!"

I grinned. "Not according to the Mexicans." He threw me a belligerent look.

We topped a small rise and saw a scatter of buildings that appeared to be houses. Women bent over beehive shaped adobe ovens. Men worked with well-groomed horses. Children herded clusters of goats and sheep. Beyond all this, closer to the Río Grande, loomed a fortress-like adobe building two stories high. Our road led directly to its massive double gates, standing open as if in welcome.

"It's a mud castle," Kendall murmured.

I turned to Ramón. "El pueblo de Santo Domingo," he said without waiting for me to ask.

Cayton Erhard frowned. "Pueblo?"

"It means town," Fitzgerald told him.

We passed more houses and through the gates. Inside, a large open space similar to the plaza at San Miguel contained a well head, a row of ovens, and a set of battered wooden stocks. It felt like the interior of a great fort, each side of the square a solid wall two stories high and pierced with small wooden doors, but few windows. Ladders led to the upper levels, where the rooms were set back from the edge, creating a sort of balcony. Another set of massive gates broke the wall opposite where we had entered.

With our guards, we were more than three hundred men, yet we didn't come near to filling the big square. We formed into long rows and stood silently as a stately old man with a brilliantly striped blanket over his shoulders came out to greet us. He carried a set of silver-topped wooden canes, cradling them like a child, but there was no softness in him. His white fur-wrapped braids gleamed in the sun.

Salazar sat on Kendall's mule, waiting. When the old man was close enough, the captain said something in Spanish. I couldn't hear the words, but the tone was demanding. The man with the canes studied him for a long moment, then shook his head, although his expression remained neutral. The two men seemed to have reached a stalemate.

"So they aren't going to feed us?" Kendall muttered. Beside him, Cayton Erhard moaned softly and rubbed his belly.

But then women began to appear, bearing platters heaped with yellow corn-flour tortillas and strips of baked pumpkin. They were followed by young men with baskets filled with ears of dark blue and red-speckled corn. The villagers moved among us, proffering their gifts, and we accepted them gratefully, wrapping tortillas around the squash and eating them on the spot while tucking the corn into our pockets to roast for dinner. All of us except Cayton Erhard, of course, who bit eagerly into his.

"You're going to break a tooth," Kendall said disapprovingly.

The boy smiled and shook his head around a mouthful of maize, juice dribbling down his chin. "Es ist gut!"

As we chuckled at him, our vehicles lumbered into the square. Amos Golpin was driving the jersey wagon, his crippled right hand in his lap. He pulled to a stop and a comely young woman carrying a basket of food moved toward him. As she reached the front wheel, a pustule-covered hand shoved aside the wagon's tattered cover. Ed Griffith's gaunt face appeared.

"He looks worn out," Fitzgerald said.

Falconer nodded. "The wound in his right thigh never did heal properly. I'm glad to see he's received permission to ride. McAllister should be there also. He was lagging behind considerably yesterday."

"He's a stubborn personage," I said. I glanced at Kendall. "And a proud one. I suspect he will find it difficult to request a place in the wagon."

But there was no time for further discussion. The cattle trotted in, then the spare horses and mules. Salazar waved his hand, the trumpet sounded, and we moved out through the southern gates and along the bank of the fabled Río Grande.

"Ah, the western Texian boundary," Falconer said with a twinkle, but Kendall ignored him.

We were perhaps ten rows back now, out of Salazar's direct line of sight, should he chance to look around. Kendall pulled out his watch and wound it carefully while the rest of us craned our necks toward the river.

Our road lay outside the shade of the gray-trunked cottonwoods, but close enough to glimpse the water now and then. The stream was placid in the afternoon sun, the sandy shallows at its edges glinting invitingly. The golden leaves of the trees moved in a breeze I couldn't feel. To our left were fallow fields neatly defined by what appeared to be shallow irrigation ditches. Some contained wheat stubble. In others, broken down cornstalks tangled with dead bean and pumpkin plants.

Kendall sniffed disdainfully. "It's very disorderly."

"Las tres hermanas," Ramón said. "Maíz, frijoles, y calabaza."

"The three sisters," I translated automatically. "Corn, beans, and squash."

Fitzgerald frowned. "How are they sisters?"

Falconer peered at the nearest field. "They appear to be sown and cultivated simultaneously in the same bit of ground. I suspect there's a unique agricultural advantage to planting them in such a distinctive manner."

Ramón cocked an eyebrow at me. When I translated what Falconer had said into Spanish, he nodded like a satisfied teacher, but Kendall shrugged. "The concept of the three sisters is not unique to Mexico. The Natives of Eastern America also grow beans, corn, and squash together in this uncivilized way, and have done so for centuries."

The rest of us ignored him. We passed another field, this one containing a cow chewing what appeared to be a dead corn stalk. She lifted her head and studied us, then returned to her work.

Falconer looked down at his hand, which still held a couple tortillas, and chuckled. "We're all eating the same thing."

"And more tonight." Kendall poked at the ear of red-speckled corn in his pocket, then glanced at Cayton Erhard. "Except for the German boy here, since he's already eaten his portion."

Cayton grimaced. "Hungrig."

Fitzgerald laughed. "What amount of food would be sufficient for you?"

Behind us, Anton Erhard chortled with amusement. "No such." Cayton gave him an annoyed look.

We continued on. More adobe walls appeared in the distance, not quite as tall as those of Santo Domingo, but still massive. As at the previous pueblo, buildings were scattered along the road to its gates, although we didn't see as many people.

"No food?" Cayton asked plaintively.

Fitzgerald nodded toward a small house just ahead. "There seems to be some there."

A young girl, perhaps ten years old, stood in the doorway holding a large wicker tray crowded with bread. The men ahead of us had also seen her. They rushed toward the house and the girl jumped back, dropping the tray. Bread toppled into the dirt. She let out a yelp, ran inside the house, and slammed the door. The prisoners plunged forward, grabbing the food.

Salazar heard the commotion and turned. A short black whip appeared in his hand. "¡Puercos!" he spat, flourishing it. "¡Herejes sin lavar!"

The crack of the whip got the men's attention. They slunk back into line, clutching their booty. Salazar gave them a disgusted look and returned to his position at the head of the column.

As our own line passed the house, I saw the girl peering out of the house's single open-air window. Fitzgerald waved at her and she lifted a hand in return, then disappeared.

"The captain called those men unwashed pigs and heretics," Falconer observed. "However, I suspect their smell probably frightened the poor child more than their religious convictions did."

I glanced at him in surprise. "You're beginning to understand Spanish."

He gave me a small smile. "There has been a certain amount of opportunity and incentive to do so. At any rate, the Spanish "lavar" and "herejes" are clear enough if one has studied much Latin."

"Yes," Fitzgerald said. "The Latin I learned in grammar school has turned out to be far more useful than the Greek and Hebrew I studied at Seminary. I was delighted to realize how it helped me pick up the local language when I was with General Evans in Spain."

Cayton Erhard gave him a puzzled look. "Seminary?"

Fitzgerald nodded. "This was prior to my enlistment in General Evans's Legion."

Kendall laughed. "We have a fighting parson among us!"

Fitzgerald grinned. "That's not quite accurate, although I suppose it is one way of describing my fragmented personality."

Another set of massive wooden gates loomed before us. We entered the expansive plaza of what Ramón told us was the Pueblo of San Felipe. We sank to the ground in clusters in front of the church while Salazar spoke to the headman, who seemed to have been waiting for him. A small boy hovered nearby.

The adobe church was a massive one and Fitzgerald was comparing it favorably to cathedrals in France when our wagons rolled into the square.

They rumbled to a stop and Salazar ordered several bundles removed and opened. The headman studied the contents, then nodded, and said something to the boy, who ran off. A few minutes later the village women appeared and began handing out food, primarily more raw corn.

Kendall looked at his with disgust. "These blue and red grains can't possibly be as healthful as the good yellow of Vermont."

Fitzgerald held his up to the light. "Look how it glows. It's quite beautiful and I'm sure very nutritious."

"Not enough," Cayton Erhard grumbled. He lifted his to his mouth and nibbled at it, then shook his head. "Needs cooked."

Falconer grinned. "Is it as hard as twice-baked trail bread?"

Erhard smiled unwillingly and tucked the corn into his pocket. Just then Salazar's trumpeter trotted up to the church front, sounded his horn, and waved his arms toward the gate on the other side of the plaza.

Cayton groaned, rubbing his belly. "Hungrig!"

But he didn't have long to wait. A few hundred yards outside the walls, we turned into a large mowed field. Small piles of firewood, perhaps twenty feet apart, had been scattered across the expanse.

"Someone was expecting us," I murmured.

Fitzgerald nodded. "They seem to be quite an organized people."

Cayton moved toward the nearest stack, collected a bit of chaff, and went to work with a small sun glass. The wood the Pueblans had left was well dried and his fire was soon hot enough for prisoners and guards alike to roast our corn while the animals rested.

However, we hadn't seen the last of San Felipe. Men appeared from the village, moving quietly among us and speaking politely. Most of us were crouched around the fires, but Kendall had sat flat on the ground and leaned forward to loosen the boot on his right ankle. The worn leather was starting to tear. As he fingered it, a man of middling age paused to watch, then turned and headed back toward the gate.

Fitzgerald chuckled. "It appears that the smell of your feet was more than the man could bear!" he said.

Kendall sniffed. "I doubt yours smell any better."

The Anglo-Irishman nodded cheerfully. "True enough. They're probably much worse."

Our corn was cooked through by the time the villager reappeared. He crouched beside the newsman and held out a pair of high-sided leather moccasins. Kendall eyed him doubtfully, but took the shoes. He turned them over and examined the double-layered rawhide sole and the flap designed to fasten around the wearer's ankle. Then he nodded and looked at me. "Ask him how much."

I turned to the San Felipe man. "¿Cuánto cuesta?" His lips tightened and he shook his head.

I looked at Kendall. "I think you've offended him."

Kendall's brow wrinkled, then cleared. "A gift?"

I looked at the man. "¿Un regalo?"

He smiled and nodded and made a pushing motion at the moccasins as if moving them toward Kendall's chest.

"I— I thank you," Kendall stammered. "Mil gracias." He looked at me. "Is that the correct expression?"

When I nodded, he turned back to the man and said it again. "Mil gracias. A thousand thanks."

The man nodded to him, then the rest of us. He rose to his feet and moved off toward the village. Kendall stared after him for a long moment before he began replacing his foot gear. Once he had the moccasins comfortably adjusted and tied, he looped the laces of his worn-out boots together, stood, and hung them around his neck.

Cayton Erhard gave him a questioning look. "I may have an opportunity further along the road to have these repaired," Kendall told him. "I'm certainly not going to leave them behind for some pickaninny to wear."

Fitzgerald's head snapped toward him, then he seemed to catch himself. He chuckled. "No, we wouldn't want to be as generous to others as our hosts are to us," he said drily.

Kendall glanced at him contemptuously and turned away.

CHAPTER 5
Wednesday, October 20, 1841
Algodones

The trumpet sounded and we moved out, continuing south. The road drifted away from the river, although we could still see its mass of trees beyond the irrigated fields that stretched between us and the stream. There were fields on both sides of the road now, which seemed wider than it had been. Salazar moved up and down the column, although he looked more at the landscape than us. His face was drawn and his chin dark with stubble.

"The captain appears to be as enthusiastic about this journey as we are," Fitzgerald murmured as we watched him go by.

Kendall sniffed. "He's doubtlessly inventing new ways to torture us."

Falconer frowned. "Were you tortured during your time at San Miguel?"

"Only in the sense that we had no real information about where you all were or what would happen next," I said.

"That was excruciating enough," Kendall said. "Especially when there was a strong possibility that 'what could happen next' was our demise."

I made a small gesture, acknowledging his point. We moved steadily on, not stopping again until it was full dark, at a place Ramón called Algodones. The moon was a mere sliver overhead, so it was difficult to make out just how many houses huddled along the road as we passed. Then, finally, there was a muffled command, and the column rippled to a stop. I peered over the heads of the men ahead of me and saw a long low building with adobe walls that curved into the darkness behind it. A much smaller building with a battered door and shutterless window stood off to the right.

Light flared from the larger building as a door opened. A young man looked out. Captain Salazar and Don Jesús swung from their mounts and crossed the porch into the house. The brightness snapped off.

The night seemed blacker now. I was suddenly aware of the cold. It had a dampness to it that I hadn't experienced before in New Mexico. Cayton Erhard had pulled his gray-brown blanket over his head, but his thin form was still shivering. His cousin leaned toward him, as if touching shoulders would generate warmth.

Don Jésus came out of the house and waved an arm toward a nearby newly harvested wheat field, directing us there, then disappeared inside. We eyed the cut stalks in the field, which was bounded by irrigation ditches. Wisps of mist rose from them, white in the night air.

"That looks most unhealthy," Falconer murmured, running his hands through his beard.

"We'll die of the cold and the damp," someone behind us said wearily. It might have been Gates. A man coughed, a long hacking sound, then groaned.

"Surely there's somewhere we can sleep with a roof over our heads," Kendall said. "That open field will send us all to premature graves."

"A fence better," Anton Erhard said, bending closer to his cousin.

I smiled a little, noting that the enclosures at Pecos and the Pino ranch had now become something to wish for. It was all a matter of perspective.

Then Falconer's face appeared beside me, a pale oval split in two by his hawk-like nose. "Van Ness, could you request someplace a bit more salubrious?" Other voices picked up the idea.

"I doubt it will make a difference," I said. "The landowner can only provide what he has available to share."

"Please try, at least."

The cough came again, one of those deep, ragged sounds that tears at the listener's chest. I turned toward the house. Ramón stood nearby, leaning wearily on his upended musket. When I explained my mission, he gave me a doubtful look, but waved me forward.

I stepped onto the porch and paused. I could hear voices inside, and perhaps the sound of glasses clinking. Light traced the edges of the closed shutters. Behind me, the cough echoed again in the night air. I balled my hand into a fist and rapped sharply.

The young man who opened the door looked at me with irritation, but he nodded when I asked for Salazar and disappeared into the room.

Don Jesús came instead. When I explained that we were concerned about the cold and the damp, he looked even more sour than usual. "Malditos tejanos," he muttered. He turned back into the room, leaving me on the threshold. I could see a long table and firelight dancing on stacks of tortillas and pots of beans. The fragrance of cooked pork hung in the air.

Then Don Jesús returned with a short stocky man who carried a large key. I followed them outside to the small building beside the house. The moon gleamed fitfully on its tired adobe, pockmarked door, and unpainted window grill.

The man lifted the wooden bar that secured the door in place and unlocked it. The wood boards creaked in protest as they swung inward. Don Jesús stepped inside, glanced around, nodded, and turned abruptly away, hurrying back to the house.

The man with the key glared after him, then moved off to tell our guards we could use the little building. I slipped inside. The window was perhaps two feet by eighteen inches. On the opposite side of the room was a doorway, the space beyond roughly the same size as the front, perhaps twelve feet by twelve. There was no window here, so it was pitch dark and the dimensions were difficult to gauge, however the entire building didn't seem large enough to accommodate all 187 of us.

I frowned as I moved back to the front room. My fellow Texians were already at the door, pushing their way in, then slowing as more entered and the crowding began. Everyone had left their walking sticks outside, but we still had our cups, water containers, and bedrolls hung about us. These and the smell of unwashed bodies added to the crush.

The crowd pushed farther in, thickening. I found myself perhaps nine feet from the outer door, with Kendall just behind me. His boots were still hanging around his neck. The sides of the soles pressed a groove into the center of my back as breath hissed between his teeth.

Ed Griffith was standing just in front of me and to my left. A final squeeze of people into the room moved him against me, his elbow digging into my ribs. "I do apologize," he said softly. At the door, a guard shouted something in Spanish and then the wooden bolt scraped into place.

"That bolt's on the outside," Kendall said.

There was a pause, then McAllister's voice. "If there's a fire, we're doomed."

Somewhere in the center of the room, there was a chuckle, then Falconer's voice. "I very much doubt there's any true danger of fire. Like most of us, I have flint, but inadequate room to strike a spark even if I could extract it from my pocket."

"No breathe." There was panic in the voice, which had a German accent. Cayton Erhard?

"Relax, friend. Easy does it," a man said soothingly. Clothes rustled. "Can we find a way to ease him a mite toward the window?"

People shifted this way and that, letting the boy pass. Once this was accomplished there was a collective silence, as we did our best to adjust to the situation. However, our combined body heat soon began to make conditions intolerable. In the back room, Curtis Caldwell's thin voice cried, "Let me out!"

"And be shot?" his father rumbled, his annoyance edged with fear.

"Let me out!"

I turned as best I could, searching for a way to ease our discomfort. The moon shed just enough light for me to make out Cayton Erhard at the window, his pale fingers yanking impatiently at the wooden bars. His cousin stood beside him.

Fitzgerald's shoulders filled the space next to Cayton. He bent toward the yard. "¡Nos estamos asfixiando!" he yelled. "We are suffocating!"

My own chest constricted, as if speaking the words made the sensation more real.

Kendall must have felt it to. "I need air," he groaned, trying to elbow me aside.

"We all need air," someone behind him said crossly. "Stop moving, damn you!"

Then Old Paint Caldwell's deep voice bellowed from the back room. "Break down the damn door!"

There was a sudden jerk of activity, as men changed places, then a shuddering sound as one shoulder, then another, hit the thick planks. The door shook but didn't move.

"That damnable bar!" Kendall said. His voice rose. "Savages! Pigs! Locking us up in here so we can smother to death!"

The Erhard boys began pulling on the window bars. "Let us out!" they howled. Other voices joined in, front room and back, becoming a chant. "Let us out! Let us out!"

Suddenly the door swung inward. The ripple effect crowded us even closer together. The breath left my lungs. I felt an irrational urge to slam forward, no matter the consequences. Sweat stung my eyes.

And then space, freedom of movement as men, including Kendall, surged past. I followed them. The air outside was icy, but delicious. I sucked its shards deep into my lungs, arms wide to embrace it.

Salazar stood on the porch, hands on his hips, looking annoyed and amused at the same time. Wordlessly, he waved an arm to the left. I could just make out a low wall behind the house. As we stumbled toward it, a door slammed, then another. A wooden bar scraped into place.

I turned back. Salazar had disappeared. The door to the little building we'd been in was shut tight. The Erhard cousins stared from the window.

"Are you all right?" I called.

Fitzgerald was at my elbow, shivering in the wind. "It will be better for them inside," he said. "Warmer, certainly."

Behind the wooden bars, Cayton nodded in agreement. "Room for sleep."

A guard poked me in the ribs. I lifted my hand to the cousins, then followed Fitzgerald around the house to our new sleeping area, a walled yard between two buildings. Chickens rustled in a small hut to one side and I could just make out a woodpile and a beehive-shaped oven. A cow stirred in one corner and Kendall muttered something about sleeping in a cow pen, but the smell of straw and the faint cedar scent of the stacked wood gave me a deep sense of satisfaction. I dropped onto the ground, wrapped my blanket around me, and sank gratefully to sleep.

Some of the guards had come in with us. They slumped against the walls, arms crossed against the cold, and heads bent to their chests. The calls of "¡Centinela, alerta!" were sporadic and muted that night.

CHAPTER 6
Thursday, October 21, 1841
Algodones to Alameda

When we rose the next morning, I saw that Thomas Gates had been one of those swept outside in the mad rush for air. He stood beside me while we waited to be counted off, his shoulders hunched under his faded brown blanket roll as if he could barely support its weight. When he bent and coughed, the racking, wet sound sent a shiver down my spine.

Fitzgerald, on his other side, gave him a concerned look. "Perhaps you should ride in the sick wagon."

Gates shook his head. "Not as long as I'm able to walk." Behind us, someone else coughed, a dry, hacking sound. He jerked his chin toward it. "I'm as well as the rest of us."

Fitzgerald grinned. "That's not saying a great deal," and Gates laughed, which sent him into another spasm of coughing. The former soldier and I exchanged a grim look.

Ramón came down the line, counting off. He was followed by a young guard, who handed us each an ear of corn, these a soft yellow.

Kendall looked at his with distaste. "Why do they persist in giving us corn fit only for cattle fodder?"

Cayton Erhard held out his hand. "I take."

Kendall handed it over and the boy bit down eagerly. I chuckled. "Your teeth must indeed be exceptionally strong."

Cayton shrugged. "Hungrig," he said with his mouth full.

The trumpet sounded. We headed out, Cayton still chomping. The road here followed a low ridge above the river, high enough that we could see beyond the treetops to the wide, shallow bed. The water glinted in the morning sun, its calm a sharp contrast to the granite mountains that loomed to our left. Their gray, pine-covered sides seemed to rise straight out of the grassland, close enough to touch. The sky was clear, an arc of solid blue.

"In some ways this country reminds me remarkably of Spain," Fitzgerald said. "The flatness, then the mountains, the dryness, the vast sky." He half-turned to study the river. "It is a beautiful place. I can understand why the Texas legislature would want to claim it."

"Have claimed it," Kendall said.

Fitzgerald lifted an eyebrow. "May I remind you that Mexico did not agree to that claim? As a result, it is unlikely to withstand a rebuttal in a court of law."

Kendall shrugged as Fitzgerald laughed. "Spoken like a true lawyer!" he teased.

We were approaching another settlement now, a place of solid adobe homes with small narrow windows that gave them the air of small fortresses. We marched through to more fields, the mountains still along side.

We'd been on the road a good two hours when Salazar called a halt outside a collection of adobe houses Ramón said was the Indian village of Sandia.

The people here seemed to be waiting for us. They spilled out of their flat-roofed houses with baskets of food. This time there was fruit as well as corn: apples and small round melons with thick rinds and juicy red flesh, one for each of us. We stabbed them open with our eating knives, cracking the spheres into jagged chunks and breaking the tender flesh apart with our fingers. It melted on our tongues, the juice running down our hairy chins. I found myself laughing with real delight.

The jersey wagon rolled in. A young woman moved toward it, proffering an especially large melon. When she saw that Golpin had only one functional hand, she sliced the rind open, separated the fruit into thick pieces, and handed them up to him one at a time, waiting until he was ready for the next section. When Griffith looked out, she gave him some as well.

There were cakes too, small and warm from the oven. A gray-haired man in a coarse white cotton shirt came by with a basket of them and stopped to talk.

"You from St. Louee?" he asked me.

I shook my head. "Vermont." I gestured toward Kendall. "He hails from New Orleans."

"I go St. Louee two, three time."

"Ah, did you go as a servant with the merchant trains?" Kendall asked.

"¿Qué?"

"You went with the wagon trains?"

"¡Si! Con los vagones."

"So you know Americans." Kendall leaned toward him. "How do we compare with your Governor Armijo?"

I pulled back and looked around anxiously. A guard moved toward us, a slight frown on his face.

The old man laughed and shook his head. "Americanos," he said. "So certain. Admirable." Then he leaned forward and lowered his voice. "Armijo, not so."

Kendall's eyes brightened. "Does the populace—"

But the guard was upon us. He waved the villager away and snapped "¡Levantaos!" at us.

Kendall looked at me. "Get up," I translated.

The guard gave me an exasperated look and nudged Kendall with his toe. "¡Vámonos!"

The trumpet sounded, reinforcing the command. As we rose unwillingly, the old man thrust more cakes into our hands. We thanked him profusely and hurried into line, this time at the end of the column.

"So the people don't admire Armijo!" Kendall said triumphantly, stuffing food into his pockets. "In fact, they despise him!"

I pursed my lips. "That is not precisely what the man said."

"That's what he meant! I'm certain of it!"

I'd learned long ago not to argue with Kendall when he'd made up his mind about something. I shrugged and nodded to Falconer and Gates as they joined us.

Almost as soon as the column started to move, Gates began coughing again.

"Have your lungs not improved at all?" I asked sympathetically.

"An old lady gave me some tea that tasted like horehound. It helped for a bit."

Kendall eyed the western sky. The sun was moving toward the horizon. "I wish we had stayed the night here," he said. "I would have liked to speak more extensively with that gentleman with the cakes."

Gates nodded. "These Indians seem to be very kind people."

"And some of the women are quite handsome, although a trifle too short and broad for my taste."

I suppressed an exasperated look, turned to gauge our distance from the sick wagon and cattle, and saw Cayton Erhard trudging along carrying a large loaf of bread. Ramón trailed after him on horseback.

An hour or so later, the sun hit the western skyline and turned the eastern mountains a soft red. As I twisted around to admire them, I saw that Cayton was still well behind us. His hands were empty now and his head and shoulders drooped wearily. Ramón remained beside him, his own head dragging. A great weariness came over me. I sighed and faced forward. The men ahead, prisoners and guards alike, also had their heads down. Our feet dragged slowly forward under the darkening sky.

We began to pass occasional buildings surrounded by knee-high adobe walls. A girl about Erhard's age appeared behind one of them. A few minutes later, I heard Ramón laugh and say something in a jesting tone. I looked back. The girl had come out of the yard and was walking beside Cayton, who gave her a sleepy, sideways look and a half smile.

She pushed her long black hair from her face and smiled back at him. Ramón was fully awake now. He laughed approvingly.

Kendall's head came up. He began walking backward, observing the girl and boy. "Say something to her, Erhard!" he called.

Cayton shook his head. "I no español."

"Try!"

Our attention had tied the boy's tongue. I faced forward again. Kendall watched the young couple a little longer, then followed my example. "My ankle aches exceedingly," he grumbled. "These moccasins provide no support whatsoever."

Behind us, Ramón began to sing some kind of love ditty, one that ended in something that translated roughly as "I have nothing more to give you than this dirty belly button." Then he began talking to the girl, calling her "Enamorada" and asking where she lived and how many siblings she had. I couldn't hear her answers.

The guard went on, inquiring whether her parents had found her a novio and, if not, whether they would allow her to marry an americano. Suddenly, he broke into exultant laughter. I glanced back. The girl was holding Erhard's hand. His face was red as a berry, but he didn't pull away.

She stayed with him until we reached our destination, a little hamlet called Alameda. It was now quite dark, the sunset a mere streak of reddish gold along the horizon. Cayton and the girl had joined us now. As we stood waiting to learn where we would sleep, she leaned in, kissed his cheek, then released his hand and slipped away into the shadows.

"De las estrellas del cielo," Ramón crooned after her.

Cayton looked at me questioningly.

"Something about the stars of heaven," I told him.

His face reddened.

Kendall laughed. "She was quite pretty. Delectable, really."

The boy glowered at him.

"How long did she hold your hand? Did you offer her your arm?"

Cayton turned his head, pointedly ignoring both Kendall and Ramón. The column began to move again and we followed, shuffling into a large yard surrounded by a low adobe wall. We found spaces near the center, a couple yards from a big adobe oven with a larger-than-usual opening.

As we unrolled our blankets, Kendall turned to Erhard. "Was her hand calloused or soft?"

Erhard scowled, wrapped himself in his blanket, dropped to the ground, and closed his eyes. Kendall poked at him with a toe, but the boy simply turned over and began to snore ostentatiously.

Kendall laughed, shook his head, and dropped down beside him. Then he sat up with a jerk. "This ground is hard as New England granite and colder than ice!"

"¡Centinela, alerta!" a guard called from the other side of the wall. Kendall groaned and covered his head.

A couple hours later, I startled awake. Kendall was thrashing around, pulling on his blanket and groaning dramatically. "This soil is unconscionably frigid," he muttered. He sat up and looked around. Many of us were huddled next to each other or sharing blankets for the sake of the extra body warmth.

Then his gaze reached the big oven. "I wonder." He stood up and flung his blanket around his shoulders. He maneuvered over to the oven and bent down to reach inside, his hair falling into his face. He pushed at it impatiently and probed further, inserting his whole arm. He frowned, his arm moving sideways, then jerked back, straightened, and put his hands on his hips. He stared at the oven for a long moment, shaking his head, then shrugged and slipped back to his former location.

"What are you doing?" I asked sleepily.

"Trying to find some protection against the ever-falling temperatures," he said as he rearranged his blanket for sleeping. "However, it seems I was preempted." He lay down, squirming into the dirt as if that would make it softer.

I raised my head and wrinkled my forehead at him.

"There are at least two people curled up inside that bit of cover."

I didn't see how this was possible, but I wasn't going to argue. In any case, he was right about how cold it was. The ground seemed to exude a stony chill. Beyond the wall, a guard called "¡Centinela, alerta!" How could they bear it? I pulled my blanket closer, rubbed my nose with my hand, tucked my face into the crook of my arm, and tried to go back to sleep.

CHAPTER 7
Friday, October 22, 1841
Alameda to Alburquerque

The sun rose clear and crisp. Captain Salazar seemed to be in a hurry. He was already in the saddle when we filed out of the yard, and Kendall's big mule moved impatiently as we were counted off. While this was going on, the guards handed out more corn, then the trumpet blew and we moved out.

I and my friends were once again at the end of the column, which made us subject to the dust our comrades kicked up. However, the walk was still a pleasant one. The road lay between fields of recently harvested corn and pumpkin, each tract bounded by well-tended irrigation ditches. Sandhill cranes stalked among the stubble. They were accompanied by flocks of white geese which rose in circles as the men ahead passed, then settled behind us.

Between the fields, buildings clustered behind tall adobe walls. We were admiring the smooth brown of the nearest one when the geese behind us to our left erupted in a great cackling.

We turned to see a man on a tall black horse racing toward us, white and gray birds rising in waves on either side.

When he reached us, he reined in, horse dancing, and lifted his broad-brimmed black hat. "¡Señores!" he cried. "¡Bienven ido a nuevo méxico!"

Everything about the man, from the brilliant green of his velvet trousers, which were slashed to show the white linen beneath, to his snug black jacket, carefully angled hat, and broad smile, bespoke a love of life that brought gladness to my heart. The silver on his high-backed saddle glinted in the morning sun. Even Kendall responded positively as the newcomer greeted us. My lips quirked. It was the first time anyone in New Mexico had called us "gentlemen". Or, for that matter, actually welcomed us.

The man bowed, replaced his hat, and moved on, prancing past our guards, nodding cheerfully to everyone he encountered, and leaving smiles behind. Even Captain Salazar, moving toward us on one of his tours of inspection, brightened when he spied the stranger. He reined in and bowed cordially. The other man doffed his hat and they spoke a few minutes, then parted, Salazar turning back to the front.

The stranger watched him go, then wheeled his horse and danced it toward us. At the end of the column, he whirled again and darted back up the line.

"What a beautiful animal!" Falconer said.

Kendall's mouth pursed. "The entire display is rather ostentatious."

I craned my neck, trying to keep the big black in sight. "The man certainly knows how to ride."

The horse slowed to a mincing walk, tossing its head. Its rider leaned forward and said something to the nearest guard, who turned and gestured to a Texian in a blue coat, a bright red blanket roll over his shoulder. More words were exchanged, then the prisoner stepped out of line to the horse. The rider leaned down, gripped the man's forearm, and swung him effortlessly up behind the saddle.

Then they galloped off, retracing the stranger's route, the prisoner's blanket roll bouncing against his back. Waves of birds flew up, calling raucously. The big black jumped first one irrigation ditch, then another.

"He's helping him escape!" Kendall breathed. He turned, walking backward to keep the horse in sight.

"Who it is?" Cayton Erhard asked.

I frowned. "I believe the Texian prisoner is Lieutenant Hornsby."

"That beast certainly knows how to jump a ditch," Kendall said enviously. He lifted a hand, greeting someone behind us. I turned to follow his gaze. Gates waved at us from the seat of the jersey wagon.

Fitzgerald waved back, frowning a little. "I don't see Griffith."

Falconer gestured ahead of us and to the left. "He's there, see?"

We peered that direction, then realized Falconer was pointing to the side of the column. Griffith was perched on the rump of a guard's mule, clutching the back of the saddle.

Fitzgerald nodded in satisfaction. "That's kind of the guard."

Kendall sniffed. "Griffith undoubtedly paid for the privilege."

Cayton was looking farther ahead, above the column. "What is?" he asked, pointing. The top of a square adobe tower was visible above the trees.

Ramón, riding beside us, studied it for a moment, then said, "La iglesia de San Felipe de Neri." He grinned. "¡Alburquerque!" he said, rolling his r's with relish.

Erhard looked at me.

"Iglesia means church," I told him. "So it's the church of Saint Philip of Neri."

"Who ever or where ever that is," grumbled Kendall.

Fitzgerald chuckled. "It's apparently in Alburquerque."

I looked at Ramón. "How far now?"

He gave me a confused look, then, before I could translate the words into Spanish, his face cleared. "Una legua," he said. Then he shrugged. "Aproximadamente."

"A league," Cayton groaned. "Three miles. Such distance." He rubbed his hips with his hands. "Such aching." He gazed at the distant tower and shook his head.

Ramón gave him a sideways look, half mischief, half serious. "Deberías haberte quedado en Texas."

Erhard looked at me.

"You should have stayed in Texas," I translated.

"We are in Texas," Kendall snapped. "At Velasco, Santa Anna ceded everything east of the Río Grande to Texas."

"As I understand it, he ceded the land that was not south of the Río Grande," Falconer said mildly. "It's not quite the same thing. But that's not truly relevant. After all, the Mexican Congress refused to agree to that boundary line."

Kendall sniffed in irritation. "Well, the United States agreed to it when they recognized Texas as a Republic. If Mexico wants to do business with our people, they will be forced to concede those boundaries and recognize Texian independence. After all, it was never truly theirs to begin with."

There was no point in rehashing this argument. We marched on. The sky was clear, the sun bright, and we were so warm that it was hard to remember the icy ground of the night before.

But we could go only so far on a meal eaten the day before. Even the beauty of our surroundings couldn't sustain us for long and we were beginning to droop again by the time we reached the outskirts of the town.

Then we straightened, almost in spite of ourselves. As we neared the town, people began pouring out of the houses along the road. They stood watching, women swathed in rebozos, only their eyes showing, silent children clinging to their skirts. Men clustered together, studying us gravely.

I braced myself. We were among the Spanish people of New Mexico now, not the Indians of Santo Domingo and the other pueblos. The Indians, suppressed by Armijo and his government, might consider us friends, but the people of Alburquerque had no reason to welcome us. We had, after all, come with guns to force their allegiance to a Republic they knew only as the men who had rebelled against their Central Government. Why should they be pleased to see us?

Then a ripple moved through the crowd. More women appeared. They bore trays of food: corn of all colors, small pumpkins, and loaves of crusty bread. They came straight to us, moving deftly past the guards and mingling with the column as they distributed their largess. This went on for some time. My arms were full by the time we reached the plaza and halted in front of the church. Here more women appeared, bringing tortillas and even eggs.

I had tucked two ears of corn, several chunks of bread, and a boiled egg into my pockets and was contemplating the pumpkin, wondering if it could be eaten raw, when a guard prodded me in the shoulder and gestured for me to follow. I handed the squash to Fitzgerald and stepped out of rank.

The guard led me to a long adobe-brick building on the other side of the square. As we stepped into the shade of its porch, Captain Salazar's tired face appeared at the nearest window. He motioned me inside, where I found Governor Armijo in a high-backed chair by the corner fireplace and looking irritable.

When he spied me, his expression smoothed out. "Ah, señor intérprete," he said. "¿Cómo ha sido tu viaje hasta ahora?" How has your journey been so far?

I glanced at Captain Salazar. There was no point in complaining and, even if I did, it seemed to me that there was little the man could have done differently.

I turned to the governor and told him what they both wanted me to say: we Texians were being treated with dignity and adequately fed and housed.

Armijo's fingers twitched on his legs, his eyes on my face. "Bueno," he said. "Bueno." He turned to Salazar. "Él es sabio."

So he considered me wise. My lips twitched in amusement.

A pretty young girl appeared at an inner door and peered in tentatively. When the governor saw her, he smiled warmly and waved her forward. She crossed to him and took his hand.

"Mi hija Ramona," he told us proudly.

She smiled at us shyly, then bent to whisper something in her father's ear. He chuckled, patted her hand, and nodded. She kissed his cheek, then slipped out of the room and reappeared almost instantly with a large cloth bundle that smelled of fresh bread and cinnamon.

She smiled at Armijo, then moved to me, and gave me a small curtsy as she presented the food. It was difficult to bow with any grace with my hands full, but I did the best I could. She flashed me a smile and slipped across the room and out the door.

Armijo watched her with an indulgent smile, but when he turned back to us his face was stony. "Bueno," he said as if he didn't mean it. He waved a dismissive hand.

Salazar and I bowed and proceeded outside. On the porch, the captain turned to me. "Gracias mi amigo."

I shrugged. "You have many men to feed and no place large enough at night to shelter them all."

He frowned, not understanding. When I turned the words into Spanish, he beamed at me. "¡Tú entiendes!"

I smiled a little guiltily. Yes, I did understand, unfortunately. But I was glad Kendall wasn't nearby to hear what I'd said. He certainly wouldn't agree with what I'd told the captain or the governor.

Salazar turned away and surveyed the plaza and its milling prisoners. He took a deep breath, tightened his jaw, and stepped off the porch to bark an order at the nearest guard. The other man nodded, turned, and bellowed the command to his fellows.

They all roused themselves and began waving us back into formation. I went to find my friends.

When I joined them, Fitzgerald gave me a curious look. "Rumor has it you were taken to see Governor Armijo."

"Yes. He wanted to know how we were being treated." I held out the bundle. "His daughter gave me food."

Cayton Erhard's nose twitched. "Zimt?" He paused, his forehead wrinkled. "Cinn—" He looked at Falconer.

"Cinnamon," the Englishman said. "Yes, it does smell like it."

I chuckled and turned to Fitzgerald. "Did you determine how best to eat the pumpkin?"

"An old woman took pity on me and explained that it should be baked. I suggest you wait until tonight and cover it in hot coals."

"You can bake it for yourself, if you like." I lifted my bundle. "I seem to be well supplied at the moment."

"Zimt," Cayton Erhard said again, rather longingly.

I turned to him. "Didn't anyone give you food?"

"Egg, one. Bread, one. Corn, two." He wrinkled his nose. "Corn hard. Needs cooked."

I stifled an urge to clutch my bundle to my chest. The boy was thin from weeks of travel. Naturally, he was hungry. But then Salazar's trumpeter rode into the square and positioned himself in front of the church steps. "We'll have to wait to see what I was given," I said.

We headed south once again. The houses began to grow farther apart. They were surrounded by low adobe walls, sometimes with children or even adults peering over them.

When this happened, we prisoners would nod politely and keep moving, but one of the yards up ahead seemed to be slowing the entire column.

As we drew nearer, I saw why. A pretty Mexican girl of perhaps fifteen stood on a section of wall balancing a large, perfectly shaped pumpkin on her head. She wasn't wearing a rebozo and her single-layered skirt of red wool and colorfully-embroidered white chemise over well-formed breasts clung nicely to her curves.

"Behold, an excellently formed young woman!" Kendall murmured.

It was her face that held my attention. She seemed completely unaware of the impression she was making. As her gaze flicked from our battered gear to our dirty faces and straggly hair, her expression held only a soft pity. Tears glimmered in her long-lashed dark eyes. She lingered on Curtis Caldwell, just ahead, then came to a full stop at Cayton Erhard's pale hair and thin chest. She lifted the pumpkin from her head and leaned forward, holding it out to him.

Cayton stared at her, confused, and Falconer gave him a little push. "When a girl like that offers, you take it!" he said, laughing.

The boy stumbled forward and clumsily took the pumpkin, nodding his thanks and almost dropping it as he turned back to us. We shuffled on, Kendall turning to watch the girl until we rounded a corner and she disappeared from sight.

"What a most exquisite beauty!" he said. "A most admirable form!" He looked at Erhard. "You are undoubtedly a most fortunate young man!"

Cayton gave him a confused look, then poked a finger at the hard rind. His brow furrowed. "Eat how?"

"Wait until we stop and can build a fire," I advised. "Fitzgerald is going to bake his. He can show you how to deal with yours, too."

Erhard looked doubtful. "Is big. Long time cook." His hands slipped on the smooth skin, trying to find purchase and he bit his chapped lips in concentration.

An hour later, he was still having trouble holding onto the girl's gift. Along this section of road, a series of sandstone blocks the size of a man's head marked either side. Rather than narrow the column to give themselves room, the guards had moved off into the sand and dirt beyond the rocks. As a result, there was no one to intervene when Erhard suddenly made an exasperated sound, darted to the edge of the road, and half-lifted, half-threw the slipping pumpkin against a squared-off stone.

The squash split in two with a wet, hollow sound. Cayton crouched down, plunged his dirty hands into the pulp-filled cavity, and began stuffing the slimy seeds into his mouth. Ramón reined in and watched, his mouth twisting with something between mirth and disgust.

Erhard looked up at him, chewing rapidly, seed pulp sticking to his chin. He gestured wildly at the remaining pumpkin, in a mute request to be allowed to eat. The guard chuckled, made a hopeless gesture, then nodded at the boy and motioned for the rest of us to go on.

When they finally rejoined us, Kendall shook his head at Erhard. "It is difficult for me to comprehend how you could be so ungrateful to that beautiful girl that you would throw a gift from her to the ground and eat it uncooked."

Erhard scowled at him. "Hungrig." He rubbed his belly and looked at my bundle of food. "Still hungrig."

Ramón's saddle creaked as he stood up in the stirrups and studied the head of the column. "Stop soon." He looked at the boy. "Maybe kill un buey."

Cayton looked at me questioningly.

"An ox," I said. "He seems to think the captain will order one to be slaughtered."

"We do still have all eighteen of them," Kendall said. Then his face changed, became suspicious. "It is somewhat puzzling that Salazar hasn't yet ordered any to be butchered."

"He hasn't needed to," Fitzgerald said. "The people of the towns have been feeding us quite well."

Falconer nodded. "Yes, and we all seem to be better for it. Despite all the walking we've done, I feel much healthier than I did when we were first captured."

Curtis Caldwell twisted toward us. "My father says we're getting strong enough to make a break for it."

I glanced at Ramón, who was studiously ignoring our conversation. The man seemed friendly enough, but he was still our guard. "Careful," I muttered.

The boy gave me a surprised look, then followed my gaze. He shrugged. "They can't speak English."

"This one can. Somewhat."

"They couldn't do anything anyway, if we all set on them at once."

I frowned and he subsided, but what he and Falconer had said prompted me to examine my fellow prisoners more closely. Except for Cayton Erhard, we all did seem more lively. Our shoulders were straighter, our heads higher. I grinned, remembering Captain Salazar's comment that keeping us hungry would make us less likely to try to escape. If he'd truly intended to deprive us of food, he hadn't achieved his goal.

He'd clearly paid for our provisions at San Felipe and perhaps the other pueblos, although the bread and other things at Alburquerque seemed to have been gifts. I wondered how long the people here could continue to share or sell us food before their own winter stores were diminished to the danger point. Their cornfields weren't infinite. Nor were the pumpkin plots, for that matter. I eyed the nearest tilled lot. The precision of the irrigation trenches along its edges were an engineer's delight.

Falconer's gaze followed mine. "It's a truly remarkable land," he said. "The potential agricultural output must be substantial."

Kendall looked up. "These particular fields are certainly well cared for, which implies that there are at least some people here who know how to work."

"What makes you think some of them don't?" I asked, trying to keep the irritation out of my voice.

Cayton Erhard gave me a puzzled look. "Poor they are."

"They live in mud houses with little or no furniture," Kendall said. "And their women have so little clothing that they wear their chemises out of doors."

Falconer nodded. "They do appear to own a minimum number of garments."

I frowned. "Perhaps they don't need more. They certainly don't hold back on their gifts of food." I shifted my bundle and sniffed appreciatively. "Cinnamon must be expensive here, and hard to come by."

"True enough," Fitzgerald said. He grinned at Kendall. "And they haven't plagued us with chiles."

Kendall frowned. "I know you thought I was terribly gauche to complain so vociferously about the amount of chile in the food at San Miguel, but you must admit it was ubiquitous there and it is definitively unkind to my American stomach."

I shook my head at this burst of newspaper hyperbole but kept quiet. After all, it was a sign that Kendall was also feeling more energetic as the result of our recent increase in calories. The more energy he had, the more he talked and the longer his words became. He was constitutionally unable to do otherwise.

We walked on. A flock of sandhill cranes rose from the river, circling over the fields and calling to each other with low, throaty cries. They settled into the stubble, but well out of our reach, moving casually away as we came closer without turning their small red-tufted heads to directly acknowledge our existence.

Kendall studied them as we passed. "The people here don't seem to hunt the meat Providence provides for them," he said. "Not even the flocks that raid their fields." He sniffed. "One imagines that the farmers would make every effort to protect what little they possess, but I have seen no evidence to support that supposition. It is quite clear to me that they are unwilling or perhaps constitutionally unable to take full advantage of this land and its capacities."

"They don't have many iron tools or guns," I pointed out.

He ignored me and turned to study the landscape east of us, where crops gave way to a grassy plain that sloped gently upward to a string of pine-covered mountains. Flocks of sheep scattered the land. "I wonder how difficult it would be to get through that row of peaks."

Cayton Erhard glanced nervously toward Ramón. "He will hear."

Kendall sniffed. "I doubt he knows enough English to be able to follow my train of thought." He shook his head. "I find it exceedingly difficult to understand how so very few of the populace here speak English. After all, American merchants have been visiting and even living among them these past twenty years."

"Perhaps the merchants found it more convenient to learn the language of the country," Fitzgerald said drily.

"Hungrig," Erhard said. He looked meaningfully at my bundle. When I didn't respond, he turned to Ramón and rubbed his stomach. The guard laughed and made a gesture as if he was throwing something on the ground, then gobbling it with both hands.

"I think he's reminding you that you had a pumpkin and wasted it," I said.

Cayton scowled. "Ate most. Long time past."

"You did eat most of it and that was hours ago," Fitzgerald agreed gently. "I'm hungry myself." He glanced toward the western horizon. The sun was perhaps a hand's width from its edge. "The sun is beginning to set. If Ramón is correct, we'll be stopping soon."

Kendall sniffed. "I doubt it will be soon enough for a beef to be slaughtered."

CHAPTER 8
Friday, October 22, 1841
Los Placeres

Perhaps thirty minutes later, the order came to halt. We had reached a small rancho Ramón told us was called Los Placeres. We milled around in the stubble of a harvested wheat field while the horses, mules, and oxen were turned into an adjacent green pasture.

"There's still time to do some butchering, if they're quick about it," Kendall said hopefully, studying the animals.

Fitzgerald hefted his pumpkin. "In the meantime, thanks to Van Ness's generosity, I plan to cook a squash." He moved off, looking for the makings of a fire.

In spite of the food we'd been given earlier, I found that I was hungry also. I crouched down to untie my gift from Armijo's daughter. Cayton Erhard hovered nearby.

Inside the cloth were two loaves of soft bread and a dozen or so cake-like cookies dusted with cinnamon. Anton huffed with disappointment and, ungrateful wretch that I am, I was inclined to agree with him. I had hoped for some meat or at least hard-boiled eggs.

"Ah, bizcochitos," a voice said from above my head.

I looked up. Salazar stood, hands behind his back, watching me. I scrambled to my feet and proffered the bundle. He took a cookie, nodded his thanks, and asked me how I did.

"Bueno," I replied. Then I patted my stomach and pulled an apologetic face. "Estoy hambriento."

He grimaced, clearly not wanting to hear about my hunger, and turned away. Kendall stood directly behind him. The captain's face hardened.

"When are we going to get some real food?" Kendall demanded, hands on his hips. "We are starving!"

Salazar's eyes flashed, then he moved his shoulders, as if calming himself, and turned to me. "Interpreta, por favor."

I tried to soften Kendall's words in translation, but I couldn't gentle his tone or stance. Salazar stared into Kendall's face as I spoke, then waved a hand at my bundle. "¡El pasto es excelente!"

Kendall gave me a puzzled look. "Pasture? For food?" He looked past me at the grazing animals, their muzzles deep in the grass. His eyes blazed. "Like cattle?"

I lifted my bundle slightly. "I believe he's referring to the food we were given earlier today."

Kendall ignored me and glared at Salazar. "You gave us only corn! Maíz!" He waved a finger in the air. "One maíz ! Only one!"

The captain didn't need a translation for this. He waved a hand, taking in the Texians scattered around the camp. Many had pulled the corn given them in Alburquerque out of their pockets and were hunched in small groups, nibbling it raw. Only Fitzgerald had made the effort to find wood for a fire.

Salazar's lip curled. "¡Comen como los lobos!" he sneered. He waved a disgusted hand and walked away muttering "¡Puercos! ¡Salvajes!"

Kendall's moccasins scuffed at the dirt. "How dare he refer to us as hogs and wolves!" he fumed. "Does he think I have no power, that he can insult me in such a way? I will remember those words and that tone!" Then his head swiveled and his spine stiffened. "What in creation is this? Have the locals come to gawk at us in our misery?"

I turned. A plump middle-aged woman with a kind face stood perhaps twenty feet away, watching us. Two round-faced girls stood beside her, each carrying a perfectly round pale-green melon. Their blue rebozos had slipped from their heads and framed glossy, red-tinted curls.

Kendall pushed his dirty hair from his face. "The fruit of the land," he muttered. "Although somewhat plump for my taste."

The newcomers moved toward us, the woman looking around the camp, the girls intent on not dropping their gifts. As the younger one handed her melon to me, Cayton Erhard moved forward, but Kendall was already reaching for the other one, muttering "Mil gracias."

The German boy looked at the fruit hungrily, then turned away with drooping shoulders. The woman put her hand out, touching his arm. "Espere por favor," she said gently.

He glanced at me.

"Please wait," I translated.

He nodded, looking confused but pleased by the attention. She turned to the nearest guard and said something in a rapid Spanish I couldn't follow. He listened politely, then nodded and moved off in the direction Salazar had taken.

A few minutes later, the sergeant of the guard came up, his fingers drumming lightly on the Spanish pistol in his waistband. Anton Erhard, Curtis Caldwell, and a couple other boys trailed after him. "El capitán está de acuerdo," the sergeant told the woman.

Cayton looked at me.

"The captain agrees," I translated. I frowned. "Although I'm not sure what it is he's agreed to."

The sergeant pointed at me. "Y tú también."

"And me also," I said. I must have looked confused, because the woman chuckled and leaned toward me to explain. I was to go with her and the five boys to her home, which was nearby, to have a proper meal. The sergeant would accompany us. As she spoke, her gaze roved the camp. Fitzgerald's was still the only fire. The smell of slightly burnt pumpkin drifted toward us and she wrinkled her nose.

I thanked her, then turned to Kendall, explained what was happening, and said he and Falconer could have the bread and cookies in my bundle. He nodded unhappily and stood watching as I, the boys, and the sergeant followed the lady and her daughters out of the field. As we reached the road, we passed Ramón. He smiled when he saw me and patted his stomach meaningfully, as if congratulating me on my good fortune.

The woman's house was a good half-mile further on, but the boys didn't seem to mind. Even Cayton moved cheerfully now that there was the prospect of home-cooked food. Only the sergeant was irritable.

The girls chatted softly with each other and smiled and spoke flirtatiously to the boys, trying to coax responses. Their mother glanced at them benevolently, then turned to me and asked where I was from, how I liked New Mexico, and what I did for a living. When I told her I was a lawyer, she laughed out loud. "¡Cuando toma cuerpo, el diablo se disfraza de abogado!" she said.

"When the devil assumes human form, he disguises himself as a lawyer?" I laughed right back at her. "I'm glad that you realize he's not always disguised as a Texian!"

She gave me a puzzled look, but when I translated the words into Spanish she clapped her hands and laughed again. The sergeant, trudging beside me, scowled malevolently, but we both ignored him.

The woman's home was quite large and surrounded by the usual adobe wall. She ushered us into the courtyard, then she and her daughters disappeared inside. The sergeant studied the enclosure suspiciously, then moved to the gate and stood beside it, hand on his pistol.

I and the boys took the liberty of extracting fat pieces of cedar from the well-built woodpile along one wall and upending them to serve as seats. We started to rise when the woman and girls reappeared with food, but she shook her head and told us to please remain where we were. When we and the sergeant had been served, the women settled themselves on a simple wooden bench beside the house door and watched us eat.

Their presence seemed to relax our guard, because he now moved away from the gate and crouched next to the bench to engage our hostess in conversation. I was too far away to hear everything he said, but he seemed to be describing the capture of the various groups of Texians as if he'd been present at each event. I didn't recall seeing him when Kendall, Fitzgerald, and I were rounded up. It was possible that he was there when the others were, but I doubted it.

The woman didn't appear skeptical about what she was hearing, although she didn't seem enthusiastic either. When the sergeant paused to take a breath, she nodded toward the boys and said something sympathetic, noting how ragged they were. She followed this with a reference to her own sons, which seemed to annoy the sergeant. He hastened to assure her that we were ill-bred as well as being a bunch of heretics and rebels.

At this, Cayton Erhard's head went up. He'd learned enough Spanish by now to understand the gist of what the man said. He glared furiously at the guard and was still scowling when we left. As we walked back to camp, he drew up beside me. "I well bred!" he hissed at me. "I not rebel! Texas is Re—" He frowned, searching for the right word. "Republik."

"That's right," I said. "It declared itself a Republic in 1836. I believe that happened before you arrived."

He nodded. "We come two year." His face dropped and he looked away.

So, 1839. And then both his parents died. I studied him, trying to decide whether to express sympathy for his orphaned state, then decided against it. "Mexico has never acknowledged Texas as a separate country," I said.

"England und Amerika do. Herr Kendall say it."

I nodded. "Yes, England and America have acknowledged Texian independence. However, Mexico continues to assert that Texas is simply in rebellion against the central government."

"Herr Kendall say land here Texas." He looked away again. "Meine familie to Texas for land frei."

"Land is never truly free. Someone has always laid claim to it. Before the Mexicans, the Indians."

He grinned. "After Mexicans, die Texianer."

I glanced at the sergeant, who was giving me irritated sideways glances. Just how much did he understand?

"Texas go to Amerika?" Cayton asked.

I slid another glance toward the sergeant. He was now focused on Curtis and one of the other boys, who were rough housing. "Yes, it's possible Texas will become part of the United States. Some people were advocating for Texas to join the Union even before it broke away from Mexico."

He grinned and waved his hand at the landscape around us. "After Texians, die Amerikaner. Und Kalifornien."

I glanced at the guard. "No one can tell the future."

Erhard nodded. Then he chuckled and patted his belly. "For now, full."

I laughed. "You wouldn't have expected that three hours ago, would you? You never know what might happen next."

As we swung off the road into camp, the man who'd kidnapped Lieutenant Hornsby rode in, the lieutenant behind his tall saddle. Hornsby slid off and bowed politely to his captor, who lifted his wide-brimmed hat, swung it in a gesture that seemed to encompass us all, then turned and galloped back toward Alburquerque.

The lieutenant watched until he disappeared from sight, then turned toward us with a chagrined expression. He held out his hands, motioning toward his clothes. His fine blue military jacket and brass buttons had been replaced with a thick weather-beaten wool coat that barely fastened across his chest. When he reached to adjust the blanket roll on his shoulder, I realized it also was different. Instead of a bright red, the wool was now a coarsely woven brown and yellow. Only his hat remained the same.

Kendall moved toward him, laughing. "Hornsby!" he cried. "You've returned to us looking for all the world like a Mexican!" Then he sobered. "What happened?"

The lieutenant shook his head. "I thought he was offering me a ride into Alburquerque, which was most kind of him. I was quite startled when I saw that we were traveling away from the road and to the northeast."

"And undoubtedly dismayed!"

The lieutenant nodded. "However, after we'd ridden a good distance, we arrived at his home. The place was quite luxurious by Mexican standards. The main room had a large mirror and several paintings."

Kendall sniffed derisively, but Hornsby shook his head. "These were real pieces of art, not cheap prints. My host ordered the servant to bring water and it arrived in a massive silver pitcher. We drank it from tumblers of beautifully cut glass." He looked around at us. "I wish you could have seen it. Not everyone in this benighted land is as poor as it appears." Then he grinned. "Although the water was refreshing, the brandy was even more so."

"Lucky dog!" Falconer laughed.

"And his wife is a pretty thing who knows how to feed a man." The lieutenant shook his head. "That was quite a breakfast. Eggs. Cheese. Beans. Warm bread." He grinned at Kendall. "Meat in a chile sauce. I haven't eaten that well since we left Austin. And there was so much of it!" He patted his belly with an air of satisfaction.

"And then?" Fitzgerald asked.

"After breakfast, my host broke out the cigars." Hornsby grimaced. "And then I learned the price of his hospitality." He gestured toward his coat. "He brought this out. He wanted to exchange it for mine. Even though he spoke no English and I have hardly any Spanish, we managed to make ourselves understood. I tried to convince him his coat wouldn't fit me and I didn't want to trade, but he was adamant. His wife attempted to stop him, but he started waving this in my face and pulling on mine, undoing the buttons. What could I do? After all, he'd given me breakfast and brandy."

"You could have simply walked out," Kendall said.

"And where would I have gone? I didn't know where I was and I didn't have a horse. He would have caught me within minutes. He seemed well disposed toward me, but how would he react if I ran away?" Hornsby shrugged. "In the end, I gave him my coat and took this in its place." He touched the cloth. "It's very rough, compared to what I had."

"And he took your blanket, too?" Franz Ernest asked, hunching his shoulders together as if the very thought made him cold.

"He did." Hornsby touched the coarse roll on his shoulder and grimaced. "This is heavy and scratchy, compared to my red one. I can't imagine what it's going to be like to sleep in it."

"You may find it's more comfortable than you think," I said. "It looks thicker than yours."

The lieutenant frowned and shrugged. "When we'd completed our trade, my host said '¡Vámonos!' just like that. I knew what that meant, of course. But I was irritated by then, I can tell you. I wasn't going just because he said to. So I crossed to the sideboard where he kept his brandy and poured myself a stiff drink. I saluted him and tossed it off and only then left the house. We mounted the horse and his wife handed me the blanket—" He tucked his hand into a fold. "She seemed a kind soul, and I've been smelling something like meat all the way here—" He pulled out a small cloth-wrapped packet and opened it carefully.

"Fleisch?" Cayton Erhard asked.

We all laughed.

"Yes, it's meat," Hornsby said. "Dried for the trail." He reached into the bedroll again. "Here's another packet, as well. Also—" He dug into his trouser pocket. "She gave me money."

"The women here are the kindest I have ever met," Kendall said.

Hornsby nodded, a soft smile on his face. Then he looked at us again. "Then we galloped back to the road and followed it until we found you."

Kendall shook his head. "And all this time we thought you'd escaped to Texas. Instead, you reappear with a too-small coat and a too-rough blanket."

"But a full meal and brandy," Fitzgerald said.

"True," the lieutenant said.

Kendall sniffed. "That's well for you, because we've had nothing this night. Salazar believes we should accommodate ourselves to eating grass."

Hornsby's eyebrows rose. "Grass?"

"That is indeed what he said." Kendall began a detailed description of his interaction with the captain, but broke it off when there was movement in the neighboring pasture. A guard drove in a good half-dozen healthy mules and several service-able horses.

Falconer looked them over appraisingly. "Those are quite decent animals. I wonder where they came from."

"They are undoubtedly stolen," Kendall said. "You have only to consider the weapons our guards carry to conclude that they are far too poor to purchase animals of any quality."

"Perhaps the men have family or friends who have lent them mounts for the journey," I said.

He gave me an irritated look. "Lawyers! It is impossible for you to contemplate the idea that not every argument has two sides to it."

As he stalked off, Falconer chuckled. "Actually, every argument does have two sides. Although, as with coins, one may be more worn than the other."

I grinned at him. "My opinion exactly. But then, we lawyers must hang together."

He looked at me, mouth grave, eyes twinkling "Please accept my sincerest apologies, but I'm not sure I want to hang with you or anyone else. Especially if I'm to be killed for my lawyerly learning, as Shakespeare's conspirators proposed."

I laughed. "I heartily agree with you!" We moved off to locate our sleeping spots, although the sun was just setting. We'd all learned that even the slightest indentation in the ground could protect a sleeper from "the icy breath of the night breezes," as Kendall liked to put it, so it paid to claim our bits of earth as early as possible.

CHAPTER 9
Saturday, October 23, 1841
Los Placeres to Valencia

Once again, the night was cold and long. We slept back to back, or even two men sharing, one blanket above and the other on the ground, doing all we could to conserve our body warmth. Kendall and Fitzgerald lay huddled together, while Falconer and I slept back to back.

When the trumpet sounded the next morning, we set off once again. My friends and I were near the head of the column this time, within sight of Salazar on Kendall's block-headed chestnut Molly. Every few minutes, the captain would look back to make sure we were all still in place.

I rubbed my belly. Even after the Señora's filling meal, my stomach wanted more. And I'd been ensconced in San Miguel for the past month with plenty of food. The men who'd been out on the plains during that time must still be feeling seriously underfed.

The thought didn't keep my stomach from grumbling. It was time to direct my attention elsewhere. I focused on the expanse of golden trees to our right. The country here was truly beautiful. It was well wooded and scattered with settlements that I found quite attractive, even if they didn't measure up to Kendall's American standards.

Our route dropped slightly to pass through a series of fields that contained neat rows of apple trees. Two enterprising

Mexicans had stationed themselves on the verge with baskets heaped with fruit. When Kendall surged toward them with his hand out, they rubbed their fingers together, indicating they wanted payment. He sniffed and moved back into line. I felt for the coins in my pocket, but the captain was turning again, checking on us, and I thought it best not to stop.

However, someone behind me took the chance. A nasal voice asked, "How much?" and a seller responded, "Dos centavos". Two cents seemed rather a lot for a piece of fruit. I was glad I hadn't given in to temptation. However, others weren't as stingy. The men behind us hung back to dicker. A voice I was sure was Cayton Erhard's offered a button from his coat and one of the sellers agreed.

But they had paused too long. A gap was forming. Up ahead, Salazar reined the mule around, saw the men and apples, and reached for his sword. "¡Vuelvan a la fila!" he yelled.

Falconer glanced at me. "Get back in line," I translated.

The captain moved toward the apple sellers, spurring the mule into a gallop and pulling out his sword. The men with the fruit moved quickly out of the way, but the prisoners stood and stared. He waved his sword in the air and swung it in Cayton's direction as the boy ducked into the ranks, clutching his purchase.

"¡Vuelvan a la fila!" Salazar yelled again. He wheeled the mule in a circle, lips tight with anger. Then he saw me. "¡Cuént ales!" he bellowed. "¡Díselo ahora o te juro que los mataré!"

I cupped my hands around my mouth. "Get back in line!" I yelled. "Do it now!" There was no need to repeat that he'd kill them if they didn't. I didn't believe he meant it and saw no reason to ruffle Texian feathers.

The men shuffled back into formation and we moved on.

I dropped back a little, letting Kendall and Fitzgerald go ahead, and found Cayton Erhard making a face as he bit into his fruit. "Deutscher is not," he said.

"Not a Dutch apple?" I asked. "Do you mean not German?"

He nodded and took another bite. He chewed unhappily. "No sweet." He looked discontentedly at what was left. "No juice full."

I was about to question him further when a guard behind us muttered, "¡Maldición!"

I looked back. Felix Ernest grinned at me sheepishly as he fumbled with the two buttons that remained on his drop front trousers. There was only one on each side now, at the very top, instead of the usual row of six.

"One button buys two pieces o' fruit," he explained. He looked down at his tattered shoes. The soles flopped from the sides with every step ."If these was any good, I'd trade 'em, too."

As I laughed and shook my head, the guard who'd sworn at him rode off the road to a small screw bean mesquite bush. He leaned down, broke two long narrow thorns from the top branch, then rode back and handed them to Ernest.

The Tennessean examined the sharp tips, then slowed down to bend forward and work the thorns into the fabric and out again. When he was done, he straightened and gave the guard a nod. "Thankee."

"De nada." The man motioned at the line ahead, which had developed another gap while Ernest slowed to fix his clothes.

We moved forward a little more quickly, trying to close the space. We weren't moving much faster, but it was enough to make the Tennessean gasp for breath and rub his chest. I looked at him more closely. His skin was white around his lips.

"Perhaps you should drop back and ride in the sick wagon with Griffith and Golpin," I said.

"I'm not used up quite yet, I reckon. Just a mite tired." His eyes twinkled in his wan face. "'Sides, Gates is ridin' too and I ain't too enthusiastic about bein' in close proximity t' his infection o' the lungs." He nodded at the wall of cottonwoods along the Río Grande. They seemed larger here, and more golden, their leaves a deep yellow that glowed in the sunlight. "If I was ridin', the wagon covers'd keep me from viewin' much o' that. I ain't never seen anything like it before. The way they're so gnarled up and proud lookin' at the same time."

I looked at him, then the trees, and nodded. We walked on, each deep in his own thoughts.

We stopped for a short break at midday, to allow the guards' animals to rest and graze. When the trumpet sounded again, Ernest and I were in the third row from the front, with McAllister, Kendall, and Fitzgerald immediately ahead, McAllister supporting himself with his crutch-like walking stick.

Kendall had used the break to surreptitiously wind his watch. As he tucked it away, Salazar rode by on the big chestnut mule, moving down the column on one of his tours of inspection.

Kendall nudged McAllister and pointed at the molly. "That's my animal."

McAllister nodded. "I remember her. She's a big one. And strong."

"She is! That mule can go on forever, no matter what she's carrying."

Salazar had turned. As he passed us, Kendall raised his voice. "However, she was bred for a pack animal, not riding."

Salazar's chin jerked in our direction. He reined in and scowled at the newsman, then looked at me. "¿Esta era su bestia?"

I nodded reluctantly. Yes, it was his beast.

The captain jerked the mule's reins. She tossed her head and danced in place. Salazar dug his big spurs into the animal's sides. "¡Un animal tejano!" he said. "¡Desobediente y de paso cruzado!"

Ramón snorted with laughter. Kendall looked back at me, "What did he say?"

"A Texian animal," I translated. "Disobedient and cross-gaited."

Ramón laughed again. Kendall gave him a bitter look and turned toward Salazar. The mule lunged sideways and forward, and the captain galloped away.

"I am pleased to see that she's still difficult to ride," the newsman said. "Be that as it may, I believe I'd still choose to ride her rather than walk as I'm now forced to do." He looked down at his feet. "If only to save shoe leather. These moccasins are wearing dangerously thin."

"Why don't you switch back to your boots?" I asked. They were still hanging by their laces around his neck.

He lifted one to show me the soles. A crack ran across the widest point. "Dirt and rocks filter in," he said. "And cockle burs of some kind, the foul beasts."

Fitzgerald chuckled. "Apparently not as foul as your old pack mule."

Kendall scowled. "Salazar and his bastard of a governor stole my passport, my goods, my horse, and my mule."

Ernest's head lifted. "Ya still got yer life." His flapping right sole twisted against a rock in the road and he jerked sideways, but I caught his elbow in time. He glanced at the guard at the end of our row and gently removed his arm from my grasp.

He needn't have worried. The man was watching Ramón, riding just ahead, who had begun singing a particularly raucous song about a female mule, a Texian, and the urge to procreate.

With the appropriate hand gestures, it wasn't hard to follow. Kendall's face darkened dangerously, but Ramón simply grinned at him and continued. When the ditty ended, he switched to loud half-English speculations about what would happen to us rebel prisioneros when we reached El Paso, suggesting mischievously that el presidente Santa Anna would have us all shot. At the very least, we'd be thrown into prison in the darkest and filthiest of holes and left to rot with no hope of seeing daylight until we reached heaven's gates.

The only appropriate response was to ignore him. However, Kendall kept turning to me, insisting that I translate, even though every time I did so, he became more aggravated. He was twisting around again, asking "What did he say?" when Salazar returned. When he reined in beside us, Ramón ceased his speculations.

The captain glanced at Kendall, then turned to me and jerked a disgusted chin toward the big mule's big head. "Ella es una bestia horrible," he said.

Kendall looked back at me.

"She is a horrible beast," I said unwillingly.

The newsman sniffed and opened his mouth to respond, but I spoke first. "Eres un excelente jinete," I told Salazar. You are an excellent rider.

He laughed. "Y usted es un caballero." And you are a gentleman. He rode beside us, looking thoughtfully at me, then suddenly turned to Ramón and fired off an order. Something about the little herd. The guard raised a sardonic eyebrow, saluted the captain, turned his horse, and trotted toward the end of the column.

Salazar stayed where he was until the guard returned leading a pretty little bay mare, already saddled. The captain gestured to the animal, then me. "¿Montamos?"

I looked at him in surprise.

"What'd he say?" Ernest asked.

"He wants me to ride with him." I frowned. "You should be mounted, not me."

The Tennessean's eyes widened in alarm. "Don't ask him! He'll know I'm fadin' fer sure and just go ahead'n shoot me!"

"¡Vámonos!" Salazar said impatiently.

"Do what he says!" Ernest said anxiously. "Please!"

I moved reluctantly out of line. The bay tossed her head as I took the reins, then settled and allowed me to swing into the saddle. The leather beneath me felt mighty comfortable. A smile lit my face. I suppressed it quickly, but Salazar had seen. His eyes twinkled, lighting up his face. "¿Se siente bien, sí?"

Yes, it did feel good. When I nodded sheepishly, he laughed out loud. Everyone within hearing swung their heads toward us.

The captain's face dropped into its usual harshness. "¡Vámonos!" he said, kicking his mule into motion.

I and the mare followed. When I glanced back at the column, Kendall was watching, a sour look on his face. I felt a momentary pang, then it occurred to me that perhaps I could use this opportunity to speak with the captain about easing the lot of my fellow prisoners.

We reached the head of the column and he gestured for me to ride on his left. On his other side, Don Jesús sent me a brief, startled look, then faced resolutely ahead, his dark middle-aged face intent on ignoring me.

The man's silence gave me the opening I needed. My little mare settled into step beside Salazar's big mule. Their size difference was offset by my height, making it possible to carry on a conversation with little strain. I began by making occasional positive comments about the landscape as well as the geese and cranes that startled up from the roadside fields as we approached.

He nodded agreeably and told me the cranes were called grullas in Spanish. The farmers left part of the crop behind for them and also occasionally placed snares. Even then, they were careful not to capture too many in the same place, as the fowl quickly grew wary of dangerous locations.

"Clever," I said.

He gave me a sideways look, as if trying to determine whether I was referring to the birds or the men, then continued to explain the various ways in which New Mexicans lived in harmony with the land instead of simply taking from it as Americanos did. I noticed that he didn't seem to differentiate between Americans and Texians.

We continued in this vein for some time, he instructing me, me making encouraging sounds. What he had to say was enlightening. I had no idea that most of the simple clothing people wore here was from wool grown, spun, and woven in New Mexico. And he confirmed what Ramón had told us about squash, corn, and beans being grown together. It ensured a more productive harvest. The captain also asserted that the advent of the Spanish in New Mexico had vastly improved the lives of the Indians, bringing as it did sheep, barley, wheat, and fruit trees. Even peaches, in season.

This gave me the chance to pursue the topic of our diet. I began by saying how much we appreciated the large ears of corn and the melons we'd received, but noted that men on foot needed meat as well. I ventured to ask when he planned to butcher an ox or two for us.

He scowled at me. "¡Cuando tengamos tiempo!" When we have time. Then his face softened. "Pido disculpas, señor. Es muy frustrante."

When I nodded, accepting his apology and acknowledging his frustration, he became more forthcoming. We had progressed much more slowly than originally anticipated, he explained. He was deeply worried that we'd be caught by the cold weather long before we reached El Paso del Norte.

He pulled his shoulders toward his chest and grimaced as he said this, demonstrating his feelings about the cold. If I thought it was bad at night now, wait until winter truly arrived! We needed to move south quickly. The sooner we arrived in El Paso, the better.

Butchering and then cooking a beef would take time we didn't have. For this reason, he'd been relying on simpler foods—corn and meal and melons and bread—from the communities along the way. He assured me rather insistently that the villages had been remunerated for what they'd provided, primarily by trading goods confiscated from the Expedition.

Then the captain's face darkened. He shook his head wearily. Unfortunately, he had found the locals unwilling to make any serious incursions into their winter supplies, no matter what he offered them. As a result, there was never truly enough food for us all. He and the guards were on short rations as well.

There was little I could say to this. It made perfect sense, although the very thought of meat made my stomach rumble. There was nothing to be done. We would simply have to cope as best we could.

We stopped shortly after nightfall on the edge of the sprawling village of Valencia and I returned to my compatriots. When I reported my conversation with Salazar, Kendall sniffed in disdain. He was perched on a piece of downed cottonwood, examining his bare feet by the light of a small cooking fire. "You spent the day riding," he said. "You have no idea what we suffered in the ranks."

I thought this was a bit harsh, given that I'd been walking up until that afternoon, but the newsman clearly didn't want to hear it. He gestured at his moccasins, on the log beside him. The leather was scuffed and dirty, and the outer layer on the right sole was almost gone. "My footwear is completely destroyed."

Fitzgerald came up just then. "The bodies of many of us are more worn out than our shoes," he said quietly. He nodded toward the far side of the fire, where Felix Ernest was huddled on the ground, his dirt-streaked brown blanket around his bent shoulders, his thin face pale with exhaustion.

Ernest lifted his head and saw us watching. "A guard give me a ride this afternoon without me payin'," he said. His eyes closed and his head dropped. "Kind o' him."

Kendall sniffed again. "You can't rely on the kindness of these people." He flicked a hand at his moccasins. "The man who gave me these knew where we were going. He should have provided me with more than one flimsy pair."

I blinked at him in surprise and Fitzgerald opened his mouth to respond, then shook his head and walked away.

Ramón appeared, distributing uncooked meal. Ernest roused enough to extend his cup for a portion, then looked down at it wearily and set it aside. He adjusted his blanket to cover his head as well as his shoulders and lay down in a fetal position, feet tucked against his thighs.

"You should cook that meal and eat it," I told him. "It only needs a little water and some fire."

"Fixin' to," he answered. His voice was so weary, I knew he wouldn't.

McAllister hobbled into the firelight, put his crutch to one side, dropped down beside Ernest, and stretched out, curving toward him to share his body warmth. "Thankee, John," the tired man murmured.

Falconer came up just then, carrying two tin mugs of cooked meal. He handed one to Kendall and sat down on the other end of the log to eat his. Kendall dug in eagerly, scooping up the food with his fingers, then looked up at me still holding my uncooked portion. "You'd better get to heating that."

I nodded. "I need to stake out a place to sleep." I looked around. We were within a stone's throw of a huddle of houses and walls. Sheep bleated behind a brush fence.

Fitzgerald appeared again, loaded down with two woolly sheepskins. His irritation with Kendall seemed to have vanished. He jerked a chin toward the nearest house. "We not only have ourselves a sleeping spot there where that bit of wall jogs inward, we have ground cover." He lifted the thick pelts. "The old lady who lives there saw me scouting around and threw me these. They'll soften our rest nicely."

"A real luxury," Kendall agreed, somewhat sourly.

"You see?" I said. "You can indeed rely on the kindness of others."

Kendall gave me an impatient look. "Not in this country."

Falconer looked up and grinned. "Not in this country? Didn't you say we're technically still in Texas?"

Kendall didn't reply. Falconer went back to his food. I moved away. Captain Caldwell and Curtis had finished with the pan they were using, so they handed it off to me and I cooked and ate my portion of meal, then settled for the night near the Erhard boys.

Cayton was having trouble getting comfortable, due to pain in his hips. "I have no fat," he complained. Anton mumbled something and the other boy finally quieted. I slept hard, worn out by the day's events. Not even the guards' periodic calls of "¡Centinela, alerta!" could disturb my slumber.

CHAPTER 10
Sunday, October 24, 1841
Valencia to Casa Colorada

I woke strangely refreshed. The sky was pale, the sun a mere idea behind the eastern mountains. I sat up and carefully rearranged my wrinkled cravat against the morning chill.

Men moved around rekindled fires, beginning the process of cooking the morning portion of meal. Kendall stood nearby, surreptitiously winding his watch.

McAllister was kneeling beside Ernest, whose blanket was still over his head. "Time to roll out," he said gently as he reached to shake him awake. Then his face changed. He leaned forward and lifted the cover from Ernest's face. His hand fell to his side. He stared down at the man in the blanket, then gulped and turned to me. "He's dead."

"Are you certain?"

He gestured toward Ernest, whose eyes stared unseeing at the fire. When I bent and pulled the blanket farther back, his chest was a dull cold. "He's been gone a good while," I said.

McAllister nodded and reached to close the staring eyes. He picked up his crutch and began pushing himself upright, but he wasn't quite steady and he lurched to one side. I grabbed his arm.

He stood, leaning heavily on the stick, and staring down at the dead man. "He oughtn't to have come on this trip. He simply wasn't strong enough."

A small crowd had gathered. Falconer and Kendall and Fitzgerald, the Erhard brothers close behind, Curtis Caldwell off to one side. The German boys held tin mugs of cooked mush.

"He's dead," I said. They all stared at me blankly, except for Fitzgerald, whose lips began to move in soundless prayer.

A guard came up. He looked down at the corpse, nudged it with a toe, and walked away.

"Abgenutzt he was at Austin," Anton Erhard said.

"Worn out?" Falconer asked. "Yes, he seemed so to me, also."

The guard came back. He pulled a large knife from his waistband, knelt beside the corpse, and turned Ernest's head to one side, exposing his ear.

"What is he doing?" Kendall asked.

No one answered. The knife sliced down, cutting through the base of the ear. Then the guard grabbed the chin and turned the head. The knife flashed again. I gulped against rising bile. Young Caldwell gagged noisily and turned away.

Kendall stepped toward the guard. "What are you doing?" He turned to me. "Ask him why he did that!"

I looked at the guard, who was standing now, ears in one hand, knife in the other. The question was clear enough on my face. I didn't have to speak it.

The guard shrugged and tucked the knife into his waist-band. "El Capitán me ordenó." He shrugged again and walked away.

"The captain ordered him to do it," I said.

"That is, after all, what Governor Armijo told Salazar to do," Falconer said, running his hands through his beard. "He said it that morning at San Miguel. We all heard him."

"But that was if we tried to escape and were caught," Curtis Caldwell's eyes slid toward the corpse and quickly away. "Not if we died."

"I suppose you could say Ernest has escaped," Fitzgerald said.

I pulled my gaze from Ernest's mutilated head. "It's a horrible thing, but the captain has little choice. When we reach El Paso, he'll be required to account for each one of us. To prove Ernest didn't escape, he'll need to show his ears, as Governor Armijo commanded."

Kendall's mouth twisted. "If he wishes to account for us, he should make more of an effort to ensure our survival!"

"Ernest was ailing when he joined the Expedition."

No one responded. They were watching McAllister. He had hobbled forward and now bent awkwardly to pull the blanket over Ernest's face. As he straightened, his good ankle twisted and he lurched sideways toward the corpse. Fitzgerald darted forward and grabbed his arm, helping him stay upright.

Two guards strode toward us. "¡Vámonos!" the taller one snapped. He waved an arm. "¡Poneos en fila!"

We moved off to gather our things. McAllister, still supported by Fitzgerald, stayed behind, staring at Ernest. The guards brushed past them to grab the blanket-wrapped corpse, one on each end, and carry it to one side. Two other men began digging a trench next to the downed cottonwood where Kendall had inspected his feet the night before. Kendall, Falconer, and I gathered our gear, then moved to stand beside McAllister and Fitzgerald and watch the burial.

Ramón came up. "Poneos en fila," he said quietly. He made an apologetic gesture toward the waiting column. "Por favor."

I nodded and we moved slowly off, followed by Fitzgerald and McAllister, whose forehead was now beaded with sweat. When I glanced back inquiringly, he shook his head. "Other ankle's twisted," he grunted.

We all placed ourselves at the end of the column and watched over our shoulders as the guards dropped Felix Ernest's body into its trench.

"They didn't dig very far down," Kendall said. "It's a mere ditch. The village dogs will dig it up before the day is over!"

I grimaced. "It would be better to dig a deeper hole and take the time for a proper farewell, but the captain must consider his duty to get the rest of us safely to El Paso before winter sets in. It would take time to locate a priest to perform a proper ceremony."

"It would be useless for him to try to find one," Fitzgerald said. "Catholic priests are not allowed to bury non-Catholics. As heretics, we're restricted from hallowed ground."

"Infidels!" Kendall muttered.

"All we can do for Ernest now is pray for him," Fitzgerald said. He sighed. "At times like this I wish I'd finished my studies and been ordained."

McAllister shifted his weight on his stick and said nothing.

Salazar came toward us on the mule, his face grim. He spotted me and waved a hand, gesturing for me to follow. We moved slowly up the waiting ranks, him riding, me walking. There was no conversation except the low buzz of my fellow prisoners as we passed.

At the front of the column, a battered, high-sided cart stood in the middle of the road. Typical of Mexican carretas, it had only two wheels, but they were made of massive tree rounds. Two Texian oxen were hitched to the front, their heads drooping. Captain Salazar climbed into the back of the ramshackle vehicle and faced the column.

"¡Para los enfermos!" he shouted, pointing at the cart. He turned to me. "Vas a interpretar." I nodded and he waited for me to climb up beside him before he turned back to the men. He'd requisitioned la carreta from the Valencia alcalde, he said. Any prisoners too weak to walk could ride in it. As soon as I'd put this into English, men surged forward.

Salazar scowled and yelled a command. The guards' sticks came out and they began forcing people back into line.

I cupped hands around my mouth. "Let only the truly sick come forward!" I yelled.

"Old Paint Caldwell!" someone called out.

The grizzled veteran moved reluctantly to the front, his hand on his side. It was clear that he didn't want to get into the cart, but felt his wound gave him no choice.

"McAllister!" someone else hollered. "He's sprained his other ankle!"

The lame man hobbled forward from the back of the column, Fitzgerald beside him. He was using two sticks now, one in each hand. His feet twisted from side to side as he tried to find the least painful way to position them, and his face was white and dazed under the road dirt and sunburn. When he reached the cart, McAllister grabbed the edge of a side plank and Fitzgerald patted his arm, then moved back into the ranks.

Other men came forward, some more reluctant than others, a dozen in all, each with their bedrolls and gear. Salazar and I climbed down and the men helped each other into the carreta, which tilted dangerously to one side. The oxen looked around anxiously and one uttered a low, disgusted moo.

Old Paint Caldwell peered over the boards and laughed. "We apologize, poor beast. Here you thought you were coming to New Mexico to get fat on rich grass!" McAllister was sitting on the bottom of the cart, his back against the side. Caldwell poked him in the ribs. "Like the rest of us!"

The other man smiled wanly. "Never thought I'd walk this much, that's certain."

Salazar turned impatiently toward the waiting column and Kendall's mule. I moved to get back in line, but he put a restraining hand on my arm. "¿Montamos?"

It wasn't a request I could deny. The man's face was drawn and there was a shadow in his eyes. I nodded agreement. Someone brought me the mare I'd ridden the day before and we moved out, Salazar and I in front with the trumpeter and Don Jesús, then the rest: rows of prisoners with guards riding alongside, the jersey and supply wagons, the cart with its passengers. Behind them, the extra horses and unyoked oxen raised an ever-spreading cloud of dust.

The road was narrow here, bounded by fields of harvested corn, yellow melons, and other crops. Tendrils of mist rose from the irrigation ditches. The cottonwoods along the Río Grande were a solid bank of gold. The captain seemed oblivious to it. His eyes were half-shut and his face grim. We rode without speaking.

We'd traveled perhaps a mile and a half when a guard came galloping up from the back of the column. The cart had broken down.

Salazar's scowl deepened, then he made a visible effort to control himself and turned politely to me. Would I be so good as to go with the guard to determine whether la carreta was still usable? He grimaced. If it wasn't, the prisoners in it must join the marching column. He looked away, then turned back to me, his eyes flat, jaw stiff. I should tell the men that if they couldn't walk, they would be shot.

My eyes widened. Surely he didn't mean it. It was entirely possible that at least some of the riding prisoners were incapable of walking at all.

The waiting guard looked at me impatiently and my mare stepped sideways, but I reined her in, watching the captain.

Salazar shook his head at me. "¡Díselo!" he said.

Reluctantly, I said I would tell them and turned to trail after the messenger. The column continued on as we rode against its flow. By the time we reached the cart, there was a significant gap between it and the jersey and supply wagons, although a number of the ambulatory walking prisoners, including Anton Erhard, had dropped back to walk beside them.

Beyond the carreta, the spare horses and oxen milled in the road, throwing up more dust. The cart itself was titled to one side. Its thick cottonwood axle had snapped in two. A big wooden wheel lay beside it in the dirt.

Most of the men who'd been riding stood just beyond, staring numbly. McAllister was slumped on the verge, clutching his sticks, his sleeping blanket on his left shoulder. He looked up as I approached. His face was milk pale now. Beads of sweat ran down his face, creating rivulets in the road dust above his dirty black beard.

I reined in, studying him, but Old Paint Caldwell limped up, claiming my attention. He gestured toward the cart. "I don't think it's repairable."

The guards apparently didn't think so either. They were unyoking the ox, who turned and trotted toward the herd.

I moved toward the cart. A guard looked up expectantly. I leaned forward. "Captain Salazar sent me to say—"

The sergeant who'd escorted me and the boys at Los Placeres trotted up, four men riding behind him. He waved an arm at the prisoners. "¡Muévanse, o dispararé!"

The prisoners looked at me. "He says move or he'll shoot," I told them. "I came to tell you that the captain—"

But I was interrupted by the sergeant, who'd pulled his heavy Spanish pistol from the sash at his waist and was waving it in the air. The long silver barrel flashed in the sun. "¡Vámonos!" he yelled. He turned in a circle, waving the weapon. When he saw the men beside the wagons ahead, now stopped perhaps two hundred feet away, he waved it at them, too. "¡Vámonos!" he shouted.

The Texians by the carreta obediently started forward. McAllister watched them for a minute, then set his jaw, lifted his sticks, and began to push himself up. I rode toward him and leaned down, offering my hand, but he shook his head.

Finally, he was on his feet. His chest heaved as we both eyed the distance to the end of the column. Griffith's face peered from the back of the sick wagon, alongside someone I didn't recognize. Surely there would be room for one more.

McAllister moved his right stick forward, gave a little hop, sucked in a breath of pain, and angled the left, the crutch, into position. I moved my horse out of his way.

The sergeant came toward us, scowling. "¿Por qué no vas más rápido?"

McAllister glanced up at me.

"Why aren't you going faster?" I translated.

He looked at the sergeant, then jerked his chin down at his sticks. "I can't."

The sergeant's scowl deepened. "¡Estás fingiendo! ¡Te dispararé!"

"¡Él es cojo!" I snapped at the guard. "He's lame, for God's sake!" I turned to McAllister. "He says you're faking. And—" I couldn't believe I was about to say it. Surely he wouldn't. "He'll shoot you."

McAllister's head jerked up, eyes blazing black in his pale face. He flung away the stick in his right hand, putting all his weight on the crutch, which bent dangerously. He didn't seem to notice. With his free hand, McAllister shoved the blanket off his shoulder and yanked his shirt open. A button popped and rolled into the dirt. "Do it, then!" he yelled.

I twisted toward the sergeant to suggest that I give McAllister a ride to the jersey wagon. The big pistol roared.

Black powder, then blood, bloomed on the lame man's chest. As he tilted sideways, his stick snapped in two. He crumpled into the dirt.

At the sound of the gun, Caldwell and the others, who were perhaps halfway to the wagons, jerked to a stop and turned toward us. The sergeant barked an order. The men with him vaulted from their animals and hurried across the road, heads down. Three quickly stripped McAllister to his shirt and drawers, then a fourth stepped forward with a knife in his hand.

He moved to McAllister's head, then paused and looked questioningly at the sergeant, who barked an angry order. The guard's lips moved as if in prayer, then he set his jaw and bent down. His knife moved once, twice, then again. I heard a retching sound—one of the guards?—and gulped against my own bile.

The man beside the corpse straightened. In his left hand were two small leathery rounds. Blood dripped along the torn edges. He wiped his face against the sleeve on his other arm and kept his eyes on the road as he crossed to the sergeant and handed them over.

The sergeant folded the ears into a large handkerchief and tucked it into a pocket, then snapped an order. The guards moved to McAllister's body, rolled him into his sleeping blanket, and dragged the resulting bundle under the carreta, out of the way of passing cattle and horses.

The sergeant barked another command and the guard who'd cut off the ear swung onto his horse and galloped back up the road. I looked at the bundle under the cart and gave the sergeant a questioning look. Was he simply going to leave it there?

"El alcalde vendrá," he said impatiently. He waved at his men. "¡Vámonos!"

They headed toward their mounts. I trotted my mare up the road to Captain Caldwell and the others, who'd been joined by Anton Erhard. "He says the alcalde will come."

Old Paint shook his grizzled head. "He'll come for a cart and discover a corpse."

Anton's face twisted."Take der wagen, leave der Körper,"

I looked at him in surprise. "Leave the corpse? I'm sure they'll find a way to bury it."

"In a ditch, like poor Ernest," Caldwell said.

"The priests are restricted—" I began.

But the sergeant was upon us. "¡Vámonos!" he bellowed.

When the men on foot began moving toward the end of the column, he trotted off. I waited a few minutes, still adjusting to what had just happened, before I followed. Yes, McAllister was weak and unable to travel on his own. But the sergeant could have allowed him to ride in the sick wagon. And I could have suggested it. Lawyers are supposed to think quickly and suggest solutions to problems. I had failed miserably. In a sense, I was as guilty of McAllister's death as the man who'd fired the pistol. I moved up the column slowly.

By the time I arrived back at its head, the sergeant had given Salazar his report and was proffering the bloody handkerchief. The captain jerked the reins of the big mule, pulling away from the other man. "¡Imbécil!" he spat. "¡Idiota!"

The sergeant's expression darkened. He thrust the ears farther out, almost waving the little packet in the air. The captain stared at it furiously, then grabbed it impatiently and shoved it into his saddle bag.

The sergeant gave him a malevolent grin and trotted off. I maneuvered my mare into place. Salazar nodded curtly and faced the road ahead, his jaw tight with anger. "¡Maldición!" he swore, letting loose a string of Spanish that seemed to be all curse words and ending with a furious diatribe against the insolent, stupido, and vulgar sergeant.

Don Jesús, who had listened impassively until now, suggested that perhaps the man should be sent home.

Salazar humphed and acknowledged that he would do so in any other circumstances. But he himself would be gone for at least another month, still on the trail. What kind of story would the sergeant take to Governor Armijo in the meantime? That he, Salazar, was not following instructions and acting as a proper leader of his men and prisoners?

There was no answer to this. Salazar fell into a black sulk and we rode without speaking, past orchards quiet in the Fall sunlight, animals grazing in the fields. A rocky black hill loomed to our left, then we were past it and moving through the plaza of a village with an impressive church on its northern edge. No one looked out to greet us, perhaps because it was Sunday.

Then came more fields, more scattered houses. The captain was as silent as the land, even more so as it changed over the course of the day, the rich alluvial soil becoming sand and rock, the mountains on our left moving farther east. The land was not irrigated here and the dryness made it formidable and bleak. The only sign of life was an occasional distant flock of sheep.

The dreariness matched my mood and gave me no respite from my self-recriminations. If I'd spoken, McAllister might still be with us, riding in the jersey wagon and nursing his ankle. How I wished Governor Armijo had found some way to house us over the winter instead of ordering Salazar to El Paso, whatever the cost.

As the sun started to set, a cluster of reddish adobe buildings appeared on the horizon. Salazar stared at them for a long while, then turned us west across country to a cotton-wood grove above the river.

When we pulled up, he stayed on his mule and gazed morosely at the dying light. I studied his face, gently bade him good evening, turned my mare over to a guard, and went in search of my friends. As I moved through the milling prisoners, I saw that they were both more subdued and more angry than usual. The news of McAllister's death, the realization that a guard truly would shoot a prisoner, was a shock.

When I found Kendall and the others, I realized that a good deal of the tension had more to do with the stories about what had happened than the actual events. The embroideries were numerous and included reports that Salazar himself had shot the man and McAllister had been stripped naked afterward, his body left in the road for the wolves. I raised an eyebrow at this. Were there wolves in this country? I had not yet heard any howling.

Even Old Paint Caldwell, who'd seen everything that occurred, and knew McAllister had dared the guard to shoot him, was caught up in the careening emotions. He stomped around growling that we Texians should rise up and slit Salazar's throat, overpower the guards, and escape across the eastern mountains. No one responded with much enthusiasm to this idea. Whether we had the capacity to overpower the guards was an open question, but we certainly didn't have the strength or land knowledge for a trek home through the New Mexico wilderness, and we all knew it.

Then the murmurs shifted slightly into something resembling hope, or at least surprise. Captain Salazar had ordered an ox butchered and the meat distributed.

Although the resulting meal eased my stomach, it didn't soothe my mind. I lay on the sandy soil late into the night, listening to the breeze rattle the leaves overhead, but finding no comfort. If only I had spoken sooner. If only—

CHAPTER 11
Monday, October 25, 1841
Casa Colorada to La Joya

The next morning, I was still feeling both regretful and stunned when a guard appeared with the little bay mare. I joined a taciturn Captain Salazar and silent Don Jesús at the head of the column. We moved slowly south, the Río Grande in sight but out of reach. Then the road turned and wound into the sand hills east of the river. We were well into the afternoon before the vegetation thickened.

The road grew thicker, too. Thicker with sand. It was hard going, and when I turned to look at the column behind, a haze of dust obscured my view.

Then we rounded the base of yet another sandy hill and I spotted a wagon train ahead, stalled in the road. Men milled on either side of the track, watching a wheelwright reset a rim.

We paused, studying the situation. The hills on either side of the road were a little farther apart here. It would be possible to get around the train if its men had the courtesy to move aside. Salazar spurred forward, chin up and jaw set. Don Jesús and I followed.

"Howdy!" A bull-shouldered teamster came out to greet us. His red hair and beard stood out in all directions and half-covered his broad, tanned face. He ran a hand through the mop on his forehead and stepped toward the captain, who kept moving, his gaze straight ahead.

The teamster turned to me. "You the Texian prisoners?"

I glanced at Salazar, who scowled. "We are," I said tersely.

The men behind us weren't so circumspect. When they spied the train, cheers went up. Salazar twisted in his saddle to bellow "¡Silencio!" then snapped an order at Don Jesús, who turned and galloped back along the line, repeating the command at the top of his voice.

The captain urged his mule forward but the teamsters watching the wheelwright didn't move. Salazar's jaw tightened as he took us left off the road around the hill. The red-headed teamster, standing on the slope, shrugged apologetically at me. My mare was having trouble with the sand, which was especially deep in this location. I smiled and nodded and focused on getting her onto firmer ground.

Once we were past the train and back on the road, I turned to Salazar. His scowl was still in place. "¡Americanos!" he spat. "¡Bastardos! ¡Impertinentes! ¡Arrogantes!" He went on, complaining about the way they'd blocked the road, had made no effort to move aside for us, and took money from the people of New Mexico, including local traders. It was evident that he spoke from long frustration. I didn't try to argue or commiserate.

He lapsed into silence as the road curved west again, treating us to a view of the setting sun. The sky was a vast palette of peach and orange behind the low black outline of the western mountains. Closer to hand, the bushes and grass on the sandy slopes cast purple shadows and brightened the adobe walls of the little village of La Joya that appeared in the distance.

The alcalde came out to greet us and showed Salazar an abandoned adobe compound where we could spend the night, then invited him to a fandango in his home. The captain brightened a little at this. He sent Don Jesús to organize food for the evening meal and allocate space in the old buildings, then disappeared to freshen up.

By the time he reappeared, I and the other prisoners had eaten and Kendall, Lieutenant Hornsby, and I were standing over a fire reflecting on McAllister's death. Our minds had adjusted to the fact of his demise, though it was still painful. We all agreed that, given the Tennessean's condition, he almost certainly would have ended by accompanying Felix Ernest to heaven before we reached Mexico City, but I still felt dissatisfied with my role in the matter.

I was startled out of my discontent by the captain. He strode toward us in his newly brushed cloak and polished boots, stopped and looked us over, then nodded as if our whiskers and rumpled, dirty clothes — even Lieutenant Hornsby's tight coat — were not as bad as they could have been. "¡Venid, venid!" he said. "¡El fandango espera!"

Kendall raised an eyebrow at me.

"Come, come, the fandango awaits," I translated. I looked at the others. "He seems to be inviting us to attend the alcalde's party with him."

"Fandango?" Kendall asked.

"I believe it's a kind of dance."

"What a capital idea!" Hornsby turned to a couple men standing nearby. "Come with us! A dance!"

More men crowded around. Salazar scowled and they backed off. He pointed at me, Kendall, Hornsby, and the two men the lieutenant had invited, then set off toward the village. We followed, feeling rather privileged but also a little anxious.

"I've never been to a Mexican dance before," Kendall said.

I grinned at him. "If the ones here are anything like those I experienced in San Antonio, you're in for a treat."

We reached the edge of the plaza and paused, orienting ourselves. The sound of violins and guitars filled the air. On the other side of the square, light streamed from an open door. We were halfway across when we heard running footsteps behind us. Salazar jerked to a stop and whirled, fists up to ward off an attack.

An American voice gasped, "Howdy!" and we saw the red-headed teamster from the wagon train, his hair and beard dripping with water in a useless effort to tame it. He grinned unabashedly at Salazar, then the rest of us. "It sure is good to see you all again!" Two men came up behind him, their eyes crinkling with laughter at their friend's enthusiasm.

"Your train made good time," Lieutenant Hornsby said.

"We did. Once that wagon wheel got fixed up, we moved at a right good clip." One of his companions chuckled and the redhead grinned. "Word is, Joya's a likely place for a fandango, so we had what you might call incentive." He looked at me. "Weren't sure we'd see you here, though."

Captain Salazar made a disgusted sound, turned on his heel, and headed toward the lit-up door.

The teamster jerked a thumb in his direction. "He the one in charge of you all?"

I nodded. "Captain Damasio Salazar."

"When we were coming through San Miguel, I heard about him. Ain't he a bigwig in the New Mexico militia?"

One of the man's friends moved forward impatiently. "We gonna stand out here and jaw all night, or we gonna dance?"

We crossed the square and entered the room. It was long and wide. The musicians took up one end while dancers crowded the center under candle chandeliers made of wood sticks. A thin red cloth was stretched over the lower part of the walls. The upper half was painted a brilliant white, which reflected the candlelight and made the space seem bigger than it was. Women, children, and men sat on thick wool cushions along the sides of the room, clapping to the tunes.

Captain Salazar was standing in a corner with a cluster of men, a pottery goblet in his hand. He tilted the drink to his mouth, then saw us, frowned, and said something to the man beside him. The man gave us a friendly look, then leaned toward Salazar and patted his arm. His lips moved. Whatever he said made Salazar's scowl deepen, but he accepted a refill.

The red-headed American teamster approached the nearest girl. "Howdy!" he said. She responded with a mere smile, but that was all he needed to seize her hand and swing her into the whirling dancers.

The rest of us followed. There was no standing on ceremony here, no need for introductions, no dance cards. Kendall hesitated, startled by the lack of formality, but soon he, too, was absorbed in having a good time.

An hour or so went by, each tune as energetic as the last. I and the red-headed teamster had no shortage of partners. The women and girls crowded around us at every lull in the music, laughing into our eyes.

"It's your hair!" Kendall told me with a grin. "Your blond and his red! They want your babies!"

I looked at him in horror. "Have you been drinking?"

He laughed and slapped me on the back, alcohol fuming his breath. "I apologize most sincerely, old friend. Did I disturb your sensibilities?"

I opened my mouth to remonstrate, but was interrupted by the furious bellow of "What did you say?" from the corner of the room. An American teamster stood, feet well-braced and a ten-inch Bowie knife in his hand, glaring at Captain Salazar.

Even with one hand on the cloth-covered wall, the captain swayed slightly. "Americano hijo de puta." His voice had an oddly flat sound.

"Son of a whore?" the teamster growled. "I've cut off a man's bollocks for sayin' less'n that!"

Salazar's chin lifted. His hand dropped to his sides. "¡Haré que te disparen!"

"You'll have me shot?" The teamster hooted with laughter. "I ain't one of your Texian prisoners!"

Salazar was so focused on the man with the knife that he didn't notice the red-headed teamster drop his dance partner's hand, move across the room, and slip into position behind him.

However, the man with the knife had. He stepped forward. "I ain't your prisoner!" he said again.

Salazar lunged, the man sidestepped, and the redhead enveloped the captain in an iron-tight bear hug, forcing his arms to his sides, and marched him to the door as the rest of us watched.

"¡Bastardos!" Salazar yelled as he stumbled on the step. "¡Hijos de puta americanos!"

The now-silent crowd looked from the teamsters to us. The girl holding my arm released it and slipped to the other side of the room. Lieutenant Hornsby and his friends moved toward the door. Kendall and I followed.

Salazar had fallen into the dirt and was struggling to rise. The stench of vomit filled the air. We circled around him without looking and headed toward the abandoned compound. "He will undoubtedly be in a foul mood on the morrow," Kendall murmured.

I shook my head, not wanting to contemplate what the next day might bring. Was the captain simply lashing out at the nearest dog or had his anger with the sergeant reshaped itself into resentment toward us Texians and all Americanos?

When we got back to the compound, the only sleeping spot I could find was in a room that included Thomas Gates. The New Yorker's cough had been deepened by the dust of the last two days. Between my churning thoughts, the rattling in Gates' lungs, and the guards' "¡Centinela, alerta!" every thirty minutes, I didn't get much rest.

CHAPTER 12
Tuesday, October 26, 1841
La Joya to La Parida

We started early the next morning, whether because we had a long trek ahead of us or because the captain wanted to leave La Joya as quickly as possible, it was difficult to tell. The half-hidden smirks of my fellow prisoners whenever he and I rode by made it clear what they thought. I glared back at them, willing them to keep their remarks to themselves, lest they spark Salazar's anger.

He had sent the mare to me, so I knew he wanted my company, but he kept his head down, as if looking into the sun made it ache, and said little beyond "¡Vámonos!" to Don Jesús and "¡Bestia torpe!" to Kendall's mule.

Although the road from the village followed the Río Grande initially, it soon swung left, through an even dryer country than the day before. The hills were higher, with a reddish cast to them, the flat spaces between pocked with dry water holes rimmed with white crystals. The very sight of them made my throat ache.

The foliage had changed, too. The grass was sparser, spread thin between the increasing soapweed yucca and mesquite trees, those givers of beans that had sustained us during our march from Austin when nothing else was to be had. These mesquites' spiky branches were bare now except for a few rattling seedpods, while the yuccas' once-majestic stalks had dried to a dull brown and canted sideways over their long spiny leaves.

There was no comfort in that thought, only bad memories. And the knowledge that the Erhards and Falconer had even worse ones. Snakes and bugs and insects. I forced my mind away from those horrors onto the dust-filled air, which produced considerable coughing and wheezing in the ranks. I wondered how Gates was coping in the sick wagon.

I was well sunk in my depressive thoughts when the captain suddenly turned to me. "¡Americanos!" he spat.

I raised a deprecating hand. "Soy tejano, no americano," I said, forcing amusement into my voice. I am Texian, not American.

He squinted at me, then his lips quirked. "¿No es lo mismo?" Not the same?

I shook my head, eyes twinkling. "No es lo mismo."

He chuckled and pointed out that, technically, we Texians were Mexicans. After all, Texas had revolted against the central government. That made everyone who fought against Mexico a traitor. He slanted an amused look in my direction. Was it better to be a traitor than an Americano?

I gulped a little at this, but his tone was friendly. How to respond? I pointed out as neutrally as possible that both Britain and the U.S. had officially recognized the Republic of Texas as an independent nation.

He sniffed at this. Both countries had incentive to do so. Texas had cotton, something Britain and the U.S. needed badly. Besides, almost everyone who called themselves Texian was originally from either the U.S. or the British isles. Except for the Germans among us. Weren't a couple of the younger Expeditionaries German immigrants?

He didn't wait for an answer. His mood changed, became more belligerent. It seemed that it was really America he disliked. America and its ever-reaching ambitions. Texas might not be part of the U.S. at the moment, but there was certainly a concerted effort to make it so. I opened my mouth to respond, but he raised a hand, indicating that he was through conversing. His head ached and he was weary of all things americano.

I nodded, acknowledging his discomfort, and subsided into further plaintive study of the countryside. I could see the Río Grande in the distance, but it was very far away and the land between its rustling beauty and the more immediate landscape was harsh indeed.

The soil along the road was more sandy than usual, and the wagons at the end of the column kept bogging down. Messengers arrived every hour or so to report that they'd fallen behind. After we'd stopped several times for them to catch up, Captain Salazar began to simply wave his hand in acknowledgement and continue on through the mesquite and soapweed yucca.

It seemed impossible that anyone or anything could live in such a landscape, so I was startled when a cluster of houses appeared early that afternoon and even more surprised to see it was surrounded by orchards, vineyards, and fields of harvested wheat and corn.

"La Parida," Salazar said with a tone of relief. He turned to the trumpeter and ordered the signal for a halt, then said something to Don Jesús, leaving him in charge, and trotted off toward the village.

Don Jesús gave me a black look, as if asking why I was still beside him, and I nodded politely and made myself scarce. The column had broken apart, prisoners and guards scattering across the hills and the rocky landscape between. I found the animal herd, handed the bay mare off to a keeper, and climbed a slope to study the village from above. A handful of residents had spotted us and were moving in our direction. Some of the guards were going out to meet them. I squinted against the bright sun. Not only the guards. Was that Kendall?

I shrugged and turned away. Prisoners were building fires using yucca stalks they'd scavenged along the way. When the flames were strong enough, others contributed dead mesquite branches. The sweet tang of the wood whispered through the air and made my mouth water.

Along with firewood, Cayton Erhard and Curtis Caldwell had collected a handful of mesquite pods. They sat back to back on a large rock, munching away. As I slowed to say hello, a village man came up and began gesturing at the boys, making eating motions. Curtis gave him a puzzled look. The man made the motions again, then nodded vigorously and tugged the boy's elbow.

Curtis scowled and yanked his arm away indignantly. The man raised his hands apologetically. "¡Ofrezco comida!" he said.

Cayton looked at me.

I couldn't help but grin. The boy who was always hungry still hadn't learned the word "comida."

"He's offering food," I said.

The boys' faces brightened. They turned eagerly toward the villager, who laughed, slapped his thigh, and moved away, motioning for them to follow.

Cayton stood up, but Curtis hesitated. "Should we find a guard to take us?"

I looked around. There were none nearby, and the ones in the distance were all occupied. If Kendall had ventured into the village, no one would complain about a couple youngsters. "Go with him," I said. "If there's a question, I'll explain."

He frowned. "I don't want to be shot. Mr. Kendall says the guards are all itching to kill someone."

I suppressed a groan. "Go. No one is going to shoot you."

He looked at me doubtfully, but the man was waiting. Curtis pushed himself from the rock.

"The kindness of strangers," I murmured, watching them go. I headed off and soon came across Falconer, who was hard at work starting a fire. He already had a battered tin pot ready with water to heat.

The flames were burning well and the water simmering, when Kendall appeared. He carried a stout pair of shoes. "Behold!" he said, flourishing them. "I have found footwear that can be worn for more than a few miles!" Then his face twisted. "Found for a price, that is. The shoemaker here knows a desperate man when he sees one and has no compassion. Not only did he take my old boots, but he tried to convince me he couldn't make change!"

Kendall glanced around to make sure no one could hear him and lowered his voice. "I used my gold piece. These shoes cost less than half that, however, I wanted to procure smaller coins in the event Salazar discovers I still have some money about me." He frowned. "Your translation skills would have been helpful, Van Ness. That damned greaser pretended not to understand anything I said, no matter how loudly I spoke or how clearly I enunciated."

Falconer and I exchanged suppressed grins. "Were you able to acquire the change?" he asked.

Kendall brightened. "I did! The priest came in and spoke some sense to the man." He patted his pocket, then glanced around uneasily. "Be that as it may, it's important that no one else know I possess them."

I turned away. Falconer was pouring meal into the water. He stirred it carefully, then added a handful of crushed mesquite beans.

"Beans?" I asked.

He nodded. "They seem to be quite healthful. Fitzgerald found them when we were collecting wood."

"At least he's good for something," Kendall said sourly.

I gave him a puzzled look, but he pursed his lips and turned away. When I raised a quizzical eyebrow at Falconer, he shrugged and focused on the pan of mush. "This includes Cayton and Curtis's portions, too," he said. "So we'll need to be sparing."

We ate, making sure there was enough left over, but when the boys came back, they weren't hungry. They'd been fed enough beans, tortillas, cheese, and miel for five. Cayton patted his belly with contentment and told Falconer he and Kendall could have his share of the cooked meal. Then he looked at me. "You also."

I shook my head. I was lying on the ground, my arms under my head, my need for rest overriding my belly's complaints. "No, thank you. Your stomach is truly content?"

"I didn't think that was possible!" Kendall laughed.

"Beans, tortillas und Melasse." The boy shook his head in wonder. Then he grinned. "And plenty!"

"So everyone has had their needs met this day," I said. "We stopped earlier than expected, Kendall replaced his worn-out footwear, and you had enough to eat."

Kendall gave me an impatient look. "You are too easily satisfied. Our need for freedom hasn't been met."

I made a small gesture, acknowledging his point, and closed my eyes. Somewhere, a guard strummed a guitar. A male voice began a low, mournful song. It was beautiful in a sad way.

"Even the guards would rather be elsewhere," Falconer said.

Kendall looked up. "Not all of them. That Ramón would rather be exactly where he is, making insulting comments and ridiculous predictions about what will happen when we finally arrive in Mexico City."

Falconer's eyes twinkled. "I notice he only makes those comments when you in particular are nearby."

Kendall sniffed and turned away. When Fitzgerald showed up a little later, he got up and left the fire to find another place to lay his head. The rest of us pretended not to notice.

CHAPTER 13
Tuesday, October 27 to Wednesday, October 28, 1841
La Parida to Socorro

Our road the next morning lay across the river, perhaps three hundred feet in width. When our mounts splashed in, Salazar's mule lurched sideways, trying to wade and drink at the same time.

"¡Maldición!" he cursed. "¡Maldita mula americana!"

On the bank behind us, there was a shout of laughter. I turned to see Kendall poking Falconer in the ribs and pointing gleefully at the mule. Fitzgerald was at his elbow, grinning widely.

The mule lurched again, tilting Salazar sideways in the saddle. Kendall clapped his hands in delight.

The captain pulled himself straight, and glared at Kendall and the others. The mule sidestepped. I moved my mare out of its way. Salazar jabbed his spurs into the molly's flanks and yanked on the reins, forcing her head up. Then he sawed them to the left, forcing her to turn and face the bank. "¡Les dispararé a todos!" he bellowed. I'll shoot you all.

Kendall straightened, his face serious, hands on his hips, but his lips quirking in sardonic amusement. Behind him, Fitzgerald's lips twitched, his eyes dancing.

Well, at least the two of them were friends again, although at the captain's expense. My mare slipped on a bit of sand and rock and I turned back to my task of getting safely across. The river was not as placid as it appeared. Though it was only perhaps two feet deep, the current was strong and the innocent-looking sand hid both buried rocks and sudden sinkholes. I was glad when we reached the safety of the cottonwoods on the other side.

I reined in beside the captain and watched my fellow prisoners and their guards. Then there was a general hush as the wheeled vehicles moved into the water. When the jersey wagon reached the middle, it gave a sudden lurch and tilted precariously. Golpin and Griffith were both on the box, managing the mules between them. Gates's face appeared behind them, framed by the tattered canvas cover. His hands were tight on the sun-bleached sideboards.

Then Golpin did something with the reins, the mules heaved, the wheels straightened, and the wagon moved toward the bank. Beside me, I heard Salazar's breath hiss in relief. He turned and motioned to his trumpeter, and we moved out again.

The road left the cottonwoods quickly and angled south-west, away from the river over a fairly level grassland. Salazar seemed less anxious now. I cast around for a neutral topic of conversation and landed on the Río Grande and its deceptive appearance.

The captain nodded and told me this stretch almost always looked calm, but its surface belied its true nature. He hated to cross it unless he absolutely had to, but he had no choice. The river curved far to the east here. Following it would lengthen our journey, which we could ill afford. Also, there were no settlements on the far side of the river between here and El Paso. Crossing put us in easy reach of Socorro. The town was larger than La Parida and the usual place to obtain provisions for the next portion of our journey. There would be no other opportunity, he added a little grimly.

When we topped a small hill an hour later, and the village of Socorro spread out before us, he brightened visibly. Light flashed from the low flat-roofed adobe buildings, although not from the square church tower above them.

I frowned in confusion and Salazar laughed, then explained that the house windows were covered with wide pieces of mica that glinted in the sun. We would have a chance to see them up close, because our supply wagons needed to be well-stocked before we moved on. It was likely to take the rest of the day to obtain all we needed.

When we halted in a field outside town and everyone realized we weren't traveling on that day, there was a general buzz of relief. I returned my mare to the herd, then milled around with the other prisoners, uncertain how to proceed. I hadn't had this much freedom in many weeks. I hardly knew what to do with myself. There wasn't any major source of water, so I couldn't wash my clothes or bathe, but I could remove my cravat and empty my canteen onto it. I squeezed the worst of the dirt out of it, then started a small fire and I held the cloth over it gingerly, just out of reach of the flames. The linen would be smoky, but somewhat cleaner than before.

My neck cloth was just at the damp-dry stage when Falconer, Kendall, and Fitzgerald came up and asked if I was interested in an excursion into the town. I raised an eyebrow. "Is it allowed?"

Ramón appeared just then. "I go also."

Kendall grimaced, but the rest of us nodded. The newsman shrugged irritably. I tied my damp cravat around my neck and we kicked out the fire and headed off, Ramón trailing behind.

It was a real pleasure to walk somewhere without guards riding on each side. Even Kendall felt it. His spirits seemed to rise the closer we got to the village. "Do you realize that we're finally in Mexico?" he asked as we wound through the narrow streets. "When we crossed the Río Grande, we finally exited the boundaries of the Texas Republic." He looked around, studying the adobe walls, the chickens scratching nearby, a little boy peaking at us from a doorway. "Be that as it may, little has changed from one bank of the river to the other."

"They're still the same people," Fitzgerald pointed out.

Kendall gave him an impatient look. "But under different jurisdictions."

"Not according to them."

I gave the Anglo-Irishman a quizzical look. He glanced at Kendall, then Ramón, still behind us. The guard gave him a half wave. "I've been talking with some of the Nuevo Mexicanos."

"And undoubtedly being seduced by fine words," Kendall sniffed.

Falconer raised a sardonic eyebrow. "Fine words? From Mexicans?"

"Yes, in fact," Fitzgerald said. "They may be poor, but they have a rich history. In fact, it's quite fascinating and not very different from that of the Irish peasants or even the people of Spain. I'm told that some of the people here descend from Jews who were expelled from the Iberian Peninsula in the late 1400s."

When Falconer nodded thoughtfully, Fitzgerald went on. "The people here are clean and industrious. They are solicitous of their animals and of each other."

Kendall sniffed. "Be that as it may, they have no Anglo go-a-headity. In fact, they appear to be incapable of utilizing the land to its fullest capacity. A goodly portion of the fields have clearly been left to return to their original weedy condition."

"They let them alone a season or two in order to recoup the soil's full strength. In addition—" He broke off as we entered a large rectangular and dusty plaza.

Ramón nodded to me as if to say "you're on your own" and walked off toward a cluster of men under a porch roof on the other side of the square. I stopped a small boy who happened to be passing and asked where we could find food. He directed us to a nearby house which also served as a cantina. The single room was dim, lit only by the light from a single milky window. It held a rough-hewn table and a scatter of stools carved from pieces of tree trunks.

Kendall raised an eyebrow. "An actual table?" He grinned at Fitzgerald. "Perhaps they truly are civilized!"

Fitzgerald didn't answer. We seated ourselves and a young boy appeared through an uncovered doorway at the back of the room. He greeted us politely and told us what was available and the price: two pesos each.

"Beans, tortillas, and goat cheese for two pesos," Kendall grumbled, when I'd translated. "High prices for a meal with no meat."

I turned to the boy and asked about the potential for meat, but he spread his hands deprecatingly. There was chicken, but it would need to be caught and dressed.

Kendall grimaced when I told him this, then shrugged and nodded to our waiter. "Very good," he said in a tone that said it wasn't. "But no chiles!" He looked at me. "Tell him no chiles!"

Fitzgerald leaned forward and told the boy we'd take what they had available, but no chiles for Kendall. The lad looked a little confused at this, but took our coins and disappeared into the back. After a few minutes he returned carrying two heaping plates,. He was followed by a round-faced thick-chested man with two more. We dug in with gusto.

The food was covered with a layer of chile sauce, which Falconer scooped up with great delight. "These people certainly know how to season their food."

Kendall shook his head. He had broken off a piece of tortilla and was using it to scrape the sauce to one side. "It's so miserably hot that I find it impossible to ascertain with any certainty where the seasoning ends and the food begins."

"Chiles do seem to be ubiquitous here," I said. "From what Cayton Erhard and Curtis Caldwell told me, this meal is almost precisely what they were given at La Parida, although they were served miel as well."

"How fortunate for them." There was a long silence, while we ate, then he added, "I have found the local molasses to be quite adequate, although it's manufactured from corn stalks, not sugar cane. The result is not as sweet as I prefer."

Fitzgerald looked up. "Is there anything about this country that you like, Kendall?"

The newsman huffed. "I must say I haven't found much to my satisfaction."

I chuckled. "The women seem to be acceptable."

Kendall pushed his plate away and leaned back, stretching his shoulders. "Ah, the women. They are beautiful and kind and generous to a fault." He shook his head. "The pumpkin that young lady in Alburquerque bestowed on Cayton Erhard was wasted in more ways than one. I would have at least tried to get a kiss along with the food."

Fitzgerald scowled at him. "The women here may smile and seem to laugh when you kiss them, but they're merely being polite."

Kendall lifted a supercilious eyebrow. "And just how did you come by that piece of knowledge?"

"I talked to a guard who has four sisters."

"And as a result, you have become an expert on all things Mexican female."

Fitzgerald's face darkened, but he was interrupted by the boy, who came in with a platter brimming with cooked chicken and fresh bread.

"Ah!" Kendall said. "That's more like it! And no sauce but its own juice!"

I grinned, my mouth watering. "And my stomach thought it was full."

"¿Y el vino también?" the boy asked.

I looked at the others "He wants to know if we'd like wine, also."

Kendall's eyes brightened. "Certainly!"

By the time we had eaten the chicken and bread, our stomachs were almost uncomfortably distended. We had a glow about us that was not entirely due to the wine, as excellent as it was.

"Some of the best I've ever tasted," Fitzgerald said contentedly. "Even in France."

We pushed back from the table, too full to eat more but in no hurry to leave.

The man who'd helped with the plates appeared, looking apologetic. "Por favor señores, el chico se equivocó."

Fitzgerald looked at me. "The boy made a mistake?"

I nodded and turned to our host, whose round face was anxious now. "El precio del pollo y el vino es de dos pesos," he said.

I looked at my friends. "The price for the chicken and wine is two pesos."

Kendall frowned. "He wants more money?"

"The chicken and wine were extra," I reminded him. "We ordered them afterwards. They cost two pesos."

The boy appeared in the doorway, looked at Kendall's irritated face, and darted across the room into the plaza, leaving the door open behind him.

"Por cada uno," the man told me quietly.

"Each," I added.

Kendall stood up and shoved his stool with his foot. It fell sideways to the floor. Kendall put his hands on his hips. "This is highway robbery!"

"It did seem like rather a lot of food for the price," Falconer observed.

"The wine alone was worth the extra," Fitzgerald said.

Kendall shook his head. "It's robbery, I tell you! We didn't agree to an additional charge!"

Our host had lost his apologetic air. He looked toward the street door. Ramón had poked his head in and was giving me a questioning look. The Texian-hating sergeant appeared behind him. He pushed past Ramón into the room, his hand on the knife at his belt.

Kendall's face darkened. "We didn't agree."

A man appeared in the doorway at the back. His shoulders filled the wooden frame. His hands were already formed into fists. "Texians?" he growled.

Our host nodded without taking his eyes from us. The newcomer flexed his hands and moved into the room. Another, slightly larger, man followed him.

"I believe we must pay the entire sum," I said quietly.

"The better part of valor," Falconer murmured, running his hand through his beard.

But Kendall was still angry. He stared at the men blocking the doors and clenched his fists.

"We have no choice," I said.

He gave me a withering look, then turned to Fitzgerald. "And you call this a civilized country!" He shoved his hands into his pockets, pulled out four coins, tossed them onto the table, and marched toward the door.

The sergeant moved to block his path and Kendall surged forward as if to push him aside, then caught himself just in time. He pulled up and turned to me. "What are you waiting for?"

Falconer, Fitzgerald, and I turned to our host and touched his hand politely as we paid our shares.

"Mil gracias," Fitzgerald said when his turn came. "Por favor, acepte mis disculpas."

Kendall scowled at this, but he waited until we were outside before he snapped, "Your apologies? What in the name of all creation were you apologizing for? Not complaining while he fleeced us?"

Fitzgerald shook his head. "I'm not going to attempt to explain to you just how wrong your behavior was. Or how discourteous."

"Discourteous! It is discourteous to myself to be taken advantage of in that way!" Kendall stalked ahead, still fuming.

We were halfway across the plaza when a cluster of Indians rode in, buckskin shirts and leggings. Falconer turned, studying them. "They almost look like the Kiowa who harassed us on the plains."

"Apache," a voice said behind us. I turned to see Ramón. He gave me a small grin and I smiled at him apologetically. Instead of enjoying his holiday, he was forced to follow us around and make sure we didn't get into trouble. He shrugged back at me and gestured toward the newcomers, who had vaulted from their horses and were heading toward the cantina, rifles in hand. "Apache," he repeated.

"They certainly have well-made firearms," Kendall said. He leaned forward, staring unabashedly. "Those are Hawken's percussion rifles manufactured in St. Louis. That short barrel and thick stock is unmistakable." He rocked back on his feet, hands on his hips, and glared at the cantina door.

"I wonder how they came by those pieces of equipment," Falconer said.

"They undoubtedly stole them." Kendall turned away. "Those guns were very likely appropriated from stout-hearted Americans like our friends on the wagon train. I know about Apaches. They're raiders. They live in continual and open warfare with everyone not of their own race, murdering and robbing whenever the opportunity offers itself." He glared at the dusty square. "Except, of course, in New Mexico, where they seem to live in peace with the entire population. They undoubtedly trade their plunder here for powder and lead, and no one inquires where they might have obtained the goods in question."

Fitzgerald frowned. "You don't know that,"

Kendall gave him a disgusted look. "I am a newspaper man. Information comes to me from many sources. I know for a fact that those Apache braves will exit that cantina as drunk as lords and then attempt to ride those horses even though they can hardly stay on their backs."

Fitzgerald shook his head and looked away. The plaza lay bare in the afternoon sun, the only movement the swishing of the Apache horses' tails. Ramón made an almost supplicating 'move along' gesture at me and Falconer saw it.

"We should probably head back to camp," he said. "I could certainly use an afternoon nap." He looked at me. "A 'siesta'? Is that the correct term?"

"I wish there was enough water to wash in," Kendall said. He scratched at his chest. "That cantina had fleas, I'm sure of it."

He was still scratching himself when we arrived back at camp to find Cayton Erhard beside the newly built fire and wearing a clean shirt.

"Did you find a way to wash your clothes?" the newsman asked hopefully.

Cayton shook his head. He was holding a chunk of twice-baked trail bread, and watching four other pieces soak in a shallow pan of water on the rocks beside the fire. "For food I trade." He examined the bread in his hand, then bit into it cautiously.

I frowned in confusion. "You traded your shirt?"

He nodded. "Five breads." He swallowed the food and pointed at his shirt. "And this."

"Five chunks of bread and a clean shirt as well?" Fitzgerald laughed. "You're quite the trader!"

Erhard grinned, then turned to Falconer and let loose a string of German.

The Englishman grinned and held up a hand. "Slowly," he said. "Could you say that again, please?"

The boy repeated himself, less rapidly this time. When he'd finished, Falconer chuckled and turned to the rest of us.

"Apparently the young man he traded with is married. He asked Erhard if he has a wife, which Cayton thought rather ridiculous, since he doesn't even own a cow."

"It doesn't take much to set up housekeeping here." Kendall dropped onto a big rock nearby. "A few mud bricks and a willing girl."

Fitzgerald frowned. "I'm told it's more complicated than that. A man must have evidence that he can provide for a wife. That might be land or a skill like weaving or herding. And he must be prepared to take in the girl's parents, if need be."

Kendall made an impatient gesture. "We do that!"

"Also, the young couple must receive permission from the church. If the prospective partners are too closely related, the priest may refuse to marry them."

"Be that as it may, there is undoubtedly a great deal of living together without benefit of clergy."

Fitzgerald bent down and picked up his blanket roll and other belongings.

"And where are you heading off to?" Kendall demanded.

"Where the inmates are kinder." He walked off, shaking his head.

"Anglo-Irish riffraff," Kendall sniffed. He looked around with a dissatisfied air. "Erhard's used up all the firewood we had and we're going to need more for our supper."

Falconer chuckled. "Are you already contemplating our evening meal? After all that we so recently ingested? Your stomach must be as hollow as Erhard's!"

The German boy grinned at him, shook his head, and pulled a piece of bread from his pan. I looked around uneasily, wondering where Fitzgerald had gone.

CHAPTER 14
Thursday, October 29 to Friday, October 30, 1841
Socorro to Fray Cristóbal

The former soldier didn't reappear that night. At any rate, he wasn't beside Kendall when we woke the next morning.

The newsman was winding his watch when Ramón came by riding a fine new horse and leading two mules. One of them had a U.S. Army brand in its hide.

Kendall stuffed his watch into a pocket and strode toward the guard. "Where did you get that animal?" he shouted, pointing at the mule.

Ramón reined in and gave him a puzzled look. I moved to Kendall's side and quickly translated, in a softer tone than Kendall's. The guard's lips twitched, but the amusement did not reach his eyes. Kendall didn't seem to notice. He stepped forward, hands on his hips, and blocked Ramón's path.

Ramón studied him, then turned to me. "Apache."

"That mule is U.S. Army property!" Kendall bellowed, pointing at the brand.

Heads lifted from nearby fires. Guards began to drift toward us. I made a calming motion at Kendall, but he fisted his hands, resettled them on his hips, and glared at Ramón.

The guard shook his head and told me he'd paid good money for the mule and he didn't care where it originated.

When I translated this into English, Kendall turned his glare on me. "He bought stolen property! Isn't that a crime in this country?"

I shrugged. "I am not versed in Mexican law or its particular permutations in New Mexico."

"Spoken like a lawyer!"

Falconer stepped forward. "Whatever the particular legal code may be here, we're in no position to insist on its enforcement," he said mildly.

The newsman sniffed contemptuously and turned away. Ramón shook his head, nodded to Falconer and me, and nudged his horse forward, mules trailing behind.

A few minutes later, someone shouted "¡Poneos en fila!" and we gathered our gear and got into line to be counted. As soon as this was completed, a guard came up with the bay mare, I joined Salazar, and we headed out.

The landscape south of Socorro reminded me a good deal of the country north of it—low sandy hills sprinkled primarily with mesquite and cactus. Craggy mountains, dark with pine, loomed to the west.

We'd traveled perhaps two miles when a small band of Apaches appeared atop the sandy slope on our right. As we drew even with them, Salazar made a gesture that almost seemed like a salute, and they moved down the hill and joined us.

Their leader was a stalwart old man with snow-white hair. He wore an ancient blue military coat with epaulettes, along with pantaloons, and a tricorne hat. The ensemble would have looked ridiculous on anyone else, but on him it seemed almost regal.

The chief's followers hung back as he came up to us and settled into place on Salazar's right. I was on the captain's left, so I couldn't see their faces as the two leaders greeted one another, but their voices were civil enough. I noted in surprise that the chief spoke fluent Spanish.

Then he leaned forward to look at me. "¿Eres tejano?"

When I answered that, yes, I was a Texian, he waved his hand at the column behind us. "¿Y todos estos son tejanos?"

I said yes, they also were Texians.

He nodded gravely, studying my face. "¿Las armas estadounidenses no pudieron vencer a los mexicanos?"

American guns could not beat Mexicans? It was a good question. How had we allowed ourselves to be captured?

My indecision about how to respond must have been evident, because Salazar broke in, mouth twitching in amusement. The Mexicans had good leadership, he told the Chief. He gave me a sly smile. And full bellies.

The Apache man laughed and nodded. Full bellies were muy importante. Then he sobered. He knew what it was to have many captives. He advised el capitán to assure that his prisoners did not eat too much.

A shadow crossed Salazar's face, but he merely nodded and said he was indeed aware of the need to maintain control.

The Chief chuckled, raised a hand in farewell, and moved his horse to the side of the road. We left him there, backed by his men, watching the column of Texians and guards go by. I wondered where the little band came from. The mountains behind them, perhaps?

The stormy peaks loomed to our right all that day as we trudged through the sand. Along with the yucca and increasing mesquite, a new plant appeared—or the seeds of it, at least—cockle burrs. Because I was riding, I didn't experience them directly, but there were periodic groans from the ranks, as someone stopped to work one out of a tattered sock.

The kinks this created in the line enabled other prisoners to dip aside to nab downed mesquite branches and pods. The guards spurred after them, their animals raising more dust to add to the pall that already hung over us.

This went on for hours. As we moved through the dry hills, I caught occasional glimpses of the cottonwoods along the Río Grande and felt a sense of real relief when the road began to trend toward them.

Although the light was dying by the time we reached them, my feelings intensified into pure gratitude when we finally passed under the big trees into a flat grassy area between them and the river.

Salazar also seemed glad to have arrived. "El valle verde", he murmured as he looked around. The green valley. Although the grass was no longer green, even in the near-dark I could see that it had been lush during the summer months. The spot was a beautiful location and a fine camping ground.

There was much grumbling the next morning when we realized we wouldn't be lingering, but the captain was intent on moving us along. He strode through the camp barking orders and looking uneasily at the sky. The air had a bite to it. We shivered as we formed up, counted off, and moved to the river, to cross back to the eastern side.

The ford here was not as deep nor the current as strong as where we'd crossed two days before. Mist drifted along the water's surface and great blue herons lifted lazily from the shallows as we approached. On the far bank, a kingfisher darted from a branch overhead, startling my mare, and Salazar laughed indulgently.

But the peacefulness of the crossing was shattered as soon as we moved onto the flats beyond. The wind came up, sweeping bitter-cold from the north. I heard imprecations behind me from the men who'd waded across, cursing their wet feet and legs and life in general.

Captain Salazar had a few choice words of his own as he hunched his shoulders together and lowered his hat over his pinched face. On his other side, Don Jesús rode without speaking.

It was another long day. Perhaps it was merely the icy wind that made the countryside seem so bleak, but the mountains that bounded both sides of the river had an implacable look, as well. My spirit was as numb as my body by the time we stopped for the night.

The road touched the river here at a campsite called Fray Cristóbal. As we swung off our mounts and out of the wind, the captain told me it was named for a Franciscan priest who'd died nearby, the cousin of an early Spanish conquistador. The place was bleak and sandy and didn't look like much, but it was the last stopping point before we began the Jornada del Muerto.

Salazar's face grew grim as he said this. The next ninety miles of our journey contained no water or sustenance for man or beast. The only way to survive it was to cross as quickly as possible. There was a reason it was called the Journey of Death.

I found myself shivering as he spoke, whether from the cold or the captain's tone, I couldn't tell. He moved away, wrapping his cloak more tightly around himself, and stared into the still-blowing wind. Thick gray clouds were descending from the mountains, closing in rapidly. Salazar looked up and sniffed, and his face darkened further. "¡Maldita nieve!"

"Snow?" I echoed. I didn't think it snowed in New Mexico. Rain itself seemed scarce. Since I'd arrived in September, I'd seen moisture from the sky only once, on the day we'd marched out of San Miguel del Bado.

The captain smiled bleakly. Oh yes. Snow. And it would be upon us this night, if his bones were as accurate as they usually were. Then he gave me an apologetic look. He and I would have to part during this next segment of our journey. He must ask me to walk with my countrymen while he rode in one of the supply wagons. Doing so would help our mounts to accomplish the Jornada del Muerto. The burden of riders would be too much for them.

He wrapped his cloak more tightly around his chest. In truth, no one in their right mind would want to ride in the cold that was coming. Walking was a much better alternative for keeping a man's blood moving.

I nodded. And yet he was going to ride in the wagon. I didn't point out this contradiction. The bay mare had been a true luxury and I appreciated being allowed to use her as long as I had. When I expressed this, Salazar's face lit up with a rare smile. "Eres un verdadero amigo," he said.

A true friend? I looked away, embarrassed.

When I looked back at him, I saw that his expression had also changed, echoing my emotions. He clapped me awkwardly on the shoulder, then turned away, calling to the nearest guard with a question about the remaining cattle.

As I moved off to find Falconer and the others, I passed the sick wagon. The mules, still in their harness, flicked their ears wearily. Someone inside coughed. It sounded as if their lungs were turning inside out. I knocked gently on the sideboards, then pulled back the tattered canvas cover and peered in.

Gates was curled on his side under his brown wool blanket and coughing into a large handkerchief that had once been white. It was spotted with blood. When he saw me, he shoved the big square under the blanket and gave me a pleading look. I nodded without speaking, agreeing to keep his secret, dropped the canvas, and moved away. How was he going to manage the trek across the Jornada? If it was as bad as Salazar had said, it would surely be the end of a man as ill as Gates.

But there was good news at the campfire. The mesquite and other pieces of debris my friends had picked up along the way burned brightly in the gathering night and word had it that the captain had ordered an ox to be butchered.

"Though it will undoubtedly be the thinnest and most worn out of the lot," Kendall grumbled. "And the best pieces will go to him and that Don Jesús."

"You don't know that," I said, thinking of Gates in the sick wagon. Hopefully, he would get a tender piece.

But when the meat arrived, it was stringy and tough.

"It's to be expected, I suppose," Falconer said. "The poor beasts are worn out. They've been traveling for the last four and a half months and have experienced little rest or good pasturage along the way."

"If Salazar had butchered them sooner, they wouldn't be quite so worn out," Kendall said. "We haven't experienced any rest, either."

I raised an eyebrow at this. He, Fitzgerald, and I had, in fact, experienced almost a month of enforced rest. But there was no point in arguing with the man and just now the smell of beef cooking on the sticks of green wood stuck in the dirt around the fire was invading all my senses.

Cayton and Anton Erhard looked as if they felt the same way. The boys' eyes were locked on the meat.

"You're like a pair of wolves," Kendall told them with a grin.

Cayton laughed, patted his belly, threw back his head, and pretended to howl. "I eat das Fleisch roh!"

"Raw meat?" Falconer chuckled. "I wouldn't advise it." Then he sobered. "Even after it's cooked, it would be wise to eat these pieces slowly, given how little fat they contain."

Anton leaned forward to examine the sticks that contained his and his cousin's portions. The meat was charred on the outside, but blood still seeped along the cut edges. When he touched it, the side gave slightly under his dirty finger.

"Enough good," he said. Both boys grabbed their sticks and bit down eagerly.

We older men held off, waiting for the food to be truly cooked. It seemed hours.

"Like a watched pot never boiling, a watched bit of meat never cooks," Falconer said wryly.

"We've forgotten how long it should take," Kendall said. He leaned forward and poked gingerly at his portion. "There's no blood seepage now, at any rate." He pulled the stick from the ground and took a small bite, his face darkening as he chewed. "This is as tough as proverbial shoe leather. It's undoubtedly going to take as long to eat as it did to cook."

I wanted to tell him he was exaggerating, but when I pulled mine away from the fire, I found that the meat really did resist mastication. However, it was still sustenance, and certainly better than more mush. The cantina meal at Socorro had only made me hungry for more like it. Or the watermelon and cakes the kind people of the Río Grande had provided.

I dreamed of cakes and melons that night, huddled into my blanket with Cayton Erhard at my back, sandwiched between me and his cousin. The wind hadn't let up and the dampness it carried didn't bode well. Even the guards' cries of "¡Centinela, alerta!" didn't seem as loud or enthusiastic as usual.

CHAPTER 15
Sunday, October 31, 1841
Jornada del Muerto, Day 1

We woke to a layer of snow.

"¡Maldición!" a guard cried irritably.

I shook cold white flakes from my head and sat up, shoving the blanket away quickly to keep the wet from my clothes.

In the distance, someone coughed, a wracking sound that tightened my own chest. I patted my cravat in a sort of defensive motion and looked around. A blanket of white, perhaps three inches of it, met my eyes. The only bright spot was a tiny fire that Cayton Erhard was carefully nurturing a few yards away. His sun glass lay beside him.

Kendall lay nearby, his back to Falconer. During the night, the Englishman had pulled his blanket over his head. He looked like a long narrow hillock mounded with snow.

Then the little hill stirred. Falconer sat up, tumbling snow onto the ground. "Damnation!" he said. He looked around, then flipped the blanket, sending little flurries into the air. He got to his feet and hurried to the fire. "I don't believe I've ever been so cold!"

Cayton grinned at him. "But you sleep warm."

Falconer's face changed. "You're quite right. I was, in fact, relatively comfortable last night."

Erhard stuck out his leg and looked down at his right foot. The dirty sock on his big toe was clearly visible through the boot leather. The boy rubbed his fingers over it ruefully.

Fitzgerald came up just then and saw what he was doing. "That looks uncomfortable."

Cayton nodded. "It is most—"

He was interrupted by a groan from Kendall as he rose, shedding snow. He stared at us, wild-eyed, then his gaze dropped to the men who were still asleep. He grinned. "They look like harvested logs waiting for the mill." Someone coughed, the sound I'd heard earlier, and Kendall winced. "Heaven protect me from such a discomfort."

"Sleep well?" Fitzgerald asked mildly.

Kendall frowned. "As a matter of fact, I did." He shook his blanket, sending the remaining ice flakes cascading to the ground. "Growing up in Vermont, we had enough sense to always sleep inside, so I've never experienced the insulating character of five or six inches of snow."

Erhard chuckled and nodded. "Mein vater—" Then his face changed. He turned away. He glanced at the fire. "More wood," he said thickly. He walked off, toward the river.

As Fitzgerald followed him, Ramón approached, smiling with pleasure. "¡Nieve!" He gestured at the sparse grass on the hillocks around the camp. "Is good!"

Kendall scowled at him. "The damnable stuff is cold!"

The guard laughed and pointed at the fire. "Cold make feel more warm!"

Kendall turned away. I chuckled. "I don't think it's possible to convince him to think positively about our current circumstances," I told the guard.

He gave me a puzzled look. When I turned what I'd said into Spanish, he laughed and shrugged. "Try!"

The sergeant came through, bellowing the order to line up. As he passed, the various mounds of snow turned into grumbling men. Were we to march off without a morning meal? When Kendall posed the question to Ramón, he pretended not to understand.

We assembled at the edge of the road, where we found Captain Salazar standing on the seat of a supply wagon, his cloak wrapped around him and his hat low over his cold-pinched face. He motioned for me to climb up beside him.

The view wasn't a pleasant one. The men were gaunt, their faces seamed with dirt and exhaustion above the blankets clutched around their shoulders. Their footwear was ragged and their clothes thin. Coats with missing buttons flapped around legs. Battered hats were tied on with bits of cloth and string.

The guards didn't look much better. The shoulders of both men and mounts were hunched against the cold.

I glanced at Salazar. I must have looked almost as unhappy as I felt. He shrugged bitterly. "Jornada del muerto," he muttered. He glanced east at the snow-encrusted mountains, shook his head, then turned back to the column. He lifted a hand. "Hombres," he called. "¡Escuchad!"

I raised my own arms. "Men!" I shouted, translating. "Pay attention!"

Guards and prisoners alike looked up warily.

Salazar began speaking, using short sentences to ease my translation. We were about to embark on the most difficult part of our journey, he said. We must prepare for it both physically and mentally. He paused here, studying the men below, then went on. The road to El Paso led across the Jornada del Muerto.

At the words "Journey of Death," there was a collective groan, prisoners and guards alike. Then someone laughed. Ramón? Yes, there he was, on his horse a few feet from Kendall, with the newsman glaring at him in disgust.

But Captain Salazar was forging grimly on. I returned to my duties. The Jornada was ninety miles long. We would cross it without stopping to eat or sleep.

The guards' animals stirred uneasily. The captain held up a hand, as if to ward off protests. The Jornada was a miserable route, he said. Crossing swiftly was the only way to survive it. He pointed at the snow on the ground, which was beginning to melt. Winter was approaching with great rapidity. We must reach El Paso before it arrived in full force. He paused, letting the words sink in.

The faces of my fellow prisoners were grim now, but they didn't seem angry. Even Kendall's face held a measure of respect for the captain's explanation and demeanor.

Then Salazar began again, emphasizing the need for everyone to carry as much water as possible. Those with gourds or canteens should fill them from the river before we set out. Men turned toward the river, but the captain held up a restraining hand. Not now. At the end of the day.

Prisoners and guards alike exchanged glances. The end of the day? We were to rest?

Then Salazar went on, and the hopeful looks faded. We would begin our crossing at nightfall. We would not stop until we had arrived at the other end of the Jornada. I gulped. Ninety miles. How long would it take us to traverse such a distance with no rest or food and only the water we carried?

But the captain was continuing. He glanced at the sky, which was as clear as if it had never thought of snowing, and noted that the moon was two days past full and the clouds had dissipated. Our journey would be well lit.

And cold, I reflected. The lack of clouds meant the temperature would drop precipitously once the sun went down. Salazar raised his hands, dismissing us, and nodded his thanks to me. As I climbed down, Don Jesús came up, and the captain turned to him with a question about the oxen.

I returned to the fire, which was bigger now, chewing through sticks the Erhard cousins had scrounged from beneath the river cottonwoods. Major Caldwell had joined us and was heating water in preparation for washing his son's feet.

"They ain't that dirty, Pa," Curtis protested.

Old Paint shook his head. "It's not the dirt I'm worried about, it's your toenails. I can't see them under the layer of soil."

The boy looked down at them. "They do hurt."

Kendall's head lifted. "Frostbite?"

The major shrugged. "That or worn-out shoes. I can't tell without seeing them." He dipped a cloth into the water.

Curtis shuddered as the warmth hit his toes. Cayton Erhard gave him a sharp look, then picked up his sleeping blanket and wrapped it around the younger boy's shoulders. "Wet feet, krank here," Cayton said, tapping his chest.

Falconer grinned. "I've always thought krank a splendid word for illness, especially in the chest."

Major Caldwell looked up. "So 'wet feet will give you a chest cold' is an old wives tale in Germany, too?"

Falconer laughed. "And an English one."

I sat down on a nearby hillock and watched the operation. Curtis' feet were merely dirty and the nails cracked. He didn't have frostbite. The guards came around with our morning portions of meal. The snow had melted into the sandy soil now and the top was relatively dry. I ate, then found a clear spot, wrapped myself in my blanket, and slept.

At noon, we ate again. This time there were portions of beef. Ramón brought them, presenting the bloody slices with great formality, a large portion for each of us, along with sharpened sticks of green wood for holding them over the flames.

Kendall eyed his with distaste. "I can only hope this is fit to eat," he said as he threaded it onto the stick.

The guard laughed. "A buena hambre no hay pan duro."

Kendall raised an unwilling eyebrow at me.

"No bread is hard when one is really hungry," I translated.

Falconer grinned. "Or, as we say in England, 'hunger is the best sauce.'"

Fitzgerald chuckled. "A Spaniard said it first. Or put it into writing, at any rate."

I swung toward him. "Truly?"

He nodded. "Miguel de Cervantes in Don Quixote."

Kendall stared at him. "That's right. I'd forgotten. It's in Smollett's translation." Then he seemed to catch himself. He leaned toward the fire and set about bracing the end of his stick against the rocks so he wouldn't have to hold it.

"Bread too hard can be," Cayton Erhard said, breaking the silence. He put his hand to his jaw and grimaced, reminding us of his bout with the twice-baked bread en route to Pecos.

We all laughed at this, including Ramón. He grinned at me and made a motion toward his mouth, indicating he was looking forward to downing his own piece of beef.

Kendall didn't need a translation for that. He scowled at the guard. "And you and Salazar and Don Jesús will undoubtedly eat the best parts."

Ramón looked at me, waiting for a translation. I hesitated, then reluctantly turned what Kendall had said into Spanish. The guard stared at me, then Kendall, and then burst into laughter. "¡Dios!" he gasped, wiping tears of amusement from his eyes. Apparently the ox that had been butchered was the sorriest of the bunch. There were no best parts. He was still chuckling as he walked away.

When I explained to my companions what he'd found so amusing, Kendall's scowl deepened. "Everything is a joke to that man. He's one of the sorriest excuses for a human being I've ever met with."

"I believe he feels obligated to try to ease our situation by introducing a little humor into it," Fitzgerald said.

Kendall's head swung toward him. "Laughter in our particular situation is not only highly overrated, it is inappropriate. I refuse to believe the man harbors any positive intention toward us whatsoever." He reached for his meat, testing whether it was cooked, and grunted in disgust. "I begin to suspect Salazar gave us the day to rest because he knew it would take that long for this stringy excuse for nourishment to cook."

Fitzgerald turned away. When his own meat was ready, he ate it in silence, then drifted off toward the river. Kendall complained throughout his own meal, then wrapped himself in his blanket and dozed by the fire, while I went over my gear, tightening knots, working a bur out of my sleeping blanket, shaking sand from my cravat, and ensuring my canteen was full.

As the sun began to drop toward the west, we ate once more, this time a double portion of meal. Our bellies were comfortably full when the captain called us together again. As he spoke and I translated, I tried not to look beyond the crowd to the lengthening shadows of the cottonwoods beside the river. The wind had come up, cold flicking its edges.

Salazar raised his voice, reminding us that our goal was to cross the Jornada as quickly as possible and reiterating that all water containers must be filled to the brim before we set out.

Then he took a breath and his tone changed. He sounded as if he was reading from a prepared speech, one he hadn't written. There would be no straying from the road. Anyone who did so or who lagged behind would be shot. Then he paused. I glanced at him, waiting for more, and was struck by the slump in his shoulders, the dread in his eyes.

He made a small gesture to indicate he was finished, then turned away abruptly, climbed down from the wagon, and walked off. The guards looked at each other, uncertain, then nodded impatiently to various prisoners who wanted one more trip to the river to fill their gourds or canteens.

The trumpet sounded a short while later. The wind was already sharper. The wagon Salazar had spoken from led the way, with him and Don Jesús bundled up in the bed behind the driver. We prisoners wrapped our sleeping blankets over our shoulders and heads and followed. Our Jornada del Muerto had begun.

I was in line with Kendall, Falconer, and Cayton Erhard. Anton and Fitzgerald walked behind us with Curtis and his father. We were well in the middle of the column where, as Kendall put it, we might get some respite from the wind. He raised an eyebrow when he realized I would be walking instead of riding. "I take it that the captain has no use for your translation services during this part of our journey."

"There's nothing left to say," Falconer pointed out. "We are marching across a waterless wasteland and that's all there is to it." He turned his head to study the landscape. "And it truly is a wasteland."

I nodded. Perhaps it was simply the approaching darkness, but the countryside seemed much bleaker now. There was almost no grass beside the road, which had already moved away from the river, winding between jagged black rocks that looked like they'd been melted into the ground. Here and there, stunted trees struggled through the crevices between them, doing their best to survive.

The only other vegetation was a species of giant yucca perhaps twice the height of a man and shaped like great shaggy trees. Their massive trunks were formed of ragged brown vegetation that had died but not fallen off, while thick green blades emerged from the top and stuck out in all directions. The things had a menacing air which grew stronger as night came on, their big fronds silhouetted against the dark blue sky.

The moon Salazar had promised us wasn't up yet, but a sharp east wind was, It smelled of snow from the mountains. I was at the end of our particular line and was grateful for the bulk of Ramón's horse between me and the worst of it.

Ramón saw me positioning myself to take advantage of this bit of protection and grinned, then peered down at me thoughtfully. A few minutes later, he vaulted from his saddle and slipped around the animal to walk beside me. He rubbed his upper arms with his hands and made an apologetic face as I moved aside for him.

I couldn't help but grin back at him. Riding was almost always better than walking, but this was clearly one case where that truism didn't apply. I glanced at the other end of our line. Sure enough, the guard who'd been beside Cayton Erhard had also dismounted.

I shivered a little, but not from the immediate cold. We were early in our journey, yet the guards were already walking. What lay ahead?

My reverie was broken by a sudden cracking sound and the gurgle of water. Kendall and Falconer stopped abruptly, snarling the column behind us.

"Tarnation!" the newsman said. His water gourd lay in pieces at his feet.

"¡Vámonos!" someone yelled from farther back. I wasn't sure it was a guard.

"And now I have no water," Kendall muttered. He crouched down to examine the gourd.

The men behind were moving forward, edging around and past. "There ain't no goin' back fer more," one of them said. "No use cryin' over spilt milk."

I turned in surprise. "Golpin?"

He stopped beside me, nodding a greeting. I noticed he was holding his right hand in his left.

"I thought you were in the wagon," I said.

He shrugged. "Mules need a break, too."

"Crying over spilt milk." Falconer grinned. "In England we say 'No weeping for shed milk'." He looked at me. "Ask Ramón what they say here."

I turned to the guard, who grinned sardonically. "Lo perdido vaya por Dios," he told me.

I winced as I translated. "What's lost is lost because God wills it."

"That's unaccountably harsh," Kendall said, rising. "I can think of no good reason why God should will that I go without water for the remainder of this miserable journey." He scowled at Ramón. "As Salazar undoubtedly wills it."

There was nothing to say to this. I busied myself with my blanket, wrapping it around my head and chin so only my eyes were visible.

I hadn't translated Kendall's words, but Ramón had caught the captain's name and understood the tone. He chuckled in amusement. As Kendall glared at him, the trumpet ahead blasted impatiently. Falconer kicked the fragments of Kendall's water gourd to the side of the road and we set off again.

The moon rose, a huge golden orb lifting over the edge of the mountains and filling the sky. The wind sharpened.

"How long march?" Cayton Erhard asked, his voice muffled. He twisted toward Falconer. "Drei stunden?"

"Three hours that we've walked, so far?" the Englishman asked. "Perhaps, though it seems longer." He adjusted his blanket, pulling it farther down his forehead.

Kendall reached for his watch pocket, then seemed to think better of it. He looked up at the sky. "I believe it's approximately nine o'clock. There's undoubtedly sufficient moonlight to ascertain the exact time, but I'm reluctant to expose the delicate mechanism of my timepiece to these temperatures." He shuddered and hunched his shoulders closer together. "I never knew a wind could be so desperately cold."

Golpin put a hand on my arm. "Am I truly seein' light up there yonder?"

I squinted against the dark and my watering eyes. There was indeed a haze of brightness ahead. Or was I imagining it? The men ahead of us had seen it too. There was a general lifting of faces and murmur of voices. Our feet moved more quickly.

Pillars of fire shot upward in the darkness just off the road. Someone had set the giant yuccas alight. Men and guards veered toward them. Flames licked up the woody bottoms of the plants, then back down, repelled by the green growth above. Lit from underneath, the fronds seemed even darker and more menacing, made grotesque by the attack against them.

We stopped in the road, watching. Fitzgerald moved up beside me, a confused look on his face. "Where did the women come from?"

I squinted, trying to see. He was right. Women in the short full skirts of New Mexico, rebozos wrapped around their heads and shoulders. One of them moved toward the fire, then back a step, and a man in a blue cloak tucked her under his arm. At first I thought he was one of our guards, then I saw his tall bearskin cap.

"Dragones," Ramón said. He frowned, then his face cleared. "From south."

Kendall pushed past him. "Perhaps they have news."

Falconer grinned. "At any rate, they have fire." When Ramón stepped toward the nearest burning plant, we and the German boys followed.

As we approached, another man in a blue cloak appeared. He flung one corner over his shoulder, exposing the red coat beneath.

"I saw that uniform at the battle for Gonzáles," Major Caldwell said. "These men are definitely Mexican dragoons,"

"Those beaver hats and long cloaks look like they'd be particularly effective against this cold," Kendall remarked enviously.

Falconer pulled his blanket closer to his shoulders. "The women don't look equipped for this weather."

"They don't need additional layers," the major said drily.

As we approached, the woman under the dragoon's cloak peeked out at us. Ramón laughed and began humming a tune that sounded reminiscent of the song he'd sung to the girl south of Sandia. The woman smiled gaily and her protector grinned and gestured us closer.

Fitzgerald lingered behind, looking up the road. "Maybe we should go on a bit." He turned to Ramón. "¿Por favor?" He pointed to the column still behind us. The men in it had stopped to stare at the pillars of heat. "They will also want some comfort from the flames. From— Incendio?" He gave me a sheepish look. "The cold has taken my Spanish."

When I explained to Ramón what Fitzgerald had suggested, he nodded and we moved on, Kendall lagging behind. We'd only gone a few yards when Cayton Erhard looked around with a small frown. "Herr Golpin?"

I looked back. The Mississippian was bent toward the licking flames, his disheveled head averted from the heat while his hands reached toward it.

The boy glanced at Ramón, who shrugged and muttered something in Spanish about Golpin not having any other place to go.

Kendall, not understanding, sniffed disparagingly. "These guards don't care what happens to the prisoners as long as they themselves keep warm."

Anton Erhard had tucked his hands under his armpits, but his head was up, studying the blackness beyond the flames. He leaned toward his cousin and muttered something in a low voice.

The older but smaller boy scowled and jerked away. "Wasser?" he snapped. "Das Essen? Die Siedlungen?"

I glanced at Falconer, who shook his head, his eyes on the boys. "Anton wants to escape under cover of the darkness," he said quietly. "Cayton wants to know where they'd find water, food, or the settlements."

Anton glanced at us, then Ramón, and leaned closer to Cayton, who shook his head and shoved the younger boy's shoulder away from him.

Falconer stepped between them. "He's quite correct," he told Anton. "You have no food, water is extremely scarce, and the land here is desolate of any habitations."

Kendall nodded. "If the Apaches didn't get you, the Mexicans would and then Salazar would have you shot and your ears severed from your body."

Cayton nodded at his cousin, who wrapped his arms around his chest and looked away. We moved on towards the next pillar of flame. Once again, the dragoons and their women moved aside for us. None appeared to speak English, but they all brightened when they realized I spoke some Spanish and told us they were heading north to assist General Armijo in fending off the Texians.

When I translated this, Kendall barked with amusement. "Don't they know we've all been captured?"

Falconer frowned. "I suppose they have no way of ascertaining whether or not there are more of us out there."

"We told them!" Kendall huffed. "Texians, unlike the inhabitants of New Mexico, don't make a habit of lying."

Ramón turned to the dragoon and asked a question I couldn't make out. The other man smiled proudly. "Nuestro líder es el Coronel Pedro José Muñoz."

The guard's face brightened. "¿El coronel vuelve a Nuevo México?"

Cayton tugged at my elbow. "What saying?"

"The dragoon says their leader is Colonel Pedro José Muñoz. Ramón asked if the colonel is returning to New Mexico."

Kendall raised an eyebrow. "He's been here before?"

The tall fire was still burning fiercely, but the men who'd been behind us in the column were now moving toward us. We said goodbye to our hosts and returned to the road. I fell in next to Ramón, and asked him about the dragoons' leader. He brightened again and explained that Colonel Muñoz, while he was still a captain, had played a role in suppressing a New Mexico revolt in 1837.

Fitzgerald, on my other side, and I nodded. We'd heard about the uprising and subsequent death of the appointed New Mexico governor and his officials. In fact, it was this rebellion, so soon after the Texian declaration of independence, that had given rise to the idea that New Mexico would want to join the Republic.

Our discussion seemed to rejuvenate Ramón, who now broke into song, repeating the tune about a guitar and a wedding day. Kendall, who was walking behind me, leaned forward and poked me in the shoulder. "Why do you feel compelled to encourage him? Whatever he's told you, it's undoubtedly untrue, and his singing voice is equivalent to an ungreased windmill."

I didn't translate this for the guard, but he seemed to understand it well enough. He turned to Kendall, grinned mischievously, and raised his voice, singing loudly until we reached the last of the big yuccas, where we stopped again to warm ourselves. The dragoons around this plant contained an officer, who nodded politely, the black horsehair crest on his helmet gleaming in the light.

After we'd introduced ourselves and warmed up a bit, I commented that our officers had been ahead of us on the road. The officer nodded. He and his men had crossed paths with Captain Sutton's party. They appeared to be doing well.

When I translated this for my companions, Kendall sniffed. "I take it they haven't received the floggings and punishment a certain person has been describing with such detail." He looked at Ramón, who shrugged and grinned at him, eyes sparkling with mischief.

I shook my head. Couldn't Kendall see that the man simply liked to tease him?

But the officer was asking politely where we were all from. I turned back to him. When I said the Erhards were from Germany, he gave them a long look. The idea that they'd come all the way from Europe to join us seemed to intrigue him.

He was about to ask another question when Ramón's head turned toward the road. The tail end of the column was approaching, followed by the jersey wagon. Behind it, cattle lowed, their smell mixing with the char of burning yucca. If we didn't move on soon, we'd be wedged between the wagon and the herd, swamped in a dusty haze.

We followed our guard to the road and fell in with the last of the prisoners, moving past yuccas whose fires were slowly dying or had subsided completely in the density of the massive fronds. The plants were mere skeletons in the darkness, thin below, where they had once been fat, the spiny leaves at the top out of proportion to their base. The moonlight brought no cheer, only a deeper sense of blackness beyond the dying yuccas.

The wind seemed sharper now and the cold deeper, perhaps because of the contrast to the bit of warmth and comradery we were leaving behind. The dust from our fellow walkers hung over us, increasing our misery. Even if I'd had anything to say, my lips were too stiff with cold to make talking worthwhile. I pulled my cravat up to cover them, tucked my hands into my armpits, and tried not to think about anything except putting one foot in front of the other.

We moved forward like this for hours, my shuffling companions also apparently lost in a dull discomfort. Kendall, who was now beside me, limped badly. I was too cold and weary to feel anything toward him except a vague awareness that he existed and flashes of irritation when his elbow bumped mine.

Only Ramón seemed to be making any effort at cheerfulness. He broke periodically into song, but the words became increasingly jumbled as the cold seeped into his face. He eventually subsided and trudged along beside us, head down.

There's something immeasurably dreary about a cold night march, especially over an unfamiliar road. There were no visible landmarks beyond the burnt yuccas. Even if there had been, they would have told us nothing about how far we had come, how long until we arrived at our destination.

The thought of destinations led inevitably to the place we were being taken. Mexico City. While it was cheering to know Sutton and his men were being well treated en route, the fact remained that they and we were all on our way to the Capitol and President Santa Anna. Regardless of how polite individual dragoons or guards might be, he alone would decide our fate. And to say he didn't much care for Texians was an understatement.

While the general's victory at the Alamo had made him a byword in Texas and the United States, his subsequent defeat and capture at San Jacinto had made him a laughing stock. No one likes to be laughed at. He'd already had plenty of time to brood over the humiliating treaties he'd been forced to sign, and he would have even more time for reflection before we reached the capital. It was still a good 1200 miles away. Four hundred leagues, as reckoned in Mexican distances.

The thought made me feel even colder, until the ache in my legs dulled my mind from even these worries. I began to feel intensely drowsy. My head drooped and my eyelids drifted shut, only to open again when I moved sideways and bumped into Kendall or slowed enough to cause Cayton Erhard, now behind me, to step on my heels.

Only when a bit of dawn began to lighten the eastern mountains, did I rouse a little and look around. I could just make out Old Paint Caldwell in the row ahead. He walked leaning sideways, as if he was drunk, Curtis clutching his arm.

I looked at the men in my own line. Their heads were down, eyes barely open, blankets over their heads and shoulders, held in place by crossed arms. Ramón's face was as drawn and gray as the rest of us.

CHAPTER 16
Monday, November 1, 1841
Jornada del Muerto, Day 2

And then the sun rose over the mountains. The trumpet blasted up ahead and our chins jerked toward it. "What the—," Kendall muttered.

I wiped dust from my eyes. Major Caldwell and the men with him were perhaps twenty yards ahead, with another gap between them and the group beyond. They had stopped to wait for us and the clusters of prisoners and guards lagging behind us. The trumpet wasn't telling us to go on, but to regroup.

We moved forward. Most of the men ahead had dropped onto the road. When we reached them, we followed their example. Cayton Erhard was so tired that he immediately pulled his blanket over his head and fell asleep. His cousin came up and dropped down beside him, nursing their water gourd.

I sat down a few feet away and stared blankly at the dirt. More men joined us, stumbling to a stop, then Golpin, his face thinner than ever, deformed hand cradled in his left. After a long while, the jersey wagon and extra animals appeared. Even at this distance, I could hear Gates' ragged cough, turning his chest inside out.

Almost as soon as the herd came up, guards appeared, counting us off. Once this had been accomplished, the trumpet sounded again and we moved out. Salazar's wagon had pulled off to the side of the road. Our heads swiveled toward it as we passed. The captain and Don Jesús were both wrapped in heavy blankets, their heads drooping.

"They sleep while we walk," Kendall muttered.

Ramón seemed to have recovered from our short rest. He grinned at the newsman. "Walking warmer."

Falconer studied the wagon. "The captain seems to be waiting to take up position at the end the column, despite the dust we stir up. He must be concerned that someone will take advantage of the way we're strung out to try to escape into the desert."

Cayton glanced at his cousin. "Too empty."

"No girls!" Ramón laughed, then began to sing the ditty that ended with "I have nothing more to give you than this dirty belly button."

When I translated the words, Cayton chuckled and nodded. "Ja, is all."

Ramón laughed and went on to serenade us with the marriage ceremony and guitar song, then began the one about the belly button again. When Kendall scowled, he broke off and started in on the tune that featured a female mule, a Texian, and the urge to procreate, accompanied by the pertinent hand gestures.

Kendall's scowl deepened. He released his blanket long enough to mimic Ramón's gestures back at him.

My breath caught, but the guard only laughed triumphantly and gave me a wink. Behind me, Cayton chuckled.

I smiled a little myself. Ramón's antics were clearly designed to keep us alert and moving forward and the strategy seemed to be working. We all had our heads up, watching Kendall and the guard, who looked quite pleased with himself.

Towards noon, we had something else to think about. Beyond the burnt yuccas was a dried-up lake bed. Thick brown grasses crowded its edges.

"Laguna del muerto," Ramón told us.

Kendall didn't need a translation for this. "Lake of death," he groaned. "Undoubtedly so called because it contains no water whatsoever." He studied the lake, the burnt plants, and our sandy road. "If the weather wasn't so cold, this lack of moisture would be unbearable."

"Thirsty," Cayton Erhard muttered.

Falconer gave him a surprised look. "I thought you had a gourd."

Erhard gestured at his cousin, who was in the row behind him. Anton held up their shared container and shook it. It made no sound.

Ramón glanced at him, then lifted his battered canteen over his head and handed it to Cayton. "Un poco."

The boy nodded, lifted the container to his lips, and dribbled in a bit of water. He rolled the liquid over his tongue, sighed a little, took a bit more, then handed it back. "Gracias."

Anton leaned forward, head following the canteen. Ramón made a comical face, then passed it to him. Cayton turned to watch. "Un poco," he said warningly. He held up two fingers and pinched them together.

Anton's face darkened. He tipped his head back and took a big gulp. Ramón's eyes narrowed. He held out his hand for the canteen. The German boy clutched it to his chest for a moment, then made a little face and returned it.

"I understand that sucking on rocks can be fairly effective in assuaging one's thirst," Falconer said.

Kendall's nose wrinkled. "And quite dirty. It's too bad we don't have any bullets."

Ramón's eyes darted toward him.

I frowned. "He's going to think you have a weapon hidden in your pockets."

Kendall's hands balled into fists. "I very much wish I did! Salazar stole everything!"

No one responded. We truly didn't need another litany of the man's woes. The sun moved higher in the cloudless blue sky and the wind died. Our muscles, bound tight by the cold, began to loosen a little.

Someone brought Ramón his mount and he climbed aboard, then pulled out the makings of a cigarillo. It was quite a feat to roll New Mexican tobacco into a square of dried corn husk while riding, but he accomplished it. However, lighting the tiny cigar was another matter. The spunk he carried for this purpose refused to cooperate.

Cayton edged toward him, digging a hand into a pocket. He held out his sun glass. "This use."

Ramón looked at me in confusion. When I explained that the boy's glass could be used to light a fire as well as a cigaril lo, he raised a disbelieving eyebrow and went back to his spunk. But it still wouldn't behave.

Cayton held out the bit of glass. "I ride?"

The guard shook his head and tucked both spunk and cigarillo away. A few paces later, Cayton lifted the glass again, turning it to spark in the sun and shine directly into Ramón's eyes.

The guard pulled back, lifting his free hand to protect his face, then realized what Cayton was doing. He gave the boy a sharp look, then chuckled and bent forward to study the glass.

Cayton moved it again, making it spark. Ramón shook his head in bemusement and slipped off his mount. He moved around the horse to walk beside Cayton and extended a hand for the glass while offering the boy the horse's reins.

Cayton grinned, handed the fire starter over, and scrambled aboard the animal. When he jiggled his heels, the horse shook its head impatiently, then half-trotted forward, moving only slightly faster than the column.

Ramón chuckled and studied the glass in his hand. He turned to me. "How?"

I demonstrated the use of the little tool as best I could while we walked, showing how it concentrated the light in one spot and produced enough heat to light the material in question. Ramón pulled out his spunk, experimented a little, and got it going again, then used it to light the little cigar. He nodded his thanks, tucked the glass into his pocket, and was puffing happily when Cayton reappeared. The boy trotted towards us, the horse still looking annoyed, and kept on going, waving as he went by. I glanced at Ramón, but he only chuckled and shrugged.

We went on, moving slowly but steadily across the barren landscape. We passed several miles of unfired yucca, then more burned ones, still smelling charred. Cayton didn't return, although we did spy him from time to time, moving up and down the column. The horse had slowed to a walk now, but the boy seemed to be thoroughly enjoying himself. Ramón watched him closely, but made no effort to retrieve his mount.

Then, as the sky began to darken toward sunset, we heard gunshots behind us. First one, then another. We all turned, jerking the column to a standstill as we tried to see over the heads and shoulders of our companions.

Cayton galloped toward us from the end of the column, eyes wide in his thin face, and reined in.

"What happened?" I demanded.

"Herr Golpin." He swallowed hard, looked away, then slid to the ground. Ramón grabbed the reins and swung into the saddle, but stayed beside us, watching the boy. The column had stopped moving.

Fitzgerald put a hand on his shoulder. "Golpin? What about him?"

"Herr walking," Cayton gasped. "Tired most." He waved a hand. "Back far." He looked uncertain, then found the English. "Behind."

"Yes?"

He plucked at his shirt, demonstrating. "Sein hemd—" he looked at Falconer beseechingly.

"His shirt?"

"Ja, his shirt for—" He motioned toward Ramón's horse.

"His shirt for a ride. He offered to trade his shirt for a ride?"

"Ja."

We all nodded encouragingly. He went on. "Walking always. His hand—"

"I would think it would be difficult for him to get his shirt off while he was stationary, much less moving," Fitzgerald said.

Cayton nodded. He turned to Falconer and rattled off a string of German.

The Englishman's face darkened as he listened. He turned to us. "Golpin stopped to wrestle with his shirt and Captain Salazar's wagon came up."

"And Salazar undoubtedly saw him and became angry and shot him." Kendall's face was a curious mixture of grimness and excitement that he could anticipate the story's outcome.

Ramón frowned, jerked his mount's head toward the end of the column, and rode off. Erhard watched him go, then refocused on Falconer, lapsing into German again.

When he had finished, Falconer gave me a somber look. "He says Salazar cried out that Golpin was trying to escape and started waving his arms at the nearest guard to stop him."

Cayton nodded. "Der guard, his gun." He gave me a confused look. "'¡No le dispares!' He say it."

"Who said it?"

"Salazar."

Fitzgerald's eyebrows lifted. "He said not to shoot Golpin?"

Kendall sniffed. "On the contrary. Salazar undoubtedly ordered the guard to shoot."

Falconer's eyes were on Cayton's pale face. "The evidence suggests otherwise."

Just then Ramón came back, a tense look on his face. "¡Muévanse!" he snapped.

Up and down the line, the other guards were issuing the same orders. We started forward. When I asked Ramón what had happened, he gave me a mulish look. The prisoner, Señor Golpin, tried to escape. The captain's orders, as formulated by el gobernador Manuel Armijo about such matters, had been clear from the beginning. Señor Golpin was dead. There was nothing further to discuss.

I sighed and turned away. He was right. Whatever had been said, and by whom, in this particular instance, the damage was done. A man was dead. Poor Golpin. Such an inoffensive, kind man.

But my grief was interrupted by Kendall gloating over the captain's guilt. "And then he undoubtedly had the prisoner's ears cut off and the body stripped and left beside the road for the wolves."

Cayton looked away. His face twisted, his mouth unsteady. He looked at me with tears in his eyes. "Ein freundlich man."

Falconer ran his hand through his beard. "He was a kind man. And not strong at all. He should have been in the sick wagon with Gates."

I made a helpless gesture. "He didn't want to make the mules pull more weight than was absolutely necessary."

"And for his mercy no mercy was extended to him," Kendall growled. "Salazar will pay for this!"

Cayton frowned. "He say no shoot."

Kendall sniffed derisively and turned away.

We walked silently on. Ramón had lost his truculence, although he was still uncharacteristically pensive. I frowned, wondering what had really happened. A command to shoot didn't seem in keeping with what I knew of the captain. Had the guard misunderstood? My shoulders sagged. Whatever had occurred, the end result was that the Jornada del Muerto had now become truly a journey of death.

The sun was moving into the west again. We had now traveled from Fray Cristóbal's campground a night and a day and were approximately halfway across the Jornada. The thought brought no comfort. Everyone was tired and their emotions frayed. Weary and hungry men are apt to do foolish and dangerous things. What more would occur before we reached the Jornada's southern boundary?

I didn't have long to ponder these fears. As the sun sank lower, an order to halt ran along the lines. We moved off the road to a sandy area tucked between low hills. On the far end was a section with a little grass, enough to allow the animals to browse while we rested.

However, darkness fell completely as we sat there and with it the cold. We huddled together for warmth and spoke in low tones, still trying to understand what had happened to Amos Golpin. The more Kendall insisted that Salazar had ordered him shot, the less certain Cayton Erhard became about what the captain had said.

The moon rose, brightening the sky, and the call came to start off again. I groaned aloud as I rose, surprised at how I'd stiffened during our short break and also at how much colder it seemed now that I was standing. The moon had brought a breeze with it, icy fingers toyed at every gap in my clothing. I pulled my cravat closer to my throat, arranged my blanket across my nose and chin, and formed up with my companions.

Ramón was once again on foot and leading his horse. He lifted the reins in my direction. "Ride?"

Giving my legs a break was tempting, but being in the saddle would expose me even more to the wind. I shook my head apologetically, and he nodded and grinned.

The row of men immediately behind us included Lieutenant Hornsby in his secondhand Mexican coat. Ed Griffith, with his wounded thigh and thin chest, stood beside him, leaning on a battered wooden stick.

I frowned at him. "Why aren't you in the jersey wagon?"

"Walking's warmer. Besides, Gates is still coughing his lungs inside out. There's no true rest there." The trumpet sounded and we moved out. The road curved up ahead. The supply wagon Salazar had commandeered rested on the verge. Griffith nodded toward it. "I figure I'm probably warmer than he is."

When we reached the wagon, we saw that its canvas cover had a significant rent in one side. Don Jesús lay inside, fast asleep, his mouth slightly open. The captain peered at us beneath heavy eyelids, then burrowed deeper into his covers.

"Look at that pile of blankets," Kendall said enviously. He looked back at Griffith. "It appears to me that riding is definitely warmer than walking, at least in this case." Then he jerked his chin at Hornsby. "You in particular are undoubtedly suffering mightily in that rough Mexican coat instead of your high-quality Texian uniform."

Hornsby patted his chest and shook his head. "I truly thought my host cheated me, but he may well have done me a favor. This old coat is surprisingly effective against the wind." He wiggled his shoulders. "And, as a result of our recent diet, it's not nearly as tight as when I first put it on."

Kendall humphed and looked away. I turned, walking sideways to speak to the lieutenant. "Did you see Golpin die?"

He shook his head. "No, and I've heard conflicting versions. Some say Salazar ordered him killed and others that he told the guard not to shoot."

Kendall looked around again, his lips tight with disapproval. "The so-called captain has been threatening us with death from the beginning of our journey."

"A man can threaten all sorts of things but not intend to follow through on them," Griffith said mildly.

Kendall gave him a disgusted look and faced forward again. A light flashed at the periphery of my vision, toward the head of the column. I turned and craned my neck, trying to see, and Ramón scrambled into his saddle. He stood in the stirrups, staring ahead, then his face split into a big grin. He bent toward us. There were yuccas ahead that hadn't been fired by the dragoons, he told us. Someone had set them on fire.

As painful as the sight of the big blackened plants had been, the thought of the resulting warmth from their flames spurred us forward. When we reached the first blaze, we crowded around it eagerly, Ramon on foot again, his horse snatching at what little browse he could find.

My toes were veritable blocks of ice. I shuffled as close to the fire as I dared. The orange tongues of the burning brown fronds licked out at me, and Kendall poked me in the ribs. "If you aren't more watchful, you'll find your whiskers well singed."

I grinned and stroked my beard. "It would appear that we're all at some risk of that danger. Your side whiskers have blended in well with the hair on your chin."

He laughed. "Yes, my facial hair has expanded considerably since we left Austin."

Ramón reached past me, stretching toward the flames, and I moved aside, almost stepping into Griffith, whose thin chest shuddered with cold even under the blanket he'd pinned around his shoulders. He leaned heavily on his stick, dirt-streaked face pale in the firelight. At the curve of the yucca's thick trunk, Fitzgerald watched him with concern.

Ramón turned, warming his backside. The smell of singed wool crept from his jacket and he leaped playfully away, making exaggerated slapping motions at his rear end, trying to raise a laugh.

A few of us chuckled, but that was all. Guards and prisoners alike, we were cold-chapped, hungry, and exhausted. Not even Ramón could get a smile from us. The jumping flames only seemed to emphasize our gaunt faces, tired shoulders, and battered footwear. The warmth from the burning yucca was merely a reprieve, and we all knew it.

CHAPTER 17
Tuesday, November 2, 1841
Jornada del Muerto, Day 3

Sure enough, Salazar's wagon came up, along with the order to move on. We headed back to the road and bent into the wind. I and my friends were now near the end of the column. Ramón had offered his horse to Griffith and the wounded man's exhaustion had overcome even the need to stay warm. He slumped forward in the saddle, his chest almost touching the horse's drooping mane.

We plodded on. When Ramón went ahead to walk with a friend, we hardly noticed. As the night sky softened into the gray of early dawn, the cold deepened. Even the body of the horse couldn't block it. It also looked worn out, poor beast. My jaw felt frozen in place. I tried to moisten my chapped lips with my tongue but found no dampness there. I lifted my canteen to my lips. Nothing came out.

Kendall twisted to watch me. "No food, no water," he said, lips barely moving.

Falconer's head was down, watching his feet. "No use complaining."

Kendall's eyes flashed. "Salazar's fault."

I raised a hand to make a dismissive gesture, but my blanket slipped as I did so. I gripped it as close as my frozen fingers would allow and plodded onward. One foot in front of the other. That's all that truly mattered.

The eastern mountains were visible now, black silhouettes against the gray. The wind grew even sharper. Then Ramón's horse jerked to a stop. We all looked up. Griffith had fallen asleep in the saddle and was leaning sideways, blinking in surprise. Then his face twisted in pain. "Help me off," he groaned.

Before I could move, Cayton Erhard stepped forward. The German boy eased the taller but frailer man out of the saddle and held his arm as Griffith lifted first one leg, then the other. He yelped in pain and clutched Erhard's arm. "I can't!"

We had all stopped while this was going on, halting the lines behind us. The sergeant approached on foot, his eyes narrowed against the wind, a musket in his hands. "¡Levantaos!"

Griffith looked up at him, shaking his head. "I can't."

"¡Dispararé!"

Griffith moved slightly, still supported by the boy. The sergeant's face darkened. He swung the musket, smacking it into Griffith's wounded side. The Texian collapsed forward, out of Erhard's grasp, and onto the ground.

"¡Levantaos!" the sergeant shouted. He swung the musket like a club, aiming for Griffith's shoulders. Instead, sick man's head came up. The musket connected with it and there was a dull crunching sound. Griffith tumbled into the dirt.

The sergeant's fury blinked out. He bent down, reaching for Griffith's skull. When he straightened, there was blood on his hands and confusion on his face. Then he shrugged.

"Murderer!" Kendall bellowed.

The prisoners and guards behind us pressed forward, then shrank back, eyeing the sergeant and the man on the ground, Cayton Erhard standing helplessly by. The horse snorted and shook his head.

"That poor man," Fitzgerald murmured. He moved toward Griffith and knelt, lips moving in prayer.

Cayton turned to the side of the road and retched soundlessly. I would have followed suit if there'd been anything in my stomach to bring up.

The sergeant's shoulders jerked back. "¡Vámonos!" he shouted. He kicked at Fitzgerald, forcing him up, then swung his weapon sideways, catching Erhard in the kidneys. "¡Muévanse!"

The boy clutched his back and lurched into line. As Fitzgerald followed, Ramón's horse snorted again, turned, and headed doggedly toward the herd behind us.

We moved reluctantly forward. When I glanced back, the sergeant was bent over Griffith's body with his knife out. He turned the head to one side.

Kendall's gaze followed mine. "Another set of ears for the captain's growing collection," he said bitterly. "I wonder who will be using Griffith's blanket tonight."

Cayton Erhard made a retching sound. He still looked green around the gills.

"And come he slow, or come he fast, It is but Death that comes at last," Fitzgerald murmured.

I frowned, then remembered where I'd seen the quote. Sir Walter Scott's *Marmion*.

Kendall recognized it, also. "Yes, everyone dies in the end," he said. "You undoubtedly find that comforting. I, for one, do not. That bastard Salazar has killed four men on our journey so far. A journey that is not yet complete. Who else among us will expire due to his bloodthirstiness?"

"Griffith was ill," I said mildly. "He could barely walk. And the captain did not kill him, the sergeant did."

"And that not intentionally, from what I could see," Fitzgerald said. "He was aiming for the man's shoulders."

Kendall ignored him. "Griffith was wounded. He should have been riding with Gates in the sick wagon."

I frowned. "He chose not to do so."

"He should have been forced to do so! That is what a leader does! He compels those who are weary to be aided and sets aside his own desires to address the afflictions of the men in his charge. This so-called captain is a murderer in both action and inaction! He rode while others walked! And died!" He turned on Fitzgerald. "You say that the sergeant did not kill him intentionally! I say you fail to see guilt where it is most manifest! You are a coward, sir!"

My head jerked toward the former Legionnaire. Those were fighting words. But Fitzgerald merely gave Kendall a long look and turned away.

The newsman looked at Falconer, then me. "Salazar is a murderer of the first degree," he muttered, as if daring us to disagree. "He undoubtedly gave orders to the guards to use every opportunity and excuse to reduce our ranks, thereby increasing his collection of ears."

There was nothing to be said to this. Once Kendall had chosen an opinion, he clung to it regardless of all evidence to the contrary. His was not a subtle nature.

And I was too stunned by Griffith's death and exhausted by the Jornada to respond anyway. Simply moving forward took what little energy I had left. The landscape had begun to change, becoming hilly and marked by more sandstone than basalt. When Falconer tried to draw my attention to these differences, I barely lifted my head.

There were more trees too, instead of cacti. The Erhard cousins began stepping to the side of the road to snatch up twigs and chips for future fires.

"Good, good!" Ramón said, coming up to join us. "Is good!" He grinned at Kendall. "A song? A happiness?" Then he peered into my face and sobered. "A sorrow?"

"Edward Griffith is dead."

He crossed himself solemnly. "Pobrecito." When I explained disjointedly what had happened, he closed his eyes, crossed himself, and looked away.

There was a long silence, then he asked tentatively, "¿Y mi caballo?"

I blinked at him stupidly. "Your horse?"

He nodded, looking a little guilty.

"Aquí," a guard said from behind us. He led the animal forward. Ramón nodded his thanks and took the reins. The horse nuzzled Ramón affectionately. He patted its muzzle. "Pobrecito," he said again.

There was a long silence, filled only with the sound of our walking. After a long while, Ramón sighed and shrugged. "No Ciudad de México, no prison," he said.

Kendall shot him a venomous glance. "Your fellow guard committed murder against a prisoner and that's all you can find to say about it?" His voice rose, became sarcastic. "Yes, Griffith is undoubtedly better off dead, since he won't now be forced to experience incarceration in Mexico City!"

"De la suerte y de la muerte no hay quien se escape," Ramón said.

"From fate and death no one escapes," I translated.

"Y tributaciones," Ramón added, smiling wryly.

Fitzgerald chuckled. "And taxes? Yes, that also."

Kendall sniffed and looked away. I felt a twinge of guilt that I and the others could not match his outrage. Were we accepting these deaths too easily? Had we faced so much killing and misery these past months, first on the plains and now on this journey south, that we had grown numb to the pain of our companions? Or were Ernest, Golpin, Griffith, and McAllister to be envied? After all, the pain was over for them. But I was too exhausted for deep thoughts. My brain couldn't function beyond the need to move my feet forward. I plodded on.

And then we rounded a bend and the Río Grande spread out below us. A ragged cheer went up. The stream sparkled in the early morning sun, a sharp contrast to the sand-colored slopes above it. Golden cottonwoods crowded its banks.

We'd made it out of the Jornada del Muerto, walked forty hours with no food and only the water we could carry, on a total of perhaps four hours rest. Exhausted as I was, there was a sudden spring to my steps, a surge of hope.

Then my step broke. Not all of us had lived to tell the tale. Amos Golpin. Edward Griffith. Both good men in their way, although inadequate to the task at hand. Despite Fitzgerald's quotations and Ramón's proverbs, the fact remained that the Jornada was well named.

I looked at my companions. Kendall was staring at the river as if he'd never seen water before. Falconer was studying the stony mountain peaks beyond it. Cayton Erhard had tears in his eyes. When he saw me watching, he turned away and wiped his dirty face with his dirtier sleeve.

Falconer looked at Ramón. "Where are we?"

"Is it over?" Kendall asked.

Neither question needed a translation. "Robledo," Ramón answered. "La Jornada del Muerto está completa." He grinned at us, then broke into almost-giddy laughter. He flung his arms open, startling his horse. "Is done! ¡De verdad! Is done!"

Another guard swung past him. "¡Comida!" he called. "¡Carne de buey!"

Ramón turned and fired a rapid question, which was answered just as quickly. Then he grinned at Cayton Erhard. "¡Carne de buey!"

The boy looked at him numbly.

"Ox meat," I translated.

Cayton nodded. He swayed from side to side and his eyes closed, although he still clutched the scraps of wood he'd collected. Fitzgerald grabbed his arm. "A little further yet," he said quietly. "Just a little more."

The boy's head nodded, whether in weariness or agreement, I couldn't tell. Fitzgerald kept his hand on his arm until we reached the river. Then Anton came up. Cayton roused a little and looked up at the trees, then dropped his collection of sticks and wandered toward the nearest grassy hillock. His cousin deposited his own scraps and followed him. They dropped onto the ground side by side and were instantly asleep.

Falconer and Fitzgerald began building a fire with the boys' contributions, while Kendall crouched off to the side, carefully winding his watch. I set about gathering more wood from downed branches.

Perhaps I gathered too many. When the meat arrived, the flames were still too high for cooking purposes.

"That butchering was completed quickly," Falconer said. "The men who did it must be as ravenous as I am."

"Or perhaps the fire isn't ready because our expert builder is asleep," Fitzgerald said with a bemused nod toward the little hill. As we watched, Anton roused, saw the meat, and got to his feet. He raised a hand, acknowledging us, said something to Falconer in German, then moved toward the river.

Kendall glanced at the British lawyer.

"He's gone to hunt up some cooking sticks," Falconer said.

The boy returned a few minutes later with sharpened sticks of green wood, then went off to refill the Erhard water gourd. We set to work threading our meat onto the sticks, then placed the ends in the soft dirt and firmed them into angles that would cook the meat without scorching it too quickly.

Just as we'd completed this task, Ramón came up, carrying an uncooked measure of meal in his tin cup. He stopped and studied the flames, then saw the meat. He laughed. "Carne first?"

I gave him a questioning look. He jerked an elbow toward the other fires, where guards were moving among the prisoners, distributing raw meal.

On the hillock, Cayton stirred, sat up, and looked around. He took in the fire and the cooking beef, then looked hungrily at Ramón's cup. "Meal?"

Ramón grinned at him and gestured toward the fires beyond ours. Cayton frowned and clutched at his belly. The guard chortled and waved his tin cup in the air.

The boy scowled and Ramón threw his head back and laughed heartily.

Cayton stood and came toward us.

"Your meat is there," Fitzgerald said, pointing to one of the larger pieces of beef.

Cayton grimaced. "Raw."

This brought another shout of laughter from Ramón. "Fleisch!" he shouted in a remarkable imitation of the boy's German. "No fleisch!"

Anton came up, the dripping water gourd in his hands.

Cayton moved closer to Ramón and eyed the meal in his cup. "I trade." He pointed at the fire, then the cup. "Fleisch for meal."

I frowned. "The meat will give you more strength."

He swayed slightly as he shook his head. "Food now."

I turned to Ramón, who was wiping tears of laughter from his cheek with his free hand. Then he sobered, peered into the boy's thin face, and handed over the cup.

Cayton took it and turned to his cousin. Anton gave him the gourd. He carefully poured water into the meal and stirred it with his finger.

"I don't know how you're going to cook that," I said. "The fire hasn't burned down to coals yet."

He shrugged and lifted the tin cup to his lips.

Kendall grimaced. "At the very least, you should attempt to heat that up. At this rate, you are undoubtedly going to give yourself an indisputably malodorous case of wind." He leaned toward the fire to poke the wood apart and allow the flames to die down. Then he tugged the stick that contained his portion of meat out of the dirt and held it over the flames. The beef sizzled and spat.

The boy turned away, gulped the last of his meal, and looked longingly into the cup.

Ramón grinned, took it from Cayton's hand, and went to the fire. He chose the largest portion of meat and bore it off, chuckling.

Kendall's eyes followed him. "The man is a pig." He glared at the guard's receding back. "¡Un puerco!"

Fitzgerald laughed. "You would have done the same thing yourself."

The newsman scowled. "Filthy soldier of fortune!"

Fitzgerald's lips tightened. He studied Kendall for a long moment, then turned away and lifted his piece of beef to the flames. Cayton had returned to his little hillock and was already asleep.

Anton chose one of the larger pieces of meat and repositioned it closer to the fire. When it was cooked, he ate half, then roused his cousin, who sat up sleepily and reached eagerly for the food. Fitzgerald and I exchanged a bemused glance, then we all settled down for a rest. If the Jornada del Muerto had taught us anything, it was to sleep whenever we had the opportunity.

When I woke, the German boys were again asleep on the little hill. It was early afternoon. My muscles were heavy and sore.

Kendall was staring into the fire. I nodded to him and Fitzgerald and Falconer, who had also just roused, and ran my hand over my hair and beard, then took off my cravat, and shook it out. I was tying it back into place when Ramón came up to say we'd be marching further that day.

Kendall looked at me. When I translated what the guard had said, his jaw dropped. "Surely he jests!" He glared at Ramón. "He undoubtedly believes this to be an appropriate joke for this time and place!"

I took a swig of water from my canteen and turned to the guard. "¿Por qué?"

He shrugged. He looked as tired as the rest of us and almost as unhappy. "Muy poca hierba."

Kendall squinted at me.

"Too little grass."

"Is there a spot in this barren land where there actually is enough grass?" Kendall demanded. He scratched at his neck.

"It seems to me that the herbage here is in direct disproportion to the abundance of insect life."

Ramón walked over to the boys and nudged Cayton with his toe. "Vámonos," he said.

Erhard sat up with a jerk. He looked around, bewildered, then up at the sky. "Is tomorrow?"

This seemed to cheer Ramón up. He broke into laughter, lifting his hands to the sky. "¡Mañana!" he crowed.

Anton sat up and gave us a puzzled look.

"We're moving on," Fitzgerald told him. He smiled at Cayton, who was now glowering at the guard. "I'm afraid it is still today. We only slept a few hours."

Kendall sniffed. "The animals' browse is undoubtedly of more importance than our rest and well-being."

The boys helped each other to their feet. Cayton looked down at his shoes. The hole in the right one had grown larger in the last two days. His big toe had eaten through its sock and was clearly visible.

Anton grinned at it. "Also hungrig."

"Well, at least we're through the grand jornada," Falconer said.

"That fact is certainly a comfort," I agreed as I pushed myself to my feet. My thighs cramped under my weight and I staggered to one side, grimacing with pain. "Perhaps a little movement would be useful, after all."

Five miles later, at a grassland which contained more fodder for the cattle and horses, I found that the exercise had, in fact, done me good. Perhaps it was merely knowing I wouldn't be roused until morning, but sleep now felt positively luxurious.

CHAPTER 18
Wednesday, November 3 to Thursday, November 4, 1841
Robledo to El Paso del Norte

I woke much refreshed. A guard brought me the sorrel mare and a request to join the captain at the head of the column. Kendall watched me go with a sour look.

As the day wore on, I was glad to be on horseback. The road lay above the river and along a series of rocky slopes covered with scree. The sun was surprisingly warm given the time of year, and there was little shade. When the captain told me the day would be a lengthy one, I was doubly grateful, although I felt guilty about the discomfort my fellow prisoners must be experiencing. The loose rock and hot sun would make walking painful.

The captain seemed aware of this issue and how it was likely to slow us all down. He periodically sent Don Jesús back up the column to assess how far the men had straggled, and became more irritated with each report. The oxen were a good mile and a quarter in the rear, the prisoners strung out between them and the sick wagon.

Salazar growled an order to tell the rear guards to have no mercy, then sank into a despondent, silent hunch. I began to wonder why he had asked me to join him. The western sky had started to color before he roused and turned to me. If all went well, we would reach El Paso the next day, he said.

When I observed that he would at last be done with us, he smiled slightly and nodded. Then his face soured. He dreaded the journey home. Not only would the cold be worse and the trip across the Jornada doubly miserable, but he'd be returning to the debts for our food. Even the cart he'd requisitioned at Valencia must be paid for, since the snapped axle had undoubtedly made it unusable.

He sighed heavily and added that the day after tomorrow we would enter El Paso and then he would be returning to Santa Fe to be held to account. He must have funds. The remaining cattle were scrawny and broken down. They would bring little in the El Paso markets. He slid me a sideways glance. Surely there were men among the prisoners with resources: coins and jewelry that could pay for their keep. Some of us clearly had funds. They'd been purchasing rides from his men.

I shook my head. Those exchanges were made with the trade of buttons or other items, I said. As to jewelry— I thought of Kendall and his watch. He'd be devastated if it was taken from him. I went on, reminding the captain that we'd all been searched when we were first captured. Armijo's men were thorough. I didn't point out that they were searching for weapons and papers at that point, not money.

Salazar accepted what I said at face value, nodded despondently, and sank back into silence. When Don Jesús returned with yet another report that the oxen were flagging and suggested we stop earlier than planned, he growled "¡Silencio!" and didn't speak again until we reached our destination, a wide spot between the rocky slopes we'd been traversing which contained a cluster of cottonwoods. It was pitch dark by this time and the moon had not yet risen over the rocky crags that surrounded us. The pale gray of the tree trunks were ghostly in the muted star light.

I left the captain and went in search of my friends. I found Falconer and Cayton Erhard crouched over a small fire and Kendall stretched out on the ground a few feet away. Falconer was stirring a serving of mush in his tin cup, being careful not to let anything spill over the sides. Erhard was staring into the flames, a small bag of meal dragging at one hand, the shared water gourd in the other. They looked up as I approached.

"Didn't they give you food rations?" I asked Cayton.

He glanced at the small bag of meal, then looked away, his head bobbing slightly. "Tired."

I looked at Falconer, who shook his head. "I couldn't convince him to make the effort even to stir water into it."

I turned to Cayton. "We don't know what tomorrow will bring. You should at least try to eat." He nodded but didn't otherwise stir.

I moved toward Kendall, whose eyes were closed. A small bag of meal lay beside him, enough for two men. "Is he asleep?"

"I'm doing my best to achieve that blessed state." The newsman opened one eye. "We're all exhausted. Although you undoubtedly aren't as weary as the rest of us, as you rode the route we were forced to travel on foot."

I forced my expression to remain neutral. "My riding may have saved you a good deal of grief."

His other eye opened.

"Captain Salazar finds himself short of the funds he will need to pay for our provisions when he returns to New Mexico. He'd like to gather the necessary resources before he reaches El Paso."

Kendall's hands went to his deepest pockets, where he kept his cash.

"He's interested in anything he can turn into coin."

The newsman sat up. "My watch?"

"And whatever else we may have in our possession."

"My breastpin!" He sprang to his feet.

"Verstecke es," Cayton said. He made a gesture of putting something in his mouth.

Falconer laughed. "Eat it? His valuables?"

Kendall made a disgusted face, then he grinned. "It would be difficult indeed to swallow my watch."

"You've managed to keep it hidden thus far," I said.

Kendall didn't appear to hear. "I must somehow hide the watch on my person. However, the money—" His eyes lit on the bag of meal. He picked it up and turned to me. "The guard gave me your portion, as well, so there's plenty here." He peered around the darkened campground. The men at the other fires were paying no attention to us. "A little water. Just enough to moisten it," he muttered. "Time is of the essence."

He turned to Falconer and nodded at the fire, his face more eager than I'd seen it in weeks. "Let that burn down to coals, and I'll bake us some bread seasoned with coin. I'll keep out some small change, so the guards can find something in their search, but we'll cook up the doubloons and other gold pieces." He grinned. "It'll look like that twice-baked bread Erhard enjoys so much."

I bit back a protest. The newsman was about to make my dinner inedible. But Cayton seemed more awake now. He held out his own bag of meal, offering to help.

Kendall grinned at him. "You mix up the dough and I'll insert the coins into it." He peered at the surrounding fires again, then turned to Falconer and me. "I don't know where that damned guard is. Keep a lookout, will you?"

Cayton was already at work, pouring meal into a cup and dribbling water into it. I shook my head in annoyance at the way my portion had been commandeered and amusement at the sudden burst of energy, but didn't complain. Falconer and I took up positions well out of the firelight, to watch for Ramón.

The thick pieces of bread-like globs were well-charred by the coals by the time he appeared. He raised an eyebrow, made a laughingly sardonic remark about the comforts of home, and went away again. I breathed a sigh of relief.

By the time he returned, the lumpy coin-filled cakes were cooled and tucked away in our deepest pockets, and we were dozing beside the dying fire. Ramón paused and studied us quizzically, then shrugged. He grinned at me. "Jornada is over." He bounced a little on his heels. "Soon I go home." He grinned at Kendall. "I go, you stay."

Kendall scowled and looked away. Ramón laughed and wandered off. Despite my hunger, my body loosened, sinking further into the ground. Even though I'd ridden all day, my bones and muscles still carried the traces of our Jornada del Muerto. Not even the guards' calls of "¡Centinela, alerta!" disturbed my sleep.

Although Kendall had been smug enough the night before, he was anxious the next morning. We'd barely risen when he pulled me several yards away from the others.

"My watch and chain are still at risk," he muttered into my ear. "Our pockets will undoubtedly be the first place Salazar's men will examine." He eyed my upper chest. "I heartily wish I still had a cravat to my name. Tucking the watch into its folds would be an excellent way to conceal it." He paused. "You are friendly with the captain. I doubt he will subject you to a search."

I turned my head, fighting to keep the irritation from my face. The man was incorrigible. He'd taken my supper the night before and now he wanted me to protect his particular treasures. But it was true that I was unlikely to be searched. And his jewelry did mean a great deal to him. I reluctantly nodded agreement.

Kendall grasped my hands gratefully. "I won't forget the assistance you have given me this day!"

"There is no guarantee that I will be exempted," I warned.

"Of course! Of course!" He glanced around to make sure we weren't being observed, then drew out his watch and chain, and handed them over. "Careful now," he said as I began rearranging the folds in my cravat around the two pieces. "Make sure they don't fall out."

As I worked at the chain, making sure it would stay in place, I gave him a bemused look. "I'll care for it as if it were my own." The metal was cold through the thin linen. I bent my chin, trying to see past my unkempt beard. The lumps under the folds seemed uncomfortably obvious, but Kendall nodded approval. "If anything, it looks better," he said. "The weight pulls out the wrinkles."

I chuckled as we turned back to the others. "It would be ironic to be accosted and searched because I looked too well-kept."

He gave my arm a comradely slap. "With that greasy hair and bedraggled beard? I doubt you're in much danger of being considered particularly well-groomed."

I ran my hand over my sticky head. "I would give a great deal for a proper bath and a shave." My hand went to the cravat, checking its contents, then I saw Ramón and jerked it away.

He gave me a quizzical look, but the order to fall in was already being passed through the camp. We got into formation, Ramón riding beside us. The count began. It appeared that we Texians would not be searched, after all. And that I was once again to march in the ranks, though when Salazar rode past on Kendall's big mule, he nodded at me politely.

Seeing this, Ramón grinned. "Como se viene, se va."

Falconer, on Kendall's other side, leaned forward and gave me a questioning look.

"As it comes, so it goes," I translated. Ramón and he laughed at the same time, which made Ramón laugh even harder. Kendall stayed rigidly silent.

The trumpet sounded and we marched out of the campground. A small pasture lay on our right. The Texian oxen were spread out over the grass, grazing peacefully beside perhaps thirty of the guards' animals.

"They with us go?" Cayton Erhard asked from the other end of our line.

I translated the question to Ramón. He shook his head. El capitán had ordered that they be left behind.

When I put this into English, Kendall's face darkened. "Salazar is undoubtedly leaving them behind so there is no record of them entering El Paso del Norte and he can do what he likes with them." He looked at me. "He has no intention of using them to raise the funds he claims to need so desperately. Not for paying off the debts he left behind in New Mexico, at any rate."

"The captain may be hoping to fatten the oxen up a little before offering them in El Paso's markets," I pointed out. I glanced meaningfully down at my chest. "We can at least be thankful he hasn't pursued other potential avenues for enhancing his resources."

"The day has not yet run its course. Be that as it may, we have no verifiable information regarding the distance that remains between us and El Paso del Norte. For all we know, we may well have another week of travel ahead of us."

I turned to Ramón and asked how far the distance actually was.

This seemed to spark his interest. He looked at Kendall, eyes twinkling. "¿A qué distancia del ejecutor?"

Kendall scowled. "Executioner? What does he mean?"

Ramón's grin widened. "¿A qué distancia del látigo?"

Kendall looked at me. "Látigo?"

I hesitated. "Whip."

Kendall's head jerked in horror. Ramón laughed out loud. Kendall gave him a disgusted look. "The man's sense of humor is astoundingly distorted."

At the other end of the line, Cayton Erhard leaned toward Falconer with an anxious look and said something in German.

I raised a quizzical brow at the British lawyer, who said, "He wants to know if they're really going to whip us."

Ramón seemed to have caught the gist of the conversation. He began laughing again and pointing at the boy.

Erhard frowned. "He know my talk?"

Falconer shook his head. "I don't believe so. He only knows that you're worried."

"Which he believes to be truly and hilariously funny." Kendall scowled at the guard. "The man is a misbegotten barbarian."

Ramón laughed again, understanding the newsman's tone, if not all his words. Then he sobered slightly and nodded at me companionably. "Son diez leguas a El Paso."

"Ten leagues !" Kendall exclaimed.

"That's only thirty miles," Falconer said. "It's a small distance considering how far we've come."

Kendall groaned dramatically. "Will this journey never end?"

Ramón burst into laughter again, slapping his thigh. I studied him out of the corner of my eye. His amusement had an almost hysterical edge. Was he, as he'd said the night before, simply glad to be almost done with us and about to return home, or had his nerves been frayed into unpredictability by the Jornada del Muerto?

At any rate, even Kendall seemed to sense that it would be best not to acerbate his strange humor. We lapsed into silence and concentrated on our rocky route above the Río Grande's eastern bank. The riverbed narrowed here, the cottonwoods along it compressed into a strip of gold made more glorious as the slope above it became more barren. Despite the stones beneath my feet, I was actually the most comfortable I'd been since we left San Miguel. This had a good deal to do with the fact that, for the first time in days, there was no wind and the air was remarkably warmer than it had been. We relaxed our grip on our blankets and soaked in the heat.

We didn't travel far. Now that we were in early November, the days were growing steadily shorter, and we'd started late. The sun was just beginning to slant into the west when we reached a kind of tableland above the river and Salazar called a halt for the night.

The mountains had receded from the far bank and opened up to give us an uninterrupted view of the setting sun. Its light streamed across the flat lands to the golden cottonwoods and then on to the jagged sandstone walls behind us, turning them a soft red. I dropped my blanket and canteen beside what would become our fire circle and moved toward the bank above the stream to get a better look.

Perhaps it was the fact that the sky was clear and the air almost warm, but the reflected glow filled with me a sense of well-being. The sun hung low on the horizon, a dark-red orb perhaps four times its ordinary size which lit the blue around with it with an orange fire. It lingered as if watching me with an indifferent, yet not unfriendly, air. I took a deep breath.

Kendall had dropped his own items beside mine. He came to stand beside me and gaze at the spectacle. After a long moment, he lifted a hand as if to test the air. "It's so warm and yet we are four days into November," he murmured. "What kind of land is this? Have we reached the end of our miseries?"

There was a sudden shout from the camp. We turned to see Cayton Erhard running toward us, his thin face anxious, blond hair flopping into his eyes.

"Señor Gates—" he gasped as he reached us. His hand clutched at his throat, demonstrating. "No breath."

We hurried toward the sick wagon, Fitzgerald joining us on the way.

"I pass, Gates call," Erhard told us. "Water, he ask." He looked at me. "Then—" He pointed at his throat and made a strangling sound, part imitation, part his own distress. We hurried on.

The jersey wagon's battered canvas covers had been rolled up. Gates lay on a thin mattress, his filthy brown blanket covering his chest. His eyes were glassy, but he seemed to recognize us. "Water?" he whispered.

The single word was enough to trigger a coughing spell, a deep hacking cough that tore at his lungs. It made my own chest hurt to hear it. When the bout had ended, he lifted a blood-spotted handkerchief and wiped at his mouth. He licked his parched lips and looked at us anxiously, as if afraid to speak again.

Fitzgerald reached for his canteen, then realized he wasn't carrying it. "He needs water!" he said. He glanced at Kendall and I, who both shook our heads. Gates made a gurgling noise and gestured toward the edge of his mattress. A battered metal canteen lay on the wagon floor.

Fitzgerald reached in, picked it up, and shook it. It was completely dry. He handed it to Cayton, whose horrified eyes hadn't left the sick man's face. "Will you fill it?"

The boy jerked into action. "Ja, I do it."

As he darted off, Ramón appeared, his musket over his shoulder and a grin on his face like he'd just heard a good joke. He looked into the wagon.

Gates turned his head. "Water?" he whispered.

The guard chuckled, leaned his musket against the wagon wheel, and held up his canteen. Moisture beaded its side. "¿Agua?" he asked teasingly. "¿Quieres agua? ¡Di por favor!"

Kendall glanced at me.

"You want water? Just say please," I translated quietly.

Kendall scowled at Ramón. "The man is dying. Give it to him!"

Something dark flashed in the guard's eyes. "Tired only. As we all." He glanced at my anxious face, shook his head, then turned to the wagon, and poured water into his cupped hand. He held it out to Gates, touching his lips with the moisture. "Bueno, bueno," he said.

The sick man's head turned toward the guard's fingers, sucking the liquid. The guard nodded at Kendall. "Bueno," he said. "Tired y thirst."

Cayton appeared with the battered canteen, now dripping wet. Ramón waved a hand, motioning him toward Gates, and moved away, calling "¡Estará bien mañana!" over his shoulder.

Kendall looked at me in confusion. "What'd he say?"

"He will be fine tomorrow."

As Kendall humphed in disgust, Cayton reached us and handed Fitzgerald the canteen. The former soldier of fortune climbed into the wagon, gently lifted the sick man's head, and dribbled water into his mouth.

Gates' lips worked, but his throat didn't seem to. Liquid slid down the side of his face. Kendall and Cayton looked away at the same time.

"Poor man," Fitzgerald murmured. He tried again. More water slipped out. Gates made a choking sound.

Ramón reappeared at the corner of the wagon and reached for his musket, which he'd left leaning against the wagon wheel. "All here still?" he asked cheerily. "Good times!" He swung the gun to his shoulder and pointed the muzzle at Gates. "¡Bam Bam!" he laughed.

Gates's eyes bulged. His mouth worked and he made a gagging sound. His hand went to his throat. His other arm thrashed out, hitting the canteen and knocking it to the floor. As liquid pooled on the boards, Gates shuddered, then went still.

Fitzgerald reached to close his empty eyes and began to murmur a prayer. Erhard choked back a sob and backed away into the night.

Kendall turned on the guard. "You killed him, you bastard!"

Ramón wasn't laughing now. He backed away, one hand in the air, the other clutching the musket. "Que era una broma." He looked at me wildly. "¡Una broma!"

I stared back at him, too stunned to speak. Perhaps it was a broma, a joke, but it had gone terribly wrong.

For the first time since we'd met the man, he didn't seem to know what to say or do. He swung in a circle, searching frantically. The sergeant of the guard appeared, crossing the far end of the campground, and Ramón's breath hitched. He ran toward him.

"And now Salazar will acquire yet another set of ears for his collection," Kendall said bitterly. "Another man dead." There was a long silence, then he looked into the wagon at the canteen. "I'll take that. I am badly in need of a water container."

Fitzgerald lifted his head and stared at the newsman. "Once again you have proven that there's more than one way for a man to be dead, Kendall." Then he patted Gates's body gently, climbed out of the wagon without looking at either of us, and walked off.

I followed, although I stayed well behind. It was clear he didn't want company, but I had no desire to watch over the corpse or to talk with Kendall. Yes, he did need a canteen, but his behavior was almost as inappropriate as Ramón's had been.

Only a few traces of red marked where the sun had fallen behind the western horizon. I stared at them dry-eyed.

CHAPTER 19
Friday, November 5, 1841
El Paso del Norte

I woke in the early dawn to birds calling from the cotton-woods along the river below, and a stony heart.

Kendall crouched beside a too-hot fire, cooking the morning meal. He had gathered our tin cups and allotted portions of meal and was attempting to turn them into gruel. The smell of scorched mush filled the air. I ate without comment while Kendall told Falconer about Gates' death. He had lost his indignation and seemed merely depressed, although he didn't mention the fate of the dead man's canteen.

Fitzgerald didn't appear and Cayton Erhard had gone off with his cousin. I presumed this was to avoid reliving what had transpired, and I couldn't blame him. I stared blankly into the fire.

But there was no time to grieve. We'd barely finished eating when the call to form up came once again. I found myself in line next to Fitzgerald, who was pensive. "I'm actually surprised Gates survived as long as he did," he said. "The man was surprisingly tough for one so sickly to begin with."

We tramped on, the only sound our gear bumping our bodies and the slap of our feet on the ground. When Fitzgerald spoke again, he was surprisingly philosophic. "What we've experienced on this journey has been horrendous," he said.

"But it was of our own making. We should never have set out to take land that wasn't ours by rights."

I glanced at him. "The Texian Congress declared it to be."

He nodded, then shook his head. "I'm devoted to the Republic of Texas, although I wish it had separated from Mexico more gently. There's no place on earth quite like it. However, I can also see its flaws. Hubris is one of them. And overreaching." He was quiet for a long stretch. "I suppose, in the end, they amount to the same thing."

I nodded. I felt much as he did, although I wasn't sure gentle separation from a mother country was ever possible. "And what will you do when this journey is over?"

He glanced at Kendall, who was just ahead of us, and smiled slightly. "You mean, if it ever ends?"

I chuckled and nodded. Fitzgerald made a small, hopeless gesture. "No one knows the future, or how events may shape our decisions, but I have no desire to return to Europe," he said. "I hope to stay in Texas. For all her faults, she's filled with great energy and opportunities. The Republic isn't bound by European caste systems. For better or worse, in Texas a man is who he says he is and what he demonstrates he can do. He's not restricted by who his grandfathers were or what they may have done."

I nodded thoughtfully. It was a good answer.

"And you?" he asked.

"I'll go back to San Antonio. I have a law practice to develop." I frowned. "I had planned to use my legal expertise as a springboard to a political career and follow my brother into the Texas Congress, make a name for myself. But now I wonder if I really wish to do so. I'm not sure I'm cut out for the give and take, the rough and tumble of political life."

He studied me, waiting. I shrugged and looked away. "I see both sides of every issue, feel the validity of every emotion expressed." I gestured toward Kendall and lowered my voice. "I envy his certainty, his sense of mission. For myself, I feel only shame for what we attempted to do, and a vast yearning for home."

He nodded.

"You would have made a good priest," I said. "You know how to listen."

He grinned at me. "I believe you are the first person who has ever made that observation about me. Certainly, my seminary professors didn't think so." He sobered. "I seemed to have learned it on this journey. Especially since we were captured." He smiled wryly. "There's been little else to do."

I chuckled and we fell into a companionable silence. Our road still lay above the river. The tableland had given way to craggy peaks, which drew ever closer now on both sides of the stream.

We'd traveled perhaps five miles through this mountain-bound wilderness when the road suddenly rounded a bend. We were at the top of a curve which dipped sharply down to the river. There was a general pause as we stood taking it in.

A low-lying waterfall lay to our right, the cascading water formidable. On the other side, the road met the water a little further on, where the current appeared to be more settled. The surface was unnervingly still. Captain Salazar and Don Jesús had reined in to consider it, the trumpeter just behind them.

"I wonder how deep that is," Falconer murmured.

"That damnable Salazar is going to drown us all before we ever get to El Paso," Kendall said. He glanced toward Ramón, then looked at me and lowered his voice. "Do be particularly careful not to get your cravat wet."

I nodded absently. The trumpet sang out up ahead, then Captain Salazar, on Kendall's big Molly, approached the stream. The mule sidestepped anxiously as she moved into the current, head up and eyes rolling.

Kendall leaned forward. "That water is up to her belly! This would be an excellent occasion for her to display her natural contrariety and dump el capitan on his head."

She stopped in midstream and stepped sideways again. Kendall laughed in delight. The captain leaned forward and spoke into the mule's ear. She tossed her head, but began moving again, onward and up the far bank. Salazar reined her around and signaled us to cross.

"It's easy enough for him," Kendall muttered. "He's riding."

Don Jesús and the trumpeter forded the stream, then the first set of prisoners entered the water. It came up to their lower chests. As they reached the center, the current jerked them sideways. Men grabbed each other's arms and shoulders to stay upright.

The guards shouted encouragement. One of them waved a sword, then his horse stumbled, and man and sword tilted toward the water. As he grabbed at the saddle horn with his free hand, his sword arm flailed and the blade slapped sideways against the horse's neck. His mount half reared, then plunged wildly toward the far bank, guard half out of the saddle.

Only I seemed to notice this. All other eyes were on the struggling prisoners. They made it across, then more men entered the water, more slowly than their compatriots, grasping each other's arms from the outset.

When we started our own passage, I found the water remarkably cold. After the first gasp of shock, no one spoke. We simply pushed forward against the side-rushing current. In one particularly deep spot, my feet lost contact. I gasped and went down, a death grip on Fitzgerald's arm. Finally, I found traction and we stumbled forward onto the bank, and off to one side, out of the way of the men behind.

Falconer and Cayton Erhard emerged and dropped down beside us. The British lawyer's sand-colored hair and beard were dripping wet. "Did you fall?" I asked.

He grinned. "I took a bit of a dip. My scalp is cleaner than it's been in months. That water is quite bracing." He glanced at Cayton. "Erhard here prevented me from taking a proper bath, though."

Erhard grinned at him. "Long one."

Falconer laughed and clapped him on the back. Kendall sloshed up, wringing out his shirt and patting his pockets. "That bread has completely disintegrated," he grumbled.

I had forgotten about the coins. I felt my own clothes. The outline of coins was sharp against my skin. I looked up at him, searching for reassuring words, but he had turned toward the river. The last of the prisoners, the weakest among us, were entering the stream. "Those poor bastards are going to have a time of it," he said. Then he frowned at me. "Are my watch and chain safe?"

I felt for my cravat and nodded as I watched the men in the river. Many were clinging to lariats the guards had lashed to their saddle horns. Others rode pillion, the animals straining to carry two men while also fighting the current.

No wagons followed. I frowned, then realized they'd been left with the grazing cattle. Since we were so close to El Paso, there was no longer a need to transport supplies. Also, with Gates dead and everyone else more or less ambulatory, the sick wagon was no longer needed. The memory of Gates' exhausted face, the canteen on the floor, filled my mind, and I looked up at the trees, trying shake it.

I felt Fitzgerald looking at me. "I wonder if Gates would have been able to cross this last barrier," he said quietly. "I doubt the wagon could have forded here and he wasn't fit to ride, even behind someone else."

I nodded. Someone shouted triumphantly and I looked toward the river. It was empty of men. We had all made it across. Men stood in clumps, squeezing water from their clothes.

Ramón came up, pressing the hem of his coat between his hands and looking irritated. We were to line up in fours. He shot an angry look at the hillock where Captain Salazar sat on Kendall's mule. "Vámonos," he said irritably, mimicking Salazar. "No time for dry."

As we watched, Salazar and Don Jesús angled their mounts across the slope and trotted up the road. Ramón let out an exasperated breath and turned back to us. El Capitán wanted us to present a respectable appearance as we entered El Paso, he told us. We were to march in lines of four and stay close together. No prisoners were allowed to ride. He and the other guards were to stay in their assigned positions beside the column with hats straight, coats buttoned, and heads up. Anyone who strayed from their place would be shot.

He looked away as he said this last bit, as if he didn't want to be reminded of guns and death. Then he turned back to us and shrugged. The captain wanted to make a good impression, he explained.

When I repeated this to the others, Kendall laughed bitterly. "A good impression? The majority of us are ill, our clothing is ragged, our footwear is full of holes, and we all need a shave." He pointed at Falconer. "Even Falconer, that prince of British law, could pass for a pirate!"

Falconer smiled self-consciously and ran his hand over his beard. "As could you."

Kendall scowled and scratched his matted head. "We're infested by bugs and in fear of our lives, yet Salazar is concerned that we appear respectable!" He spit into the dirt. "May he rot in hell!"

The trumpet sounded. We shuffled into lines four men wide, guards at either end, and marched out. I walked with Kendall, Falconer, and Cayton Erhard. Ramón, beside me, stared straight ahead. He seemed to have lost all his delight in the proximity of our journey's end.

This section of road bordered an irrigation channel wider than anything we'd seen upriver. Falconer studied it and the plots of corn and other crops with great interest. Kendall's head was down, as he stared at his feet.

We approached a succession of well-tended vineyards which lay on both sides of the road. "They seem to cultivate a good many grapes here," Falconer observed.

Kendall glanced up. "I wonder if the vines are strong enough to hang rebels with."

Cayton Erhard's head jerked. "Rebels hang?"

"We are not rebels," Falconer said. "We're prisoners of war."

I raised an eyebrow. This was quite different from his prior assessment of our situation.

"Those of us who are Texian could be considered rebels," I pointed out.

The British lawyer glanced at the boy. "Prisoners of war," he said firmly. "As such, we cannot be summarily hanged as rebels. We will be exchanged or paroled."

I nodded my understanding of why he'd said this and hoped he was right about the distinction in punishments, but didn't pursue it.

Kendall's head had jerked upward again. "I am a tourist!"

This drew a snort from Ramón, though he didn't acknowledge me when I turned toward him. There was no amusement in his face.

The vineyards came to an end as the road ahead curved sharply. Trees lined both sides, so we were at the bend before we could see beyond it. Kendall's breath whistled between his teeth. "A real town!"

I was so struck by the change that I almost stopped walking. The dirt track had widened into a street. The houses on either side were substantial and surrounded by well-kept adobe walls. Trees stretched above them while red and pink roses bloomed at their edges.

"Flowers in November," Falconer marveled.

Kendall had gone back to scowling at the dirt under his feet. "What does it matter? Death undoubtedly awaits us all."

Cayton Erhard was studying the road ahead, a hand shading his eyes. "See!" he said. "Das dache—" He looked at Falconer. "Roof?" He waved toward a building on our right. "Texians!"

We followed his pointing arm. A cluster of men stood on the flat roof of a house a little farther along, staring down at us. One of them wore the blue coat of a Texian officer. As we marched closer, the prisoners behind us spied the house and men. A ragged cheer went up.

Then we turned a corner and the rooftop vanished. A small canal ran beside us, carrying water into the town. Trees lined its bank. Where our street intersected with others, small bridges spanned the stream. One of them held a cluster of men in Texian uniforms. There were no guards in sight, in fact no Mexicans at all, except for a woman in a European-style bonnet.

Kendall's head had finally lifted. "That appears to be General McLeod," he murmured. We drew closer. "They're clean shaven!" His shoulders straightened. "And neatly dressed!"

Falconer gave him a sympathetic look. "They are officers," he pointed out. "The Mexicans may well accord them special privileges not allowed to the ranks."

"I am not—" Kendall stopped, then waved a hand, brushing away his usual protest, and nodded reluctantly.

I felt my own hopefulness drop. Falconer was right. It was simply too soon to get our hopes up. After all, we were still prisoners, whether rebels or otherwise. We had no idea what lay ahead, either here or in Mexico City.

We reached the town plaza, a good sized square, and marched across it to a large enclosure, a kind of walled courtyard with a covered porch that ran along three sides. A cluster of Mexican officials stood waiting for us. We formed up facing them. Captain Salazar rode to the porch, saluted a man in a blue coat with scarlet lapels and gold epaulettes, bowed to the others, then swung toward us, and barked a lengthy order.

Beside me, Ramón's head jerked. He frowned slightly, then shrugged, nodded to us politely, and turned his mount toward the gate.

The other guards were taking the same abrupt leave of the men they'd traveled with the last three weeks. Salazar waited until they had all disappeared, then saluted his counterpart once again and spurred Kendall's mule into a canter.

"My molly," Kendall muttered as the captain rode by. His face darkened and his hands balled into fists. "He will pay for what he's done."

I gave him an impatient look. Had he really thought he'd somehow retrieve the big mule? Did he truly believe all our trials were over and the time for revenge was at hand? However, this was not the time to try to talk sense into Kendall. The man with the epaulettes had stepped up onto a block of wood, the better to look us over.

He was of medium height but carried himself with the calm air of inherited privilege as well as command. He studied us, one hand on the hilt of his sword, his face touched with sadness. Then he bowed slightly, turning as he did so to direct the action to all of us. We stirred uneasily, bracing ourselves for whatever might come next.

"You are most welcome!" he said.

I opened my mouth to interpret, then realized he'd spoken in English. A sense of relief washed over me, followed by surprise at how much I'd felt the burden of translation. Then I caught myself. This was one man. Who knew what lay ahead?

"We were not expecting so many of you!" he said with a smile. "Allow me to introduce myself. I am called Lt. Colonel José María Elías González Romo y de Vivar and I am the comandante of the presidio here at El Paso del Norte." His eyes twinkled. "It is a long and cumbersome appellation, is it not? You may refer to me as General Elías." He turned to the little cluster of officials. "Señor Alcalde, would you do us the honor of speaking a few words of welcome to our guests?"

A tall, thin, slightly stooped man with thick gray hair moved forward. He also spoke English, though it was heavily accented. He greeted us politely, then explained that we'd be billeted in small groups with the families of the town, as there was no space large enough to house us under one roof. He smiled and spread his hands. "In addition, the food of our women's cocinas is far superior to anything we military men could provide you!"

There was laughter from the men behind him. We smiled uneasily. Surely it was too good to be true.

But it wasn't. In fact, for Kendall, Falconer, and I, the situation was better than most. We were assigned to lodge with General Elías himself.

While the assignments were going on, Anton Erhard had edged forward to hover near his cousin, apparently hoping to increase the chances they'd be billeted together. The boys bade us goodbye with an envious air. I wished we could invite them along, but we were, after all, still prisoners. We had no control over our destiny.

As the three of us moved toward the gate, we passed Fitzgerald, standing near Captain and Curtis Caldwell. They nodded and we returned the greeting, though I noticed Kendall responded to the Caldwells, but not Fitzgerald.

Falconer had seen it also. "Has my countryman offended you to the point that he is no longer due the common courtesies?" he asked mildly as we entered the plaza.

Kendall pursed his lips. "The man has the insufferable habit of judging others. It has become quite offensive."

I opened my mouth, then shut it again. Now was not the time. Besides, we were almost to the Commandant's house.

It was a substantial one, with thick adobe walls and arranged in the Spanish or Roman style so that the rooms all faced an inner courtyard. This peaceful space featured roses, two acacia trees, and a tile-lined fountain. High-backed carved benches decorated with bright-colored cushions were grouped in inviting clusters.

We stood gazing as if we'd been transported to another realm. The Commandant came out of a far room and hastened toward us. He'd changed out of his uniform but still had that air of effortless authority. He held out welcoming hands to each of us in turn, introduced himself and asked our names.

Kendall was the last to be greeted. "Don General González," he said. "I salute you with great pleasure and the hope of finding redress for my plight."

The commandant's left eyebrow lifted slightly, but he merely smiled and said, "Please, call me General Elías." He gestured to the nearest set of benches. "Let us be seated." As we moved toward them, a girl appeared in a doorway. He said something to her in rapid Spanish. By the time we were seated, she and a companion had reappeared with refreshments—tumblers of cold water with slices of fruit floating in them.

Kendall took a long drink. "Ah, delicioso." Then he turned to our host. "As you may know, I am a newspaper man. My writing implements were stolen from me prior to our journey to your fair city, but my mind is trained to retain details, and I wish to report to you the excesses to which we have been subjected."

General Elías surveyed him politely. Kendall took this as interest and plunged on. "From the beginning of our journey, we were fed primarily on corn. This, despite the fact that we had with us the remainder of the Texian cattle herd. In fact, the majority of that herd has been hidden away by Salazar in a meadow north of El Paso, along with animals undoubtedly stolen from the American military."

The Commandant raised a hand. "A point of clarification, if I may. This is Captain Juan Damasio Salazar of whom you speak? The man who escorted you here?"

Kendall nodded impatiently. "He did not feed us properly, either in terms of types of food or size of portions, and this lack of sustenance led directly to the most recent demise of a gentleman named Thomas Gates. Although Gates was already emaciated from the difficulties of the trek across the Eastern Plains, after his capture by New Mexican troops, he was subjected to the harshest of conditions, which resulted in a subsequent inflammation of the lungs." Kendall paused to sip his drink. "As ill as he was, Señor Gates might well have lived to see El Paso and regain his health in your salubrious climate if he hadn't literally been frightened to death by one of Sala zar's guards."

The general stirred slightly. "Ah, then it is the guard of whom you complain. And what is his name?"

Kendall shook his head. "It is Captain Salazar of whom I complain. He ordered the guards to shoot all of us if any one individual tried to escape. In addition, following the demise of my unfortunate compatriots, he cut off their ears and retained them as a kind of personal trophy."

Elías nodded, his face inscrutable. "How many died?"

"Five in all."

"And you say that there are cattle from the Texian herd still alive?"

Kendall nodded. The general gazed at the burbling fountain for a long moment. "This is all most unfortunate and must be investigated closely." He peered at Falconer and I. "And you, gentlemen? Do you have anything you wish to add to this tale?"

Falconer straightened a little. "We have walked for many days and have a far distance to travel before we reach Mexico City, which we understand is our final destination in your country," he said politely. "We hope to recoup our strength before we proceed south."

The Commandant smiled, his eyes twinkling. "I understand you to say that you would like confirmation of your destination as well as a sense of how long you might expect to be my guests." Then he sobered. "My expectation is to give you a good three days rest before you set off again. And you are correct, my orders are to place you on the road to Ciudad de México." He rose to his feet. "However, for the time being, allow me to show you to your chambers, so that you may begin your recuperation in earnest."

He escorted us to our room, then left, saying dinner would be served at eight. The space was filled with light from two glazed windows and a half-open door to a small balcony. It held three beds, each made up with white sheets and a gaily embroidered bedcover. I crossed to the nearest one and looked at it with bemusement, comparing its pristine beauty to my grimy self.

A flowered pitcher and bowl stood on a nearby sideboard with an elaborate red-and-gold-framed mirror on the wall above. The pitcher was full and the water was warm. I quickly filled the bowl and lavished liquid over my hands and face while Kendall and Falconer watched.

"Be careful not to get my watch wet," Kendall said.

I grinned, pulled his jewelry out of my cravat, handed it to him, and turned back to the basin.

Falconer chuckled. "I see you don't plan to save any of that for us. I hadn't realized you were so vain."

I cupped more water over my face. "I hadn't realized how much I craved clean skin." I grinned at him. "I didn't take a river bath earlier today." He laughed and ran his hand over his beard as I examined myself in the mirror. "Although I could certainly use a real bath. My hair is so filthy it looks like mud."

There was a knock on the door, then a maid entered and invited us to the room next door. When we saw what it contained, Kendall chortled, "We're in a fairy tale. Van Ness asked for a bath, and here it is!" Three hip baths filled with steaming hot water gleamed back at us.

Falconer grinned at me. "It appears that you were precipitate in the washing of your hands and face."

I laughed. I was already stripping off my clothes. "As a result, my water won't get quite as dirty as it would have!"

We stepped into the tubs and immersed ourselves luxuriously. I had come up for air the second time and was contemplating the filthy clothes on the floor, wondering if I should wash them as well, when there was another knock on the door. A young man entered this time, carrying an armload of fresh clothes—light-colored cotton trousers, shirts, and clean linen—for each of us.

"What glory!" Kendall exclaimed. "This is what I call true hospitality!" When we were dressed and back in our rooms, he went to the window and looked out. "What a fine city!"

Then his face darkened. He stepped onto the balcony, bent over the railing, and glared at the street below. "You there!" he bellowed. "You, Ramón!" He made a rude gesture with his hands. "¡Bastardo! ¡Hijo de puta!"

"Kendall!" Falconer objected. "That seems a bit harsh."

Kendall drew back into the room, eyes blazing. "I may be clean now, but I have suffered immeasurably over the course of the last three weeks from that man's vitriol and coarse language and I do not intend to expunge any of that from my memory! In addition, as surely as I stand here before you, I swear I will inform the world that the cowardly bastard killed Thomas Gates! He will pay for what he has done!"

I studied him. Did he still not understand that much of Ramón's teasing was a response to Kendall's own bristling reaction? Or that the guard's singing and garrulousness were strategies to keep us alert and marching, especially across the Jornada del Muerto? Ramón may have precipitated Gates' death, but the death itself had been inevitable. And he had been as remorseful about it as a man could be.

But none of these arguments would seem reasonable to the newsman. "We are still prisoners," I said mildly. "It wouldn't be wise to presume too much or complain too vociferously about our treatment up to this point."

Falconer nodded agreement. "We cannot predict what tomorrow will bring. We're still a good distance from Mexico

City and any dispositions President Santa Anna might choose to make regarding our fate."

"Dispositions regarding our fate?" Kendall sneered. "Spoken like a lawyer." He dropped onto the nearest bed and stretched out, his wet hair marking the white pillow. "My stomach is hollow."

Falconer turned away. He moved to a bed, eased onto it, and fingered the bedclothes. "These are very fine."

"Only the best for the general's guests," Kendall said sleepily.

"And to think that last night we slept on the ground," I said. I headed toward the third bed but was interrupted by a knock on the door. I opened it to a young woman carrying a silver tray laden with a plate of small cakes and a steaming silver pot with small matching cups.

Kendall roused instantly. "Do I smell chocolate?"

She smiled at him as she set the tray on a table by the door, her cheeks dimpling. "Si, señor, chocolate."

"Chocolate in the afternoon?" Falconer asked.

She smiled again, as if she'd heard the question before. "Es nuestra costumbre."

He glanced at me.

"It is our custom," I translated.

"A most excellent one!" He turned to her. "Mil gracias, señorita."

She dimpled at him and went out. Kendall's eyes followed her, then went to the table.

We ate, drank, and returned to our beds for a siesta, but were up and ready for dinner when another servant girl appeared a little before eight to escort us. We found General McLeod in the dining room with General Elías, and greeted him with delight.

The presidio commander smiled at our enthusiasm, then introduced his cousin-housekeeper, nephew, and other guests, who all nodded at us with great goodwill. Kendall seemed to expand with pleasure at the company we were keeping. I dared to hope he would keep his emotions under control and recriminations against Captain Salazar and anyone else to a minimum. This was not the time or place. His outburst from the balcony had startled me and I wasn't sure he'd be able to restrain himself.

But then the food began to come in. The plates were large, the portions substantial, the chile sauce was served separately so we could partake according to our taste, and the milky-white glass tumblers for the sweet El Paso wine were as large as the cider mugs of New England.

When we were satiated, the commandant produced a finely shredded fragrant tobacco and taught us how to create cigarillos. "Oh thou weed!" Kendall rhapsodized. "As the great Shakespeare put it so aptly, 'thou art lovely fair and smell'st most sweet.' Indeed, I would go so far as to designate you the very essence of civilization."

We all chuckled at his extravagance, then leaned back in our chairs and puffed and talked, sharing bits of information about our backgrounds and catching up on the national and international news while carefully avoiding any reference to events in New Mexico since mid-September. Several times, Kendall seemed about to burst forth with diatribes against

Captain Salazar and our guards, but Falconer and I managed to direct the conversation into other avenues.

It was quite late when we retired to our room and beds. "True sheets," Kendall murmured as he slid between them. He stretched luxuriously, then rolled over to press his nose into the pillow. "And they smell of soap, not sweat and other human odors."

"Or dirt," Falconer said. "There are no rocks under the mattresses, either."

"There are mattresses," I said as I sank into mine. "What small things can give so much pleasure."

Kendall rolled onto his side and repositioned the pillow under his head. "I hope Captain Salazar is sleeping on iron spikes tonight." He closed his eyes. "For every rock that jabbed my back, for every thorn that pierced my foot, I desire nothing more than that an iron spike is stabbing deep into his skin."

I lifted my head. "That seems a rather vindictive wish."

He opened his eyes. They were pinpricks of anger. "The man is a beast sent by Manuel Armijo to make my life a living hell. I will not forget and I will be revenged."

"I have a great deal of trouble believing he targeted you specifically. As for the actions he took on the road, he had his reasons. Including his orders from the governor."

Kendall sniffed. "Spoken like a lawyer." He turned over, facing the wall.

CHAPTER 20
Saturday, November 6 to November 7, 1841
El Paso del Norte

A good night's sleep seemed to do wonders for the newsman's attitude. When I roused the next morning he was in front of the mirror, smoothing his wavy brown hair and beard. He saw me watching and patted his whiskers. "I had intended to shave this off, but I am beginning to think better of that idea."

He stood back, hands on his hips, watching himself. "Not even my mother would recognize me as I am now, and this is how all the Mexicans know me. If I find a way to escape, I can visit a barber and instantly be made incognito."

There was a knock at the door. The dimpled servant girl entered with a tray of cakes and chocolate.

Falconer stirred and sat up. "That is the most delicious smell."

She smiled at each of us, set the tray on the table nearest Falconer's bed, then backed away, curtsied, and went out.

"What a delightful custom," Kendall said.

Falconer grinned. "The chocolate or the smiling servant girls?"

I chuckled. "I think we all know how Kendall feels about the women of Mexico."

The newsman turned back to the mirror. "I believe I will let it remain as it is," he said thoughtfully.

Two hours later, we were invited to breakfast. At the end of the meal, General Elías asked how we planned to spend our day. Falconer nodded toward a silver-framed mirror on the opposite wall. "I have been observing the state of my chin and have discovered that I am more vain than I thought. I want very much to visit a barber and indulge in a shave."

Our host's eyes twinkled. "And you, Señor Kendall?"

The newsman ran his fingers through his hair and caught them on a tangle. "It may be beneficial to have the worst of it taken off."

The Commandant's gaze moved to me. My hair, being so fine, was long but still somewhat presentable and my beard lay smoothly enough. And something in his gaze told me he wished for a private conversation. "I have no plans."

"If you would join me in the courtyard after your friends have departed, perhaps you would be so kind as to provide me with an American legal opinion regarding your recent experiences."

"I would be honored." I could feel Kendall's eyes on me, but I didn't look his direction. I knew what he thought I should tell the Commandant, and how forcefully. However, Kendall's view was based on highly colored emotion, not considered fact. I was a lawyer and General Elías had asked for my input from that perspective.

I was a little trepidatious when I went to meet him. Where to begin? How to explain all that had occurred? Would he ask me to justify the action of the Texian legislature in claiming territory to the Río Grande and its headwaters?

But when we'd settled onto a bench beside the fountain, the Commandant set politics aside almost immediately. He wasn't actually interested in my legal opinion. He wanted to know what I knew of Armijo's orders to Salazar. Then he moved on to the various deaths along the road. Could I provide him with the facts in each case?

I went through each situation carefully. He listened with a neutral expression. I couldn't help but think that he would make an excellent judge. When I noted that Governor Armijo had ordered Salazar to shoot anyone who lagged or tried to escape and to bring him their ears, he nodded, as if this was to be expected.

I paused and gave him a questioning look. He smiled slightly. "It can be an effective method for maintaining an accurate tally."

When he didn't expound on this statement, I went on, noting that, to my knowledge, Captain Salazar had not been directly responsible for any of the five deaths on the road. Indeed, he'd been visibly upset after John McAllister and Amos Golpin were killed.

When I finished, the general nodded. "And the animals?"

I frowned, confused, then realized he was referring to the Texian oxen. I repeated what Salazar had told me about our need to move swiftly in order to reach El Paso before winter set in.

"And you believed him?"

I paused, considering, then nodded. Salazar had seemed a somewhat beleaguered and unwilling leader as we moved south, I said. And sincere in his dealings with us, although rather rhetorical and impatient at times.

General Elías's eyes twinkled for the first time since we'd sat down. "You appear to be an excellent judge of character, Señor Van Ness." He looked down at his hands, then at me. "And your fellow prisoners? This newsman, Señor Kendall?"

I stirred uneasily. "As you say, he is my fellow prisoner. With your leave, sir, I am unwilling to discuss my comrades and their motivations and actions with a member of the government which still holds us in its power."

His smile widened. "Spoken like a true lawyer." He slapped his knees and rose to his feet. "I thank you for the information you have provided me and will take it into due consideration." He bowed courteously, turned, and went out, leaving me beside the burbling water.

We did not meet again until the midday meal, when General McLeod joined us once more. The first course was a delicious clear broth, followed by mutton and a chile sauce. There were also beans fried in fat and patties of thickened sheep's blood which were surprisingly delicious. Falconer noted that these were quite different from the blood pudding of his homeland, and much tastier. Even Kendall liked them.

We had finished our dessert of sweetmeats and were sitting back to enjoy more hand-rolled cigarillos when Captain Salazar was announced. Kendall's chair scraped against the floor and I looked at him. He sat ramrod straight, eyes glittering.

"Ah yes," General Elías said from the head of the table. "Please send him in."

We all turned toward the door. Salazar stepped through, then stopped abruptly. His glance flicked from me to Falconer, then Kendall. He straightened, nodded to me, and approached General Elías.

"Buenos tardes, Comandante," he said politely. "Deseo informar—"

The General placed his cigarillo on the edge of a small plate, frowned at the captain, and rattled off a question in rapid Spanish.

Salazar made a sorrowful face. "No, comandante. Lo siento."

Our host turned to me. "I had forgotten that he speaks no English. Would you be so kind as to translate for the rest of the company? To do so myself will be cumbersome." Without waiting for my reply, he turned back to the captain. "¿Qué tienes que decir por ti mismo?"

"What do you have to say for yourself?" I translated, my eyes on Salazar's face, which had blanched a little at the general's sharp tone.

He began what seemed to be a prepared speech, explaining that in mid-October Governor Armijo entrusted him with the responsibility of conveying the largest of the three groups of Texian prisoners to El Paso del Norte. This he had done to the best of his ability.

He glanced at me, to assure I had translated all this, and went on. It had been a difficult undertaking. He had no time to gather the necessary provisions and winter was approaching rapidly. He was forced to march men and guards at an uncomfortable rate of speed and with a minimum of rations.

He paused again, waiting for me to catch up, then turned back to the general. Unfortunately, five prisoners expired en route. He hastened to assure the Commandant that the men had not escaped. To confirm this was so, he had followed Governor Armijo's instructions and secured the appropriate evidence.

Here he produced the ears of the dead prisoners, strung together on a narrow piece of rawhide, and laid them on the table. The older ones were beginning to shrivel, while Gates's were still waxy, the cut edges dark with blood.

The Commandant studied them for a long moment, then looked at Salazar. "Three were murdered," he said neutrally. "Perhaps not by you, but by your guards." His eyes rested on Kendall, then returned to the captain. His chin jerked. "¡Asesinado!"

Salazar took a step back, raising his hands in protest. "¡No, ciertamente no!" He shook his head vehemently and launched into a description of how the various groups of Texians had been captured and his role in those events. "¡Soy un hombre honorable!" he said. "¡Me aseguro de que Su Excelencia duerma en seguro!"

Kendall leaned toward me. "What did he say?"

"That he's an honorable man and Armijo trusts him."

The Commandant spoke again, in a cool voice that conveyed just how much he outranked the captain both in private and military status. "Todo eso es irrelevante," he said. "Hablamos de tres muertos, asesinados sin razón."

"All that is irrelevant," I murmured. "We speak of three dead men, killed for no reason."

Salazar opened his mouth, then shut it with a snap. Kendall snickered. Salazar turned and gave him a contemptuous look. Then his eyes met mine. His face changed, became reproachful. I looked away.

But the commandant was speaking again. "¿Qué pasa con el ganado?"

Kendall jogged my elbow.

"He's asking about the cattle," I said.

Salazar frowned in confusion, but the Commandant didn't give him a chance to answer. Instead, he continued, rather theatrically, "¡Te los guardaste para ti!"

"You kept them for yourself," I translated.

Salazar shook his head and opened his mouth, but General Elías cut him off. "Y los caballos y mulas robados."

"And the stolen horses and mules," I translated.

The general glanced at me, then muttered something about the citizenry of El Paso sleeping safely in their beds and gave Salazar a stern look. Until said animals had been brought in and examined, the captain could consider himself under arrest.

Salazar's face twitched in dismay, but he pulled himself together, nodded, saluted, and went out. I studied the table.

As the door thudded shut, Kendall chuckled and poked me in the ribs. "I would advise you not to go out after dark," he said. "The look he gave you just now promised a good dose of revenge."

The Commandant smiled faintly. "Señor Van Ness is in no danger. The captain will be kept under close watch until the court martial and then he will return to Santa Fe." He reached for his cigarillo, once more the genial host. "You yourselves will be well on your way to sunnier climes before that occurs! How do you propose to spend the time you have remaining in my fair city?"

"Falconer and I thought we'd take a walk around the square," Kendall said. He smiled mischievously. "The girls here are quite pretty."

The commandant laughed and shook a playful finger at him. "Do not allow yourself to become so distracted that you miss supper tonight. Padre Ortiz will be joining us and he desires very much to make your acquaintance."

Falconer chuckled. "I, for one, will be back well before then, in order to enjoy the afternoon chocolate and cakes."

"Until then, señores." General Elías took a last puff from his cigarette, ground it out, and rose from his chair. "I must meet with my officers and see to the wines for our evening's entertainment. I hope to make it a pleasant one."

And it was indeed a pleasant meal. The priest was a young man with urbane manners and exquisite English. Captain and Curtis Caldwell were quartered with him, he explained, and he'd found them so interesting that he wished to expand his knowledge of other Texians and Americans, as well.

He apparently didn't learn enough in that one evening, because he appeared at breakfast the next morning, with an invitation for Kendall and me to spend the day at his home. Kendall accepted with alacrity but I begged off. I wasn't happy about the exclusion of British citizens from the invitation, although Falconer seemed unruffled by it and said he planned to spend the day further recuperating from our recent experiences.

I couldn't bring myself to be so gracious. I wasn't feeling particularly celebratory or in need of company. The scene with the captain the day before kept repeating itself in my head. There was something there I didn't understand, a sudden current of showmanship in the Commandant's expressions and gestures that seemed at odds with his reaction to our discussion by the fountain.

Kendall had been more than satisfied with the outcome of the scene in the dining room, but I wasn't. The general appeared to have decided to take a more aggressive course of action than I had expected. If so, it was surely my fault, something I had left unsaid. Salazar's reproachful look had certainly indicated he thought so.

It all left me feeling unsettled and I was not at all confident that I could show the priest the best of either Texian or American attitudes. Kendall could play those roles better than I.

Padre Ortiz sent for a horse while Kendall ran back to our room to get ready. I followed at a more leisurely pace and found him tucking his watch and chain into one pocket and his silver breastpin into another. "I want to show them to the padre," he explained. "They are all excellent examples of our fine American craftsmanship."

"Why don't you simply wear them?"

He shook his head. "We are, after all, still prisoners. I don't know who might spy them and decide they should be confiscated during subsequent phases of our journey." He patted his pantaloons pockets. "I'm carrying all my coins, too. I know you and Falconer don't think there's any danger, but the servants here are quite poor by our standards. I wouldn't want to put temptation in their way."

My lips quirked. So it wasn't that he didn't trust them, he was keeping them from harm. I was debating whether to point out this bit of hypocrisy when Falconer came in. He crossed to his bed and laid down, hands behind his head. "Are you going to rest as well?" he asked me.

I went to the mirror and stared at my reflection. "I think perhaps I do need a haircut after all. And perhaps a shave."

Falconer closed his eyes. "Please be so good as to close the door gently."

Kendall and I laughed and went out. A horse waited for him outside the house, resplendent in silver-ornamented saddle and bridle. Padre Ortiz stood beside it. He bowed when he saw Kendall, then vaulted onto his own mule. He looked at me invitingly and patted the animal's rump. "There's room here, if you like."

I shook my head and thanked him. He turned toward Kendall, who was now mounted. "I thought we could take a tour of the city en route to my home."

Kendall nodded enthusiastically and they set off. I wandered into the plaza and considered my options. The square was a good deal larger than those in Alburquerque or San Miguel del Bado, and anchored on one end by a two-story church taller than any I'd seen in New Mexico. The rest of the buildings were the usual flat-roofed, one-story structures. Some were clearly homes while others held small stores or cantinas. On the long, covered porches that shaded their windows and doors, small groups of people chatted or promenaded, some-times both.

Despite all the fine food the general had furnished, I still felt a little hungry. I headed to the nearest cantina, where I found a number of my fellow prisoners. They all looked clean, relaxed, and much better clothed than when I'd seen them last. Fitzgerald sat in a corner, looking content, and I joined him.

I ordered a small plate of food and some wine and was just finishing up when the Erhard boys came in. They greeted us enthusiastically and expressed their satisfaction with their accommodations. They'd been housed together, with a family whose women seemed intent on fattening them up.

I waved a hand at our surroundings. "Then why are you here?"

Cayton looked sheepish. "Also die kinder hungrig."

Fitzgerald laughed. "So you're worried you're going to eat them out of house and home?"

As Cayton nodded, Anton gestured toward my drink. "Wein is gut."

"Ah, yes, the wine," Fitzgerald said. "It is excellent, indeed."

I hesitated, not wanting to insult the boys, but their poverty had been evident throughout our journey. "Do you have Mexican coins?"

They grinned at each other, then me. "El padre is kind," Cayton said. So they also had encountered Padre Ortiz. A young man approached to take their order and I left them to it.

Fitzgerald followed me out and headed toward the church. I meandered across the plaza, soaking in the warmth of the

November day, the sight of children playing, the shadows the covered porches cast on the brown adobe walls.

Eventually, I found a barber and submitted myself to his ministrations. When I came out, the sun had begun to set. The plaza had more people in it now, family groups and young people out for a promenade. I spied Fitzgerald looking out the window of a small store. Captain Salazar and Don Jesús stood a few yards away, talking with a cluster of other uniformed men.

I stopped where I was, uncertain how to proceed. Should I acknowledge the captain? Would he wish to be greeted, to be reminded of the scene in the commandant's dining room? My eyes touched Fitzgerald's and he nodded an acknowledgment.

Then Kendall and Padre Ortiz rode into the square. The newsman was resplendent in brilliantly white linen and a new waistcoat. His silver breastpin glittered on his lapel and his watch chain was strung ostentatiously across his chest. His head was up, scanning the plaza. It stopped at Salazar and his friends.

Kendall pulled his horse to a halt, leaned toward the priest, and said something I couldn't hear. The other man nodded and smiled, and Kendall vaulted from his saddle. He handed his horse's reins to the padre and stalked toward the store, head up and chest out. A few yards from the porch, he slowed and put his hands in his pantaloons pockets. I could hear the jingle of coins from where I stood.

Salazar and his friends fell silent. The captain's face was perfectly still.

Kendall continued forward, looking straight ahead. He stepped onto the porch, stopped, cleared his throat, then drew his watch out with a flourish and clicked the cover open. He studied it for a moment, glanced at the store window, shrugged, and turned away. "No time," he said with satisfaction. "General Elías will be waiting."

He spun on his heel and headed back to his horse. As he mounted, he saw me and flashed a gleeful smile. I turned toward the captain.

The impotent rage on his face, the malicious triumph in Kendall's, the grave sorrow of Fitzgerald beyond, haunt me to this day.

AFTERWARD

The Texian prisoners and Mexican soldiers left El Paso del Norte for Chihuahua around noon the day after Kendall's final interaction with Salazar. The leg to Chihuahua seems to have gone well, but the journey to Mexico City was not trouble-free. The Texians, the majority of them still weak from their ordeal en route to New Mexico, were stricken by various ailments, including smallpox.

When the prisoners arrived in the capitol in early February 1842, Mexican President Antonio López de Santa Anna was not as sympathetic to their plight as the people of El Paso had been. He considered the Texians rebels against his government, and the supporters of rebels. He refused to negotiate with the Republic of Texas and reacted negatively when the United States Minister to Mexico attempted to intervene.

Santa Ana scattered the Texians among various prisons in the Mexico City area as well as at Puebla. The ill, including Kendall, who'd come down with a fever, were sent to San Lázaro, the capital's hospital for lepers.

A few men—British citizens such as Falconer and Fitzgerald, and prisoners with connections in Washington D.C. like George Van Ness—were released early on. George Kendall was not. He remained at San Lázaro, where he, although vaccinated against smallpox, came down with it again. He had recovered by mid-April 1842, and was released along with half a dozen other Americans.

More Texians, including Anton Erhard, were freed later that month. The bulk of the prisoners, which included the Caldwells and may have included Cayton Erhard, had to wait until June 13.

On his return to New Orleans, George Wilkins Kendall immediately went to work writing his version of the Texas Santa Fe Expedition's experiences. The first installment appeared in the *New Orleans Picayune on* June 1, 1842. This and subsequent chapters were reprinted in newspapers across the country. The two-volume edition was published in 1844 and went on to become a best seller, with more than 40,000 copies sold over the next eight years.

Kendall went to great lengths to draw an inflammatory picture of Damasio Salazar, describing him as a monster and villain with a vendetta against Americans and Kendall in particular. He also portrayed Mexican men as shiftless, Mexican women as "kind" and susceptible to the charms of the "blue eyes, light hair, and fair complexion" of the Americans, and the Mexican Army as weak and poorly armed. His *Narrative of an Expedition Across the Great Southwestern Prairies, from Texas to Santa Fe* helped shape public opinion about Mexico and its people and was instrumental in rallying popular support for what Americans call the Mexican-American War. Many soldiers carried his books with them into Mexico.

By the time that war began, Texas had given up its status as an independent Republic and become a part of the U.S. However, its legislators still insisted that their western boundary extended to the Río Grande and north to its headwaters. This claim was the basis for the 1850 settlement between the

U.S. Congress and Texas which formally established New Mexico's eastern boundaries where they'd been all along and provided $10 million to pay debts Texas had incurred as a Republic.

NOTE TO READER

The Texian Prisoners is biographical fiction. All the characters in it participated in the events portrayed. That being said, it's impossible to know what may have motivated them or exactly what they did from moment to moment. This novel seeks to portray what the historical record tells us as accurately as possible, while allowing for imagined conversations and events which bridge the gaps in that record.

In the case of the Texas Santa Fe Expedition, the records themselves raise some interesting conundrums. The only English-language sources were written by members of the Expedition. The most famous of these is George Wilkins Kendall's *Narrative of an Expedition Across the Great Southwestern Prairies, from Texas to Santa Fe.* Other sources, such as Cayton Erhard's reminiscences forty years after the fact, often quoted Kendall's book verbatim.

If the study of history has taught me anything, it is to be wary of any account's assertion that it contains the absolute truth. This is especially the case with Kendall's *Narrative,* whose biases and outright inventions are sometimes blazingly clear. His biographical portrait of New Mexico Governor Manuel Armijo is so outrageous and his sweeping statements about the New Mexican populace are so racist (even the best of the men are untrustworthy, and the women's faces aren't "comely" because they contain a mixture of Spanish and Indian blood) that I was initially inclined to disbelieve anything he said.

However, Thomas Falconer's *Letters and Notes on the Texan Santa Fe Expedition, 1841-1842,* also written shortly after the events in question, corroborates key elements of Kendall's story, including the food distributed, the lengthy marches, the five prisoners' deaths, and the misery of the trek across the Jornada del Muerto. This and Cayton Erhard's reminiscences, including the incident in which the Alburquerque girl gives him a pumpkin, led me to believe that much of what Kendall reported was, in the main, accurate.

However, that didn't mean it happened exactly as he described. In fact, Kendall, Falconer, and Erhard often differ on details. For example, they give three different accounts of John McAllister death's south of Valencia. One says he was stabbed by Captain Salazar, another that Salazar shot him, while the third says a sergeant killed him. Since none of them were present at the event, it's anyone's guess what might have actually occurred.

In the case of Amos Golpin's death, all three accounts agree it originated in the crippled man's attempt to take off his shirt in exchange for a ride. While Erhard simply paraphrases Kendall's account, Falconer implies a misunderstanding on the part of the guard and doesn't implicate Salazar. Kendall, however, blames the captain to the exclusion of everyone else. Given Kendall's rather over-the-top descriptions of Salazar throughout the *Narrative* (he's specifically targeting Kendall, he's a brute whose only delight is in cruelty and blood, and so forth), I'm inclined to place more credence on Falconer's report and have imagined this scene based on that account.

This kind of sifting through the sources and trying to find a plausible middle ground was an ongoing effort during the development of *The Texian Prisoners,* an issue inherent in any study of the past. As New Mexico historian Marc Simmons put it, "Unhappily, faithful [historical] testimony is not the rule, since human beings are prone to falsify their statements, either deliberately or unconsciously."

Bearing this in mind, my interpretation of the sources available to me is that in the Fall of 1841, New Mexico militia Captain Damasio Salazar was hell-bent on getting his Texian prisoners south to El Paso and off his hands as quickly as possible. This may have led him to push them faster than was wise, given that many were still weak from their disastrous trek from Austin to New Mexico.

However, winter was closing in. Those of us who have spent much time in New Mexico know just how quickly that can occur. One day it's sunny and warm, and the next day, the crops in the fields are frozen and icy snow is pelting down. Travel becomes difficult and potentially fatal, especially on foot or horseback.

Salazar's most puzzling action during this journey, and the one Kendall returns to again and again, is the taking of the dead Texians' ears. My initial impulse was to view this as Kendall's invention, but Falconer also reports that it happened. I couldn't discount it.

As I began digging deeper, I was reminded that body parts have been taken as war trophies in the Western hemisphere since antiquity. In addition, there is evidence that it was widespread in the Americas at one time or another. American forces cut off the ears of British soldiers during the Revolutionary War, a fact which makes Kendall's horror rather ironic.

However, Kendall may have known this. What seems to especially appall him is that Salazar wasn't taking the ears as trophies, but as a kind of accounting method to prove that none of the prisoners had escaped en route to El Paso del Norte. I was bemused to discover that the severed-ear method of recording the dead actually originated with El Paso presidio commander, Lt. Colonel "General" Elías Gonzáles, the man whom Kendall complained to. During the 1835 Mexican conflict with Apaches in Sinaloa and Sonora, Gonzáles ordered the ears of killed rebel Indians to be cut off so he could use them as proof that the Apaches were indeed in armed conflict with Mexico.

This bit of information clarified Kendall's description of what happened when Salazar gave Gonzáles the string of severed ears. The Presidio commander didn't question the presence of the ears, but instead turned to the disposition of the Texian cattle. Neither charge seems to have been of deep concern. Although Kendall tells us Salazar was placed under arrest, we know he wasn't incarcerated. If he had been, he wouldn't have been in the plaza and available for Kendall's final interaction with him.

Other sources besides Kendall indicate there was a subsequent investigation into Salazar's conduct, but the outcome must not have been very severe, because the captain returned home to serve in the New Mexico militia. In fact, he was reportedly a Mexican officer five years later when the Americans invaded. He was arrested a few months later in connection with a plot against the occupying army, but was found not guilty and released. He eventually settled north of San Miguel del Bado, in Sapello, New Mexico, where he spent the rest of his life.

I gathered this additional information about the captain from New Mexico census and other data, including Father Francis Stanley's delightful *The San Miguel del Bado, New Mexico Story*. I do my best to locate these types of biographical details for all my historical characters, although sometimes there are few available.

In the case of *The Texian Prisoners*, there were two characters for which I could find no information. The first was the name and background of the guard Kendall says bedeviled him all the way from San Miguel del Bado to El Paso del Norte, predicting dire outcomes once the prisoners reach Mexico City, singing rude songs, and generally harassing him.

Kendall never names this man. However, he does name the guard who teases Thomas Gates with a gun as he lays dying. Kendall calls this person "Ramón." Because I have no other information, and for the sake of consistency in the story, I combined the singing and teasing guard with Ramón. I think it's plausible they were the same person, although I have no way of proving or disproving that theory.

I had even less to go on when it came to the sergeant who accompanied Van Ness and the boys to dinner at the home of the woman in Los Placeres. Kendall's *Narrative* mentions a sergeant a number of times, but it's impossible to tell whether he's referring to one man or several. I chose to combine these mentions into one person whom I refer to as "the sergeant." Again, it's possible they are the same person, but I have no way of knowing this for certain.

I also have no way of knowing whether I have accurately portrayed the motives and thoughts of any of my characters. For example, I don't know that George Van Ness was haunted the rest of his days by the role he played in the conflict between Kendall and Salazar. I also don't know that Archibald Fitzgerald, for all of his training for the ministry, was a deeply spiritual man. However, I do know Kendall's *Narrative* hints at a rupture in his friendship with Fitzgerald somewhere between Valencia—where they shared a blanket and sheepskin against the cold—and Socorro, when Fitzgerald simply disappears from Kendall's account. This break may have occurred any time between the two locations and for any reason. I have chosen to see it as building over time and culminating in Socorro, where Kendall claimed he and his friends were cheated into paying twice for their meal.

I don't know what really happened. Do we ever? But I hope that my fictional retelling of this particular portion of the Texians' experience will encourage you to ask questions, both about the events of 1841 and those currently swirling around us, to look at the evidence, and draw your own conclusions.

LIST OF CHARACTERS

Armijo, Manuel (circa 1790 – 1854) The only person to serve as Governor of New Mexico three times. His terms of office were 1827–1829, late 1837–1844, and 1845–1846, when he relinquished New Mexico to the invading Americans without a fight.

Bustamante, Tomás (?? – ??) San Miguel del Bado man who acted as the Kendall group's agent and news source during their incarceration there.

Caldwell, Curtis (circa 1828 – ??) Son of Matthew Caldwell and possibly the youngest participant in the Texas Santa Fe Expedition. He became ill with smallpox at Celeya and was nursed back to health by the Mexican governor there. He and his father returned to New Orleans in August. He died young, apparently never marrying.

Caldwell, Matthew "Old Paint" (1798 – 1842) Captain of Texas Santa Fe Expedition Company D. He was called "Old Paint" because his beard and hair were black with white patches. He became ill with smallpox en route to Mexico City, and was left behind in the Guanajuato hospital while his son went on with the other prisoners. They were reunited in Mexico City and returned to New Orleans in August 1842. In September, he commanded the Texian troops at the Battle of Salado and died four months later.

Erhard, Anton (circa 1824 – ??) Cayton Erhard's younger cousin, who accompanied him on the Texas Santa Fe Expedition.

Erhard, Cayton (1822 – after Fall 1882) German orphan and member, with his cousin Anton, of the Texas Santa Fe Expedition. After his release from Mexican prison, he returned to Texas and eventually settled in Bastrop, where he owned a drugstore. His memories of the events of 1841/42, which drew heavily on Kendall's *Narrative,* were published in a local newspaper between Nov. 16, 1882 and July 24, 1884.

Ernest, Felix (?? – October 1841) First member of Texas Santa Fe Expedition to die on the journey between San Miguel del Bado to El Paso del Norte. He passed away in his sleep, apparently from exhaustion. A small, quiet man, Ernest was originally from Tennessee.

Falconer, Thomas (1805 – 1882) British barrister who participated in the Texas Santa Fe Expedition as historiographer and scientific observer. His *Letters and Notes on the Texan Santa Fe Expedition, 1841-1842* provide a calmer and shorter perspective on the events covered by Kendall's *Narrative.* Falconer's Texas experience seems to have generated an interest in North American boundary issues in general. In 1844, he published a detailed examination of the Sieur de La Salle's exploration of the Mississippi River and the resulting implications for American claims to Texas and Oregon. The research for this and his 1845 book, *The Oregon Question,* led to his 1850 involvement in establishing the boundary between Canada and New Brunswick. The following year he was appointed judge of the Welsh county courts of Glamorganshire and Brecknockshire as well as the district of Rhayader. He died in Bath at age 77.

Fitzgerald, Archibald (1816 – 1843) Former member of General Evans's Legion in Spain who participated in the Texas Santa Fe Expedition. The grandson of Irish patriot Archibald Hamilton Rowan, Fitzgerald was educated for the Anglican ministry at Boulogne, France. He left school in 1834 and enlisted for Spain against the Carlist Revolution. Afterwards, he drifted to Texas, where he joined the Expedition to Santa Fe. After his release from Mexican prison, Fitzgerald returned to Texas, where he was captured at the battle of Mier in late December 1842 and died during a subsequent escape attempt.

Gates, Thomas (?? – 1841) New York-born member of the Texas Santa Fe Expedition. Already weakened by the brutal trek from Texas to New Mexico, Gates died the night before the prisoners under Salazar reached El Paso del Norte.

Golpin, Amos (?? – 1841) Merchant with the Texas Santa Fe Expedition who identified as American, not Texian. Golpin had a crippled right hand and a delicate constitution, which put him in the Expedition sick wagon at least a month before the Texians were captured. He was shot by a guard during the trek across the Jornada del Muerto.

Gonzáles, Jose María Elías González Romo y de Vivar (1793 – 1864) Presidio Commander at El Paso del Norte in late 1841 when the Texas Santa Fe Expedition prisoners under Salazar arrived there. Gonzáles, aka General Elías, held various political and military posts in Mexico from 1812 until his death in Sonora in 1864.

Griffith, Edward (?? – 1841) Man wounded by Kiowa during the Texas Santa Fe Expedition to New Mexico. Following the Expedition's capture, he was killed by a guard during the crossing of the Jornada del Muerto.

Hornsby, C. C. (?? – ??) Lieutenant of Santa Fe Expedition Company B) who Kendall says was the best dressed man on the journey. Hornsby was "kidnapped" by a Mexican gentleman just north of Alburquerque and returned to his fellow prisoners later that day with a Mexican coat that would prove useful during the trek across the Jornada del Muerto.

Kendall, George Wilkins (1809 – 1867) Co-owner of the *New Orleans Picayune* and member of the Texas Santa Fe Expedition who subsequently wrote a highly colored account of that experience. Kendall's *Narrative* provided fuel to the fire that would become the U.S. war to extend its boundaries to the Pacific Ocean. After participating in that conflict as an embedded correspondent and publishing an illustrated book about it, Kendall settled in Texas, where he died in 1867.

Lucero, Jesús (circa 1794 – ??) Ensign, or alférez, presumably of the San Miguel del Bado militia who I believe was Captain Damasio Salazar's second in command during the journey between San Miguel del Bado and El Paso del Norte. This identification is tentative because Kendall only refers to Salazar's lieutenant as "Don Jesús."

McAllister, Thomas (?? – 1841) Tennessee-born man who participated in the Texas Santa Fe Expedition despite a lame ankle, which he'd injured in childhood. McAllister died south of Valencia, New Mexico during an altercation with a guard about his inability to keep up with his fellow prisoners.

McLeod, General Hugh (1814 – 1862) Leader of the Texas Santa Fe Expedition. Raised in Georgia, he attended West Point, where he graduated last in his class of 56. After graduation, McLeod was assigned to Louisiana, but deserted to Texas. There, he served as President Houston's adjutant general and participated in battles against the Caddo, Cherokee, and Comanche. Following the Texas Santa Fe Expedition and his subsequent incarceration at Puebla and Perote, McLeod returned to Texas. He supported William Walker's 1850s takeover of Nicaragua and served the Confederacy during the Civil War, rising to the rank of Colonel.

Muñoz, Pedro José (?? – ??) Mexican military leader who, as captain of the Vera Cruz dragoons, was instrumental in putting down the 1837/38 New Mexico rebellion described in my novel *There Will Be Consequences*. He returned to New Mexico in late 1841 as a full Colonel, to assist Armijo against further Texian threats. Muñoz and his men remained there until at least September 1845, when they assisted in repelling a Ute attack on the Santa Fe plaza.

Ortiz, Ramón (circa 1813 – 1896) Priest of Nuestra Señor de Guadalupe in El Paso del Norte when the Texas Santa Fe Expedition arrived there. Although friendly with the prisoners during their stay and instrumental in providing them relief, he did not approve of the 1846 American invasion and opposed the treaty of Guadalupe Hidalgo. He served in El Paso until his death.

Ramón the guard (?? – ??) The only New Mexican guard named in Kendall's narrative, although Kendall provides no other details about him. As a result, Ramón is a composite character. See Note to Reader for more details.

Salazar, Juan Damasio (1797 – circa 1865) Leader of the men who escorted the group of Texian prisoners that included George Wilkins Kendall. Following an inquiry into the charges Kendall leveled against him, Salazar returned to New Mexico and continued his military career. After the U.S. seized New Mexico in 1846, he was arrested in connection with a plot to kick the Americans out, but no evidence was found against him and he was reluctantly released. Salazar died in the mid-1860s and is buried at Sapello, New Mexico.

Santa Anna, Antonio (1794 – 1876) President of the United Mexican States during the period covered by this novel as well as various other times during his forty-year career in Mexican politics.

Sergeant of the Guard (?? – ??) Man who acted as sergeant of the guard for the contingent of Texian prisoners escorted to El Paso del Bado by Damasio Salazar. This man is a composite character, as none of the sources available to me name him. See Note to Reader for more details.

Shoemaker's Wife (?? – ??) San Miguel del Bado woman who befriended the Kendall group in September 1841. Kendall says her name was Francisca and that she was married to the San Miguel shoemaker. However, neither of the two shoemakers listed in the San Miguel 1841 Census records had a wife named Francisca. Did Kendall deliberately misname her, perhaps to shield her identity from invading Americans?

Van Ness, George (circa 1822 – before 1856) Secretary to the Civil Commissioners on the Texas Santa Fe Expedition who was captured, along with Kendall, during an attempt to procure supplies for the starving Texians. Van Ness served as translator to Captain Damasio Salazar during the journey between San Miguel del Bado and El Paso del Norte. After his release from Mexican incarceration, he returned to

Texas and eventually settled in Eagle Pass, near the border with Mexico.

PARTIAL BIBLIOGRAPHY

Chacon, Richard J. and David H. Dye. *The Taking and Displaying of Human Body Parts as Trophies by Amerindians.* New York: Springer, 2007.

Copeland, Fayette. *Kendall of the Picayune.* Norman: University of Oklahoma Press, 1943.

Dixon, Ford. "Cayton Erhard's Reminiscences of the Texan Santa Fe Expedition, 1841." *The Southwestern Historical Quarterly,* Jan. 1963, Vol. 66, Nos. 3 & 4, 424-456, 547-568.

Falconer, Thomas. *Letters and Notes on the Texan Santa Fe Expedition, 1841-1842.* Edited by Thomas F. W. Hodge. New York: Dauber & Pine Bookshops, 1930.

Kendall, George Wilkins. *Narrative of the First Texan Santa Fe Expedition.* New York: Harper, 1847.

Loomis, Noel M. *The Texian-Santa Fe Pioneers.* Norman: University of Oklahoma Press, 1958.

Scurlock, Dan. "The Río Grande Bosque: Ever Changing." New Mexico Historical Review, April 1988, 131-140.

Stanley, Francis. *The San Miguel del Bado (New Mexico) Story.* Pep, Texas: 1964.

Sunder, John E. *Matt Field on the Santa Fe Trail.* Norman: University of Oklahoma Press, 1995.

Vigil, Cipriano Frederico. *New Mexican Folk Music: Treasures of a People.* Albuquerque: University of New Mexico Press, 2014.

Vigil, Julián Josué. *San Miguel del Bado, 1841 Census.*
Springer: Editorial Telaraña, 1984.

VOCABULARY

Note: Most of the non-English material in this novel is translated in the text or have English cognates. The list below contains terms that don't fit either of these categories.

adobe - unburnt brick dried in the sun. Common building material in New Mexico prior to 1846. (Spanish)

Alburquerque – City south of Santa Fe which is now the largest in New Mexico. This is the original Spanish spelling, which changed some time during the 1800s, when it lost its first 'r' and became "Albuquerque." I've chosen to use the older form in this book.

alcalde – a magistrate who served as head of a municipal council and justice of the peace (Spanish)

aquí – here (Spanish)

auch – also, too, likewise (German)

Bienvenido a nuevo méxico – welcome to New Mexico (Spanish)

bueno – very well, all right (Spanish)

buenas tardes – good afternoon

cantina – restaurant (Spanish)

cocina – kitchen (Spanish)

comen como lobos – you (plural) eat like wolves (Spanish)

comida – food, nourishment, victuals (Spanish)

de nada – you're welcome, don't mention it (Spanish)

deseo informar - wish to report (Spanish)

Dios le guarde - God be with you (Spanish)

Dios – God (Spanish)

díselo - tell them (Spanish)

Don – Mister, Sir. Spanish title for gentleman used only before the Christian, or first, name, (Spanish)

español– Spanish/Spaniards (Spanish)

Gracias – thanks, thank you (Spanish)

herr – mister (German)

hija – daughter (Spanish)

incendio – fire, conflagration, burning (Spanish)

ja – yes, certainly (German)

kinder – children (German)

lo siento – I am sorry (Spanish)

maldición – damnation (as imprecation) (Spanish)

maldito/maldita – accursed, damned (Spanish)

novio – fiancee (masculine)

para los enfermos – For the sick ones!

patrón – master (Spanish)

pobrecito – poor little one (Spanish)

por favor – literally "if you will," please. (Spanish)

por qué – why (Spanish)

presidio – military garrison (Spanish)

querida – sweetheart (Spanish)

Qué – What? Interrogatory. (Spanish)

rebozo – a kind of long woven shawl used by women in New Mexico and Mexico. (Spanish)

río – river, (Spanish)

salvajes – savages (Spanish)

señor – Sir, lord, mister. Also used in the sense of "gentle-man." Not capitalized except as part of a name. (Spanish)

señora – Madam, lady. Also used in the sense of "gentle woman." Not capitalized except as part of a name. (Spanish)

señorita – young lady, Miss. Not capitalized except as part of a name. (Spanish)

sí – yes, (Spanish)

tejano – Texan, or (as the Texans called themselves, "Texian"). Also a term applied disparagingly to any white stranger coming into New Mexico. (Spanish)

Texian – Texan. A term people from Texas applied to themselves during this period.

Un poco – a little (Spanish)

verdammen – damnation, damn it (German)

y – and (Spanish)